ULADZIMIR KARATKEVICH

KING STAKH'S
WILD HUNT

KING STAKH'S WILD HUNT

By Uladzimir Karatkevich

Second edition

First published in Belarusian
as "Дзікае паляванне караля Стаха"
in "Вока тайфуна. Апавяданні і аповесці".
Minsk, "Mastatskaya Litaratura", 1974 г.

Translated by Mary Mintz

Edited by Camilla Stein

© Alena Sinkevich, 1974

© 2012, Glagoslav Publications

www.glagoslav.com

ISBN: 978-1-909156-11-1
ISBN: 978-1-909156-10-4

ULADZIMIR KARATKEVICH

KING STAKH'S
WILD HUNT

TRANSLATED BY MARY MINTZ

GLAGOSLAV PUBLICATIONS

CONTENTS

INTRODUCTION

I am an old man, a very old man. No book can give you any idea of what I, Andrey Belaretsky, now a man of ninety six years, have seen with my own eyes. People say that fate usually grants long life to fools so that they should have time enough in which to acquire rich experience, experience that will make up for their lack of wisdom. Well then, I wish I were twice as foolish and might have lived twice as long, for I am an inquisitive fellow. How much that is interesting will occur in this world in the coming ninety six years!

If someone should tell me that tomorrow I shall die, so what of it? To rest is not a bad thing. Some day people will be able to live much longer than I have lived, and they will not know any bitterness in their lives. In mine I have experienced everything – life has not always been a bed of roses – what then is there to regret? I can lie down and fall asleep, sleeping calmly and even with a smile.

I am alone. As Shelley puts it:

When the lute is broken,
Sweet tones are remember'd not:
When the lips have spoken,
Loved accents are soon forgot.

She was a good person and we lived together, as told in a fairy tale, happily ever after till death did us part. However, enough! I have overtaxed your heart with sorrowful words. Having already said that my old age is a happy one, I better now tell you of those remote days of my youth. Here it is demanded of me that my story brings to an end my reminiscences of the Yanovskys and their decline, and the extinction of the Belarusian gentry. Evidently, I have to do it, for indeed what kind of a story would it be without an ending?

Besides, the story closely concerns me, and there's no one else left but myself to tell it. You will find it interesting to listen to this amazing story to its very end, only to say that it greatly resembles fiction.

So then, before we begin, I must say that all this is the truth and nothing but the truth, although you will have only my word for it.

CHAPTER ONE

I was travelling in a hired carriage from the provincial city M. to the most remote corner of the province, and my expedition was coming to an end. Some two more weeks remained of sleeping in barns or under the stars in the carriage itself, of drinking water from clay pots, water that made one's teeth and forehead ache, of listening to the long, drawn out singing of the old women sitting in the yards in front of their houses, singing of the woe of the Belarusians. And of woe there used to be plenty in those days – the cursed eighties were coming to an end.

However, you must not think that the only thing we did at that time was to wail and ask of the muzhyk "Where are you running to, muzhyk?" or "Will you awaken in the morning, strong and hearty?" The real compassion for the people came later. It is well known that a man is very honest until the age of twenty five. He cannot in his heart of hearts bear injustice when young. However, young people are too preoccupied with themselves. Everything is new to them. They find it interesting to watch the development of new feelings that settle in their souls, and they are certain that no one has ever previously experienced anything equal to their emotions.

It is only later that the sleepless nights will come, when bending over a scrap of newspaper you'll read a notice in the same print as all the other news, that three were taken to the scaffold today – three, you understand, alive and merry fellows! It is only then that the desire will come to sacrifice yourself.

At that time, though considered a "Red", I was convinced in the depths of my soul that the forests which grow on Earth are not only forests of scaffolds which was, of course, true even during the times of Yazafat Kuntsevich and the Belarusian "slander" inquisition, and that it was not only moaning which we heard in the singing. For me at that time it was much more important to understand who I was and which gods I should pray to. My surname, people said, was of a Polish origin, though even today I do not know what is so Polish about it. In our high school – and this was at the time when the dreadful memory of the trustee, Kornilov, who was Muravyov's associate, had not yet been forgotten – our ethnicity was determined, depending on the language of our forefathers, "the eldest branch of the Russian tribe, pure blooded, truly Russian people!" That's right, even more Russian than the Russians themselves!

Had they preached this theory to us before the beginning of the century, then Belarus would inevitably have overpowered Germany, while the Belarusians would have become the greatest oppressors on Earth, going on to conquer vital Russian territories of the not so Russian Russians, especially if the good gods had given us of the horn of plenty.

I sought my people and began to understand, as did many others at the time, that my people was here, at my side, but that for two centuries the ability to comprehend this fact had been beaten out of the minds of our intelligentsia. That is why I chose an unusual profession for myself – I was going to study and embrace this people.

And so, I graduated from the gymnasium and the university and became an ethnographer. This kind of work was only in its beginning at the time and the reigning powers considered the occupation dangerous for the existing order.

Contrary to the expectation, I met with eager helpfulness and attention wherever I went, and only this circumstance made my work easier for me. Many people offered their assistance. A clerk of our small district being a man of modest education, who later on mailed me and Romanov our notes on tales; or that village teacher who worried over his loaf of bread. My people lived even in the persona of one governor, an exceptionally benign man, a rarity and perhaps even a gem among his kind. He gave me a letter of recommendation in which he ordered under threat of severe punishment that I should be given every aid I needed.

My thanks to you, my Belarusian people! Even now I offer prayers for you. What then can be said about those years?

Gradually I arrived to the understanding of who I was. What was it that instigated the process?

Perhaps it was in the lights of the villages so dear and their names which even to this very day fill my heart with a sort of longing and pain. Linden Land, Forty Tatars, Broken Horn, Oakland, Squirrels, Clouds, Birch Land Freedom...

Could it have been the nights in the meadow when children told you stories and drowsiness was crawling up under your sheepskin coat together with the cold? Or was it the heady smell of fresh hay and the stars shining through the barn's torn roof? Perhaps none of these, but simply a teapot filled with pine needles and smoky black huts where women in their warm, long skirts, made of homespun fabric, sung their song. An endless song, more like a groan.

All of this was mine, my own. Over a period of two years I had travelled – on foot or in a carriage – across the Miensk, Mahilow, Vitsebsk provinces and part of the Vilnia province. And everywhere I saw blind beggars and dirty children, saw the woe of my people whom I loved more than anything else in the world – this I know now.

This region was an ethnographic paradise then, although the tale, especially the legend, as the most unstable product of a people's fantasy, began to retreat farther and farther into the backwoods, into the most remote, forsaken corners.

There, too, I went. My legs were young, and young was my thirst for knowledge. And oh the things that I saw!

I saw the ceremony, an extraordinarily important one, called in Belarusian "zalom", that is, if an enemy wished to bewitch somebody's field, he had to tie together a bunch of wheatears into a knot.

I saw the stinging nettle yuletide, the game 'pangolin' otherwise known as 'lizard', rare even for those days. Yet more often I would see the last potato in a bowl of soup, bread as black as the soil and the tear stained sky wide eyes of the women, and I would hear a sleepy "a-a-a" over a cradle.

This was the Byzantine Belarus!

This was the land of hunters and nomads, black tar sprayers and quiet and pleasant chimes coming across the quagmires from the distant churches, the land of lyric poets and of darkness.

It was just at this time that the long and painful decline of our gentry was coming to an end. This death, this being buried alive, continued over a long period, a period of almost two centuries.

In the 18th century the gentry died out stormily in duels, in the straw, having squandered millions. At the beginning of the 19th century their dying out bore a quiet sadness for their neglected castles that stood in pine groves. There was already nothing poetic or sorrowful about it in my days; it was rather loathsome, at times horrifying even in its nakedness.

It was the death of the sluggards who had hidden themselves in their burrows, the death of the beggars, whose forefathers had been mentioned as the most distinguished nobles in the Horodlo privilege; they lived in old, dilapidated castles, went about dressed mostly in homespun clothing, but their arrogance was boundless.

It was a savage race, hopeless, abominable, leading at times to bloody crimes, the reasons for which one could have sought only in their eyes set either too closely or too far apart, eyes of vicious fanatics and degenerates.

Their stoves faced with Dutch tile they heated with splintered fragments of priceless Belarusian 17th century furniture; they sat like spiders in their cold rooms, staring into the endless darkness through windows covered with small fleets of drops that floated obliquely.

Such were the times when I was preparing for an expedition that would take me to the remote provincial District N. I had chosen a bad time for the endeavour. Summer, of course, is the most favourable time for the ethnographer; it is warm and all around there are attractive landscapes. However, our work gets the best results in the late autumn or in winter. This is the time for games and songs, for gatherings of women spinners with their endless stories, and somewhat later – the peasant weddings. This period is a golden time for us.

However, I had managed to arrive only at the beginning of August, which was not the time for storytelling, but for hard work in the fields. Only drawn out harvesting hymns were being hummed in the open air. All August I travelled about, and September, and part of October, and only just managed to catch the dead of autumn – the time when I might find something worthwhile. In the province errands were awaiting me that could not be put off.

My catch was nothing to boast of, and therefore I was as angry as the priest who came to a funeral and suddenly saw the corpse rise from the dead. I never had a real chance to examine a particular feeling that tormented me, a feeling that in those days stirred in the soul of every Belarusian. It was his lack of belief in the value of his cause, his inability to do anything, his deep pain – the main signs of those evil years, signs that arose, according to the words of a Polish poet, as a result of the persisting fear that someone in a blue uniform would come up to you, and say with a sweet smile: "To the gendarmerie, please!"

I had very few ancient legends, although it was for them that I was on the hunt. You probably know that all legends can be divided into two groups. The first are those that are alive everywhere amidst the greater part of the people. In the Belarusian folklore they are legends about a snake queen, about an amber palace, and also a great number of religious legends.

The second type are those which are rooted, as if chained, in a certain locality, district, or even in a village. They are connected to an unusual rock or cliff at the bank of a lake, with the name of a tree or a grove or with a particular cave nearby. It goes without saying that such legends, being linked to a minority, die out more quickly, although they are sometimes more poetic than the well known ones, and when published they are very popular.

Such was, for instance, the legend of Masheka – I was hunting a different group of legends when I stumbled on this one. I had to hurry, as the very notion of a legend and a tale was dying out.

I don't know how it is with other ethnographers, but it has always been difficult for me to leave any locality. It would seem to me that during the winter that I had to spend in town, some woman might die there, the woman, you understand, who is the only one who knows that particular enchanting old tale. This story will die together with her, and nobody will hear it, and my people and I shall be robbed.

Therefore my anger and my anxiety should not surprise anyone.

I was in this mood when one of my friends advised me to go to the District N., which was even at that time considered a most unwelcoming place.

Could he have foreseen that I would almost lose my mind because of the horrors facing me there, that I would find courage and fortitude in myself, and what would I discover? However, I shall not forestall events.

My preparations did not take long. I packed all necessary things into a medium sized travelling bag, hired a carriage and soon left the hub of a comparatively advanced society, putting the civilization behind me. And so, I came to the neighbouring district with its forestry and swamps, a territory which was no smaller than perhaps Luxemburg.

At first, along both sides of the road I saw fields with several wild pear trees, resembling oaks, standing scattered here and there. We came across villages on our way in which whole colonies of storks lived, but then the fertile soil came to an end and endless forest land appeared in front of us. Trees stood like columns, the brushwood along the road deadened the rumbling of the wheels. The forest ravines gave off a smell of mould and decay. Sometimes from under the very hoofs of our horses flocks of heath cocks would rise up into the air – in autumn heath cocks always bunch together in flocks – and here and there from beneath the brushwood and heather brown or black caps of nice thick mushrooms were already peeping out.

Twice we spent the nights in small forest lodges, glad to see their feeble lights in the blind windows. Midnight. A baby is crying, and something in the yard seems to be disturbing the horses – a bear is probably passing nearby, and over the trees, over the ocean-like forest, a solid rain of stars.

It is impossible to breathe in the lodge. A little girl is rocking the cradle with her foot. Her refrain is as old as the hills:

> *Don't go kitty on the bench,*
> *You will get your paws kicked.*
> *Don't go kitty on the floor,*
> *You will get your tail kinked.*
> *A–a–a!*

Oh, how fearful, how eternal and immeasurable is thy sorrow, my Belarus!

Midnight. Stars. Primitive darkness in the forests.

Nevertheless, even this was Italy in comparison to what we saw two days later.

The forest was beginning to wither, was less dense than before. And soon an endless plain came into view.

This was not an ordinary plain throughout which our rye rolls on in small rustling waves; it was not even a quagmire... a quagmire is not at all monotonous. You can find there some sad, warped saplings, a little lake may suddenly appear, whereas this was the gloomiest, the most hopeless of our landscapes – the peat bogs. One has to be a man-hater with the brain of a cave man to imagine such places. Nevertheless, this was not the figment of someone's imagination; here before our very eyes lay the swamp.

This boundless plain was brownish, hopelessly smooth, boring and gloomy.

At times we met great heaps of stones, at times it was a brown cone. Some God forsaken man was digging peat, nobody knows why. At times we came across a lonely little hut along the roadway, with its one window, with its chimney sticking out from the stove, with not even a tree anywhere around. The forest that dragged on beyond the plain seemed even gloomier than it really was. After a short while little islands of trees began coming into view, trees covered with moss and cobwebs, most of them as warped and ugly as those in the drawings that illustrate a horribly frightening tale.

I was ready to growl, such resentment did I feel.

As if to spite us, the weather changed for the worse. Low level dark clouds were creeping on to meet us. Here and there leaden strips of rain came slanting down at us. Not a single crested lark did we see on the road, and this was a bad sign – it would rain cats and dogs all night through.

I was ready to turn in at the first hut, but none came in sight. Cursing my friend who had sent me here, I told the man to drive faster, and I drew my rain cloak closer around me. The sky became filled with dark, heavy rain clouds again and a gloomy and cold twilight made me shiver as it descended over the plain. A feeble streak of lightning flashed in the distance.

No sooner did the disturbing thought strike me that at this time of the year it was too late for thunder, than an ocean of cold water came pouring down on me, on the horses and the coachman.

Someone had handed the plain over into the clutches of night and rain.

The night was as dark as soot, I couldn't even see my fingers, and only guessed that we were still on the move because the carriage kept on jolting. The coachman, too, could probably see nothing and gave himself up entirely to the instincts of his horses.

Whether they really had their instincts I don't know – the fact remains that our closed carriage was thrown out from a hole onto a kind of a hillock and back again into a hole.

Lumps of clay, marshy dirt and paling were flying into the carriage, onto my cloak, into my face, but I resigned myself to this and prayed for only one thing – not to fall into the quagmire. I knew what these marshes were famous for. The carriage, the horses, and the people, all would be swallowed up, and it would never enter anybody's mind that somebody had ever been there. That only a few minutes ago a human being had screamed there until a thick brown marsh mass had blocked his mouth, and now that human being was lying together with the horses buried six metres down below the ground.

Suddenly there was a roar, a dismal howl. A long, drawn out howl, an inhuman howl... The horses gave a jerk. I was almost thrown out... they ran on, heaven knows where, apparently straight on across the swamp. Then something cracked, and the back wheels of the carriage were drawn down. On feeling water under my feet, I grabbed the coachman by the shoulder and he, with a kind of indifference, uttered:

"It's all over with us, sir. We shall die here!"

But I did not want to die. I snatched the whip from out of the coachman's hand and began to strike in the darkness where the horses should have been.

That unearthly sound howled again, the horses neighed madly and pulled. The carriage trembled as if it were trying with all its might to pull itself out of that swamp, then a loud smacking noise from under the wheels, the cart bent, jolted even worse, the mare began to neigh! And lo! A miracle! The cart rolled on, and was soon knocking along on firm ground. Only now did I comprehend that it was none other than me in my own person who had uttered those heart wrenching howls. I now was deeply ashamed of myself.

I was about to ask the coachman to stop the horses on this relatively firm ground, and spend the night there, when the rain began to quiet down.

At this moment something wet and prickly struck me in the face. "The branch of a fir tree," I guessed. "Then we must be in a forest, the horses will stop on their own."

However, time passed, once or twice fir tree branches hit me in the face again, but the carriage slid on evenly and smoothly – a sign that we were on a forest path.

I decided that it had to lead somewhere and gave myself up to fate. Indeed, when about thirty minutes had passed, a warm and beckoning light appeared ahead of us in this dank and pitch-dark night.

We soon saw that it was not a woodsman's hut and not a tar sprayer's hut as I had thought at first, but some kind of a large building, too large even for the city. In front of the building – a flower bed, surrounded with wet trees, a black mouth of the fir tree lane through which we had come.

The entrance had a kind of a high rooflet over it and a heavy bronze ring on the door.

At first I and then the coachman, then again I, knocked on the door with this ring. We rang timidly, knocked a little louder, beat the ring very bravely, stopped, called out, then beat the door with our feet – but to no avail. At last we heard somebody moving behind the door, uncertainly, timidly. Then from somewhere at the top came a woman's voice, hoarse and husky:

"Who's there?"

"We're travellers, dear lady, let us in."

"You aren't from the Hunt, are you?"

"Whatever hunt are you speaking of? We're wet through, from head to foot, can hardly stand on our feet. For God's sake let us in."

The woman remained silent, then in a hesitating voice she inquired:

"But whoever are you? What's your name?"

"Belaretsky is my name. I'm with my coachman."

"*Count* Belaretsky?"

"I hope I am a Count," I answered with the plebeian's lack of reverence for titles.

The voice hardened:

"Well then, go on, my good man, back to where you came from. Just to think of it, he *hopes* he is a Count! Joking about serious things like that in the middle of the night? Come on, off you go! Go back and look for some lair in the forest, if you're such a smart fellow."

"My dear lady," I begged, "gladly would I look for one and not disturb people, but I am a stranger in this area. I'm from the district town; we've lost our way, not a dry thread on us."

"Away, away with you!" answered an inexorable voice.

In answer to that, anybody else in my place would have probably grabbed a stone and begun beating on the door with it, swearing at the cruel owners, but even at such a moment I could not rid myself of the thought it was wrong to break into a strange house. Therefore I only signed and turned to the coachman.

"Well then, let's leave this place."

We were about to return to our carriage, but our ready agreement had apparently made a good impression, for the old woman softened and called us:

"Just a moment, wayfarers, but who are you, anyway?"

I was afraid to answer "an ethnographer", because twice before after saying this I had been taken for a bad painter. Therefore I answered:

"A merchant."

"But how did you get into the park when a stone wall and an iron fence encircle it?"

"Oh! I don't know," I answered sincerely. "We were riding somewhere through the marsh, fell somewhere through somewhere, we hardly got out... Something roared there too..." Truth to tell, I had already given up all hope, however, after these words of mine the old woman quietly sighed and said in a frightened voice:

"Oh! Oh! My God! Then you must have escaped through the Giant's Gap for only from that side there's no fence. That's how lucky you were. You're a fortunate man. The Heavenly Mother saved you! Oh, good God! Oh, heavenly martyrs!"

And such sympathy and such kindness were heard in those words that I forgave her the hour of questioning at the entrance. The woman thundered with the bolts, then the door opened, and a dim orange-coloured stream of light pierced through the darkness of the night.

A woman stood before us, short of stature, in a dress wide as a church bell with a violet-coloured belt, a dress which our ancestors wore in the times of King Sas, wearing a starched cap on her head. Her face was covered with a web of wrinkles. She had a hooked nose and an immense mouth, resembling a nutcracker with her lips slightly protruding. She was round like a small keg, of medium height, with plump little hands, as if she were asking to be called "Mother dear". This old woman held tremendous oven prongs in her hands – armour! I was about to burst into laughter, but remembered in time how cold and rainy it was outside, and therefore kept silent. *How many people even to this very day keep from laughing at things deserving to be laughed at, fearing the rain outside?*

We went into a little room that smelled like mice, and immediately pools of water ran down from our clothes onto the floor. I glanced at my feet and was horrified – a brown mass of mud enveloped my legs almost up to my knees, making them look like boots.

The old woman only shook her head.

"See, I told you it was that scary thing! You, Mr. Merchant, must light a big candle as an offering to God for having escaped so easily!" And she opened a door leading into a neighbouring room with an already lit fireplace. "You've had a narrow escape. Take off your clothes, dry yourselves. Have you any other clothes to get into?"

Luckily, my sack was dry. I changed my clothing before the fireplace. The woman dragged away our clothes – mine and the coachman's – and returned with dry clothing for the coachman. She came in paying no attention to the coachman being quite naked, standing bashfully with his back turned to her.

She looked at his back that had turned blue and said disapprovingly:

"You, young man, don't turn your back to me. I'm an old woman. And don't squeeze your toes. Here, take these and dress yourself."

When we had somewhat warmed up at the fireplace, the old woman looked at us with her deep sunken eyes and said:

"Warmed up a bit? Good! You, young man, will retire for the night with Jan at his quarters, it won't be comfortable for you here... Jan!"

Jan showed up. An almost blind old man about sixty years of age, with long grey hair, a nose as sharp as an awl, sunken cheeks and a moustache reaching down to the middle of his chest.

At first I had been surprised that the old woman all alone with only oven prongs in her hands had not been afraid to open the door to two men who had appeared in the middle of the night who knows from where. However, after seeing Jan I understood that all this time he had been hiding somewhere behind her and she had counted on him for help.

His help would be "just grand". In the hands of the old man I saw a gun. To be exact, it wasn't a gun. "A musket" would be a more correct name for the weapon the man was holding. The thing was approximately six inches taller than Jan himself, the gun barrel had notches in it and was bell-shaped at the end, the rifle stock and butt stock were worn from long handling, the slow match was hanging down. In other words, the item's rightful place was long ago in an Armoury Museum. Such guns usually shoot like cannons, and they recoil on the shoulder with such a feedback that if unprepared for the shock a person drops down on the ground like a sheaf.

For some reason, perhaps unrelated, I recalled with pleasure the marvellous English six-shooter, now sitting tight in my pocket.

Hardly able to move his unbending legs, Jan led the coachman to the door. I noticed that even his hands were trembling.

"Dependable aid for the mistress," I thought.

But the mistress touched me by the shoulder and invited me to follow after her into the "apartments". We passed through yet another small room, the old woman opened another door, and I quietly gasped in surprise and delight.

Meeting our gaze was a great entrance hall, a kind of a drawing room, a customary thing in noble castles of the old time. And oh! The beauty there!

The room was so enormous that my gloomy reflection in the mirror somewhere on the opposite wall seemed no bigger than the joint of my little finger. The floor was made of oak "bricks" already quite worn. The exceptionally high walls were bordered at the edges with shining fretwork that was blackened by the years and the windows were sitting almost under the ceiling, small ones in deep lancet niches.

In the dark we had evidently hit on a side porch, for to the right of me was the front entrance, a wide lancet door, divided by wooden columns into three parts. Flowers, leaves and fruit carved on the columns were cracked with time. Behind the door in the depth of the hall was the entrance door, a massive piece of oak, bound by darkened bronze nails with square heads. And above the door I saw an enormous dark window, looking into the night and darkness. The window was embraced in a ship of forged iron, a masterpiece of workmanship.

I walked along the hall in amazement of this kind of splendour, and how all had been neglected. There was massive furniture along the walls – it squeaked even in answer to footfalls. Here an enormous wooden statue of St. George, one of the somewhat naive creations of the Belarusian national genius, and at the feet of the statue a layer of white dust, as if someone had spread flour over it; this unique work had been spoiled by woodlice. And here hanging down from the ceiling was a chandelier, also of surprising beauty, but with more than half of its pendants missing.

It might have seemed that no one lived here, were it not for an enormous fireplace, its flames lighting up the space around it with an uncertain flickering light.

Almost in the middle of this splendid entrance hall a marble staircase led up to the first floor, where everything was almost the same as on the ground floor. The same enormous room, even a similar fireplace also lit, except that on the walls the black wood, probably oak, alternated with shabby coffee coloured damask wallpaper and on this wallpaper in all their splendour hung portraits in heavy frames. In addition, a small table and two armchairs stood near the fireplace.

The old woman touched me by the sleeve:

"Now I'll lead you to your room. It's not far from here along the hall. And afterwards... perhaps you would like to have supper?"

I did not refuse, for I hadn't eaten anything all day.

"Well then, sir, wait for me..."

She returned in about ten minutes with a broad smile on her face and in a confidential tone delivered the following:

"You know the village goes to bed early. But we here don't like to sleep. We try to go to bed as late as possible. The mistress doesn't like visitors. I don't know why she suddenly consented to admit you into her house, and even lets you share her supper table. I hope, sir, you will excuse me. You are evidently the most worthy of all those who have been here in the last three years."

"You mean then," I said, surprised, "that you are not the mistress?"

"I'm the housekeeper," the old woman answered with dignity. "I am the housekeeper. In the best of the best houses, in a good family, understand this, Mr. Merchant. In the very best of the best families. This is even better than being the mistress of a family not of the very best."

"What family is this?" I asked imprudently. "Where am I?"

The old woman's eyes blazed with anger.

"You are in the castle of Marsh Firs. And you ought to be ashamed of yourself not to know the owners. They are the Yanovskys. You understand, the Yanovskys! You must have heard of them!"

I answered that I had, of course, heard of them. This statement of mine must have reassured the old woman.

With a gesture worthy of a queen, she pointed to an armchair, approximately as queens do in the theatre when they point to the executioner's block ready for their unlucky lover: "There's your place, you ill fated one". Then she asked to be excused and left me alone.

The change in the old woman surprised me greatly. On the ground floor she moaned and lamented, spoke with that expressive intonation of the people, on the first floor she immediately changed, became the devil alone knows what. Apparently, on the ground floor she was at home, whereas on the first she was nothing but the housekeeper, a rare guest, and her demeanour changed accordingly.

Remaining alone, I began to examine the portraits. About seventy of them, they gleamed on the walls, some were ancient and some quite new – and a sad sight they made.

Here on one of the oldest pictures, a nobleman dressed in something like a sheepskin coat, his face the face of a peasant, broad, healthy, with thick blood in his veins.

Here another, this one already in a long silver-woven tunic with a girdle, a wide beaver collar falling across his shoulders. *A sly weasel you were, young man!* Next to him a mighty man with rocks for shoulders and sincere eyes, in a red cloak, at his head a shield with the family coat-of-arms, the top half smeared with black paint. Farther on the wall others just as strong, but with oily eyes, lopped off noses, their lips hard.

Beyond them portraits of women with sloping shoulders, women created for caresses. Faces were such that would have made an executioner weep. Most likely some of these women did actually lay their heads on the executioner's block in those hard times. It was unpleasant to think that these women took their food from their plates with their hands, and bedbugs made their nests in the canopies of their beds.

I paused at one of the portraits, fascinated by a strangely wonderful, incomprehensible smile, a smile that our old masters painted so inimitably. The woman looked at me mysteriously and compassionately.

"You there, you little man," her look seemed to say. "What have you seen in life? Oh! If only you could have seen the torches ablaze on the walls of this hall during our parties, if only you could have known the delight in kissing your lovers till they bled, to make two men fight a duel, to poison one, to throw another to the executioner, to aid your husband in firing from the tower at the attackers, to send yet another lover to the grave for love of you, and then to take the blame on yourself, to lay your head with its white wide forehead and intricate hair-do under the axe."

I swear upon my honour that that is what she said to me, and although I hate aristocrats, I understood, standing before these portraits, what a fearful thing is 'an ancient family', what an imprint it leaves on its descendants, what a heavy burden their old sins and degeneration lay on their shoulders.

I understood also that uncountable decades had gone by since the time when this woman sat for the painter. Where are they now, all these people with their hot blood and passionate desires, how many centuries have thundered over their decaying bones?

I felt the wind of time whistling past my back, and the hair on my head stood on end. I also felt a kind of cold that reigned in this house, the cold that the fireplaces could not drive out even if they burned day and night.

Enormous, gloomy halls with their dusty air, with their creaking floors, their dark corners, their eternal draughts, the smell of mice, and their cold. Such a cold that made your heart freeze, a cold of which centuries had gone into making, a cold created by an entailed estate, the exclusive right of inheritance belonging to the eldest son, by an enormous, now impoverished and almost extinct family.

Oh! What a cold it was! If our late decadents, once singing praises to the dilapidated castles of the gentry, were left here overnight, for just one night, they would very soon ask to be taken out and put on the grass in the warm sunshine.

A brave rat ran diagonally across the hall. I winced and turned to more of the portraits. These portraits were of a later period and altogether different. The men had a kind of a hungry look, a discontented look. Their eyes like those in old seladons, on their lips an incomprehensible, subtle smile and an unpleasant causticity. The women were different too. Their lips too full of lust, their looks mannered and cold. And very obvious were their hands, now much weaker hands. Beneath their white skin, both in the men and the women, one could visibly distinguish blue veins. Their shoulders had become narrower and were thrust forward, while the expression on their faces showed a markedly increased voluptuousness.

Life, what cruel jokes you play on those who for centuries live an isolated life, and come into contact with the people only to bring bastards into the world!

It was difficult and unpleasant for me to look at all this. Again that feeling of a sharp, incomprehensible cold...

I did not hear any steps behind my back, it was as if someone had come flying through the air. I simply felt all of a sudden that someone was already standing behind me, piercing my back. Under the influence of this look, I turned around. A woman stood behind me, staring at me with an inquiry in her eyes, her head slightly bent. I was stunned. It seemed to me as if the portrait that had just been talking to me had suddenly come to life and the woman in it had stepped down from it.

I don't even know what the two had in common. The one in the portrait – and I made sure to confirm that she was in her place – was tall, well built, with a great reserve of vitality, quite cheerful, strong and beautiful. At the same time the one that stood in front of me was simply a puny creature.

Still there was a resemblance, a kind of a prompt that can force us to recognize two men in a crowd as being brothers, although they may not have too many similarities, one a dark haired and the other a blond.

Yet, there was more. The women's hair was exactly alike, their noses of the same form, their mouths with the same kind of slit and their identically white even teeth. Add to this a general resemblance in the expression on their faces, something ancestral, eternal.

And nevertheless I had never before seen such an unpleasant looking person. Everything alike, and yet everything somehow different. Short of stature, thin as a twig, thighs almost underdeveloped and a pitiable chest, light blue veins on the neck and hands, in which there seemed to be no blood at all – so weak she appeared, like a small stem of wormwood.

Very thin skin, a very fragile neck, even her hair styled in a near inexpressive fashion. This seemed so very strange because her hair was actually of the colour of gold, voluminous and surprisingly beautiful. Whatever for was that absurd knot at the back of her head, escaped me.

Her features were so expressive, sharply defined, regularly proportioned that they would have served as a model for even a great sculptor, but I doubt whether any artist would have been tempted to use her as a model for Juno; seldom does one see such an unpleasant face, a face to be pitied. Crooked lips, deep shadows on both sides of her nose, pale greyish complexion, black eyes with a fixed and incomprehensible expression.

"The poor thing is devilish in her ugliness," I thought, sympathizing with her, and I lowered my gaze.

I know many women who would never to their dying days have forgiven me my lowered eyes, but this one was probably accustomed to seeing something similar on the faces of the people she met with. She paid absolutely no attention to my behaviour.

I was unpleasantly surprised by this frankness of hers, to put it mildly. What was it, a subtle calculation or naivety? But no matter my effort to analyze this distorted face, I couldn't see in it any ulterior motive.

No doubt her face was artless, like that of a child. But her voice was most convincing. Slow, lazy, indifferent, at the same time timid and broken like the voice of a forest bird.

"To your knowledge, as a matter of fact, I saw you before!"

"Where?" I was frankly amazed.

"Not that I know for sure. I see many people. It seems to me that I've seen you in my sleep... Often... Didn't you ever happen to feel as if you had lived somewhere formerly and long ago... and now you discover you are looking at something you had seen a long, long time ago..?"

I am a healthy man. And I had not yet known then what I know now, that something similar sometimes happens to nervous people with a very keen perception. The connection between primary concepts and subsequent notions is somehow disturbed in the memory, and things that might be very much alike seem identical to them; in objects entirely unknown to them they uncover something long known and known solely to them. Whereas the consciousness – ever a realist – resists this. And so it happens that to them an object appears simultaneously unfamiliar and mysteriously familiar.

I must emphasize I had not known this fact of medical science at the time. And even though a thought that this girl could tell a lie never even for a moment entered my head, sincerity and indifference that I felt in her words alerted me.

"I have seen you," she repeated. "But who are you? I do not know you."

"My name is Andrey Belaretsky, Miss Yanovsky. I am an ethnographer."

She wasn't at all surprised. On the contrary, on learning that she knew this word, it was I who was surprised.

"Well, that is very curious. And what interests you? Songs? Sayings? Proverbs?"

"Legends, Miss Yanovsky, old local legends."

I got terribly frightened. It was no laughing matter for she suddenly straightened up as if an electric current had been passed through her, torturing her. Her face became pale, her eyelids closed.

I rushed over to her, supported her head, and put a glass of water to her lips, but she had already come to her senses. Her eyes sparkled with such indignation, with such an inexplicable reproach in them that I felt as if I were the worst scoundrel on Earth; I hadn't had the faintest idea why I should not have spoken about my profession. A vague thought flashed through my mind that something was connected with the old rule to never speak of woe in the house whose master has been hanged.

In a broken voice she said:

"And you... And you, too... why do you torture me, why does everybody..?"

"My dear lady! Upon my word of honour, I had nothing harmful in mind, I don't know anything... Look, here is my certificate from the Academy. Here is a letter from the governor. I've never been here before. Please forgive me, for heaven's sake, if I have caused you any pain."

"Never mind," she said. "Never mind, calm yourself, Mr. Belaretsky... It's simply that I hate what savages can create in the minds of savages. Perhaps you, too, will someday understand what it is... this gloom. Whereas I understood that all too well long before. But I'll be long dead prior to everything becoming clearer to me."

I realized it would be tactless of me to question her any further, and I kept silent. It was only after a while, when she had calmed down, that I said:

"I beg your pardon for having disturbed you, Miss Yanovsky, I see that I have immediately become an unpleasant person for you. When must I leave? It seems to me the sooner the better."

Again that distorted face!

"Ah! As if that were the trouble! Don't leave us. You will offend me deeply if you leave now. And besides," her voice began to tremble, "What would you say if I asked you to remain here, in this house, for at least two or three weeks? Until the season of the dark autumn nights are over?"

Her look began to wander. On her lips a pitiful smile appeared.

"Afterwards there will be snow... And footprints in the snow. Of course, you will do as you see fit. However, it would be unpleasant for me were it to be said of the last of the Yanovskys that she had forgotten the custom of hospitality."

She said 'the last of the Yanovskys' in such a way, this eighteen year old girl, that my heart was wrung with pain.

ULADZIMIR KARATKEVICH

"Well then," she continued, "If this awful stuff interests you, how can I possibly object? Some people collect snakes. We here have more spectres and ghosts than living people. Peasants, shaken with fever, tell amazing and fearful stories. They live on potatoes, bread made of grasses, porridge without butter, and on fantasy. You mustn't sleep in their huts: it's dirty there and congested, and all is evilly neglected. Go about the neighbouring farmsteads, there for money that will be spend on bread or vodka, warming up for a moment the blood that is everlastingly cold from malaria, they will tell you everything. And in the evening return here. Dinner will be ready, awaiting you here, as well as a place to sleep in, and a fire in the fireplace. Remember this – I am the mistress here, and the peasants obey me. Agreed?"

By this time I was already quite certain that nobody obeyed this child, nobody was afraid of her, and nobody depended on her. Perhaps, had it been anybody else, I might have smiled into her eyes, but in this "command" of hers there was so much entreaty that I did not yet quite understand that I answered with my eyes lowered:

"Alright. I agree to your wish."

She did not notice the ironic gleam in my eyes and for a moment even blushed, apparently because somebody had obeyed her.

The leftovers of a very modest supper were removed from the table. We remained in our armchairs before the fireplace. Yanovsky looked around at the black windows behind which the branches of enormous trees rubbed against, and said:

"Perhaps you are ready for sleep now?"

This strange evening had put me into such a state of mind that I had lost all desire for sleep. And here we were sitting side by side looking into the fire.

"Tell me," she suddenly said. "Do people everywhere live as we do here?"

I glanced at her, puzzled. Hadn't she ever been anywhere outside of her home? As if she had read my thoughts, she said: "I've never been anywhere beyond this plain in the forest... My father was the best man living on Earth, taught me on his own for he was a very educated man. I know, of course, what countries there are in the world. I know that not everywhere do our fir-trees grow, but tell me, is it everywhere so damp and cold for man to live on this Earth?"

"Many find life cold on this Earth, Miss Yanovsky. The people who thirst for power are to blame for that, they wish for power that is beyond their ability to exert. Also money is guilty, money for the sake of which people grab each other by the throat. However, it seems to me that not everywhere is it so lonely as it is here. Over there, beyond the forests, there are warm meadows, flowers, storks in the trees, as well as impoverished and oppressed people; but there the people somehow seek escape. They decorate their homes, women laugh, children play. While here there is very little of all that."

"I suspected just that," she said. "That world is alluring, but I am not needed anywhere except at Marsh Firs. And what should I do there to earn my living should I be in need of money? Tell me, such things as love and friendship, do they exist there, at least now and then? Or is it so only in the books that are in my father's library?"

Again I did not for a moment suspect that this was an equivocal joke, though I was in quite an awkward position, sitting at night in a room and conversing with a young lady whom I hardly knew, talking about love, the subject having been brought up by her...

"Sometimes those things happen there."

"There, that's what I say. It's impossible that people lie. But here we have nothing of the kind. Here we have the quagmire and gloom. Here we have wolves... wolves with fiery eyes. On such nights it seems to me that nowhere on this Earth, nowhere does the sun shine."

It was terrifying to see a dry black gleam in her eyes, and to quickly change the subject, I said:

"It can't be that your father and mother did not love each other."

Her smile was enigmatic:

"Our people do not love. This house sucks the life out of its people. And then who told you that I had a mother? I don't remember her, nobody in this house remembers her. At times it seems to me that my appearance in this world was of my own doing."

In spite of the naivety of these words, I understood that this was an unknown scene from *Decameron* and one must not laugh; it was all so terrible. A young girl was sitting near me talking of things that she had long been hiding in her heart and which, however, had no greater reality for her than angels in heaven had for me.

"You are mistaken," I growled, "love nevertheless, even though rarely, does come our way on Earth."

"Wolves cannot love. And how can one love, if death is all around? Here it is, beyond the window."

A very thin, transparent hand pointed to the black spots on the windows. And again her fine voice:

"Your books lie that love is a great mystery, that love is happiness and light, that when it comes to a man and there is no reciprocation, he kills himself."

"Oh no, love happens!," I answered, "Otherwise there would be neither men nor women."

"A lie. People kill others, not themselves. I don't believe in it, I've never experienced it, which means that it doesn't exist. I don't wish to kiss anybody like in those books of yours, – people bite each other."

Even now such talk frightens some men, what then is there to say about those times? I am not an unfeeling sort of person, but I felt no shame; she spoke about love as other women do about the weather. She did not know what love was, she had not been awakened, was still quite cold, as cold as ice. She could not even understand whether love was shameful or not. And her eyes stared frankly into mine.

This could not have been coquetry. This was a child. No, not even a child, but a living corpse.

She wrapped her shawl around her and said:

"Death reigns on Earth. That I know. I don't like it when people lie about what has never existed on our Earth."

Beyond the walls the wind kept howling. She shrugged her shoulders and said quietly:

"A terrible land, terrible trees, terrible nights."

And again I saw that same expression on her face that I did not understand.

"Tell me, they are large cities – Vilnia and Miensk?"

"Rather large, but Moscow and Petersburg are larger."

"And there, too, the nights bring no comfort to people?"

"Not at all. Lights burn in the windows, people laugh in the streets , on skating rings, under shining street lamps."

She became thoughtful.

"That might be so over there. But here not a single light in the dark. Surrounding this old park by two miles on every side, lonely huts are asleep, sleeping without any lights. In this house there are about fifty rooms, many halls and passages with dark corners. It was built so long ago... And it is a cold house, for our ancestors forbade laying stoves, they allowed only fireplaces in order to be unlike their common neighbours. The fireplaces burn day and night, but even so there is dampness in the corners and cold everywhere. And in these fifty rooms there are only three people. The housekeeper sleeps on the ground floor and the watchman also. And in one of the wings behind the alleys and the park lives the cook and the washerwoman. They live well. And in the second annex to this house, with its separate entrance, lives my manager, Ihnat Bierman–Hatsevich. Whatever we need this manager for, I do not know, but such is the order of things. And in this house, on the entire first floor with its thirty rooms, I am the only one. And it is so uncomfortable here that I'd like to get into some corner, wrap myself up in my blanket as a child does, and sit there. Now for some reason or other it feels good and so quiet here as it has not been for two years, since the time my father died. And it is all the same to me now whether there are lights beyond these windows or not. You know, it is very good when there are people beside yourself..."

She led me to my room. Her room was only two doors away, and when I had already opened the door, she said:

"If old legends and traditions interest you, look for them in the library, in the bookcase for manuscripts. A volume of legends about our family must be there. And some other papers as well."

And then she added: "Thank you, Mr. Belaretsky."

I don't know what she thanked me for, and I confess of not thinking about it much when I entered a small room without any door bolts, and put my candle on the table.

There was a bed there as wide as the Koydanov Battlefield. Over the bed was an old canopy. On the floor a threadbare carpet that had properties of a wonderful piece of work. The bed, evidently, was made up with the help of a special stick, as they used to do two hundred years ago, and what a big stick it was. The stick stood near the bed. Besides the bed there were a chest of drawers, a high writing desk and a table. Nothing else.

I undressed, lay down under a warm blanket, having put out the candle. And immediately beyond the window the black silhouettes of the trees appeared on a blue background, and sounds were heard, sounds evoking dreams.

For some reason or other a feeling of abandonment overcame me to such a degree that I stretched out, drew my hands over my head and, almost beginning to laugh, so happy did I feel, I fell asleep, as if I had fallen into some kind of a dark abyss over a precipice. It seemed to me I was dreaming that someone was making short and careful steps along the hall, but I paid no attention to that, and as I slept in my dream I was glad that I was asleep.

This was my first night and the only peaceful one in the house of the Yanovskys at Marsh Firs.

The abandoned park, wild and blackened by age and moisture, was disturbed for many acres around, filled with the noise of an autumn rain.

CHAPTER TWO

The following day was a usual grey day, one of those that often occur in Belarus in autumn. In the morning I did not see the mistress of the house. I was told that she slept badly at night and therefore got up late. The housekeeper's face, when I was having breakfast, was a kind of a vinegar sour face and so sulky and haughty, it was unpleasant to look at her. Therefore I did not stay long at the table, took my tattered notebook, five pencils, put on my cloak that had dried overnight, and having asked the way, set off for the nearest project for myself that I could think of – one or two huts in a forest, the beginning of a future village.

I immediately felt better, although nothing in the surroundings made for merriness. Only from here, from this wet footpath, could I take a good look at the castle. At night it had seemed smaller to me, for both of its wings were safely hidden in the thicket of the park and the entire ground floor was completely overtaken by the lilac flower that had grown completely wild. And beneath the lilac grew yellow dahlias, pulpy burdock, dead nettle and other rubbish. Here and there as in all very damp places, greater celandine stuck out its web footed stalks, and sweetbriar and solanum grew wild as well. On the damp soil amidst the various herbs lay branches, covered in white mold, broken off, apparently, by the wind.

Traces of the human touch were seen only in front of the entrance where late dark purple asters shone in a large flower bed. And the house looked so gloomy and cold that it wrung my heart. It was a two-storeyed building with an enormous belvedere, with turrets along the sides, though not very large ones. Striking was the lack of architecture characteristic of the magnificent constructions of those days when our ancestors ceased building castles but nevertheless demanded that their architects should erect mansions resembling this old lair under all that moss.

I decided to go to the farmstead only after I had examined everything here, so I continued along the lane. The devil alone knows what kind of a fool had thought of planting fir trees in such a gloomy place, but it had been done, and the park which must have been hundreds of years old was only a little pleasanter than Dante's famous forest. The firs were so thick that two persons together could not have encircled them with their arms, and they approached the very walls of the castle, their branches knocking at the windows, their blue-green tops rising above the roof. Their trunks were covered by a grey border of moss and lichen, the lower branches hung down to the ground like tents, and the alley was a reminder of a narrow path between hills. Gigantic, gloomy almost bare linden trees could be seen here and there at a close proximity to the very house, dark from the rain. And only one thick oak tree, evidently well looked after, for its top was several metres higher than those of the tallest firs.

My feet stepped softly along the coniferous path. Smoke came from the left and I went in the direction of the smell. Soon the trees were not so dense anymore and an overgrown wing with boarded-up windows came into view.

"About half a mile from the castle," I thought. "If, let's say, someone took it into his head to kill the owners – nobody would hear anything, even if a gun were fired."

ULADZIMIR KARATKEVICH

At the very windows a small cast-iron pot stood on two bricks, and an old hunchbacked woman was stirring something in it with a spoon. The stoves produced too much smoke and therefore the food was prepared in the open air until the late autumn.

And again the green but dismal alleyway of trees. I walked until I came to the place where we had entered the park the night before. The marks that our carriage had made were still visible. The forged iron fence, a surprisingly fine piece of work, had fallen down long ago, and broken into pieces it lay there thrown aside. Birch trees had grown through its curves. Behind the fence, where the alleyway turned to the left and dragged on leading to nobody knew where, lay a brown endless plain with twisted trees here and there, enormous stone boulders, and the green windows of the quagmire, into one of which we had, evidently, almost fallen yesterday. At seeing this I grew cold with terror.

A lonely crow was circling above this distressing place.

I returned home from the farmstead towards evening, so exhausted I could hardly pull myself together. I began to think that this would last forever. These brown plains, the quagmire, the people more dead than alive from feverish mania, the park that was dying of old age – all this hopeless land was nevertheless my own, my native land, covered in the day by clouds, and in the night by a wild moonlight, or else by an endless rain pouring down over it.

Nadzezhda Yanovsky awaited me in the same room and again that strange expression on her distorted face, that same indifference to her clothes. There were some changes only on the table where a late dinner was served.

The dinner was a most modest one and did not cost the mistress a kopeck, for all this food was prepared from local products. In the middle of the table stood a bottle of wine and it too was apparently from their own cellars. The rest was a firework of flowers and forms. In the middle stood a flower vase and in it two small yellow maple branches. Beside it, though probably from another set, a large silver soup bowl, a silver salt cellar, plates, several dishes. However, it was not the layout of the table that surprised me, not even that the dishes were all from different sets, darkened with age, and here and there, somewhat damaged. What surprised me was the fact that they were of ancient local workmanship.

You no doubt know that two or three centuries ago, the silver and gold dishes in Belarus were mainly of German make and were imported from Prussia. These articles, richly decorated with "twists and turns", with figures of holy men and angels, were so sugary sweet that it was nauseating, but nothing could be done about it, it was the fashion.

But this was our own. The clumsy stocky little figures on the vase, a characteristic ornament. And the women depicted on the salt cellar had even the somewhat wide face of the local women.

There stood also two wine glasses of iridescent ancient glass which today cannot be bought even for gold. The edge of one wineglass, the one standing at my hostess's place, was somewhat chipped.

The last and the only sun ray that day shone in through the window, lighting up in it dozens of varicoloured little lights.

The mistress had probably noticed my look and said:

"This is the last of three sets which were left by our forefather, Roman Zhysh-Yanovsky. But there is this stupid belief that the set had probably been presented to him by King Stakh."

Today she was somehow livelier, did not even seem to be so bad-looking, she evidently liked her new role.

We drank wine and finished eating, talking almost all the time. It was a red wine, red as pomegranate, and very good. I became quite cheerful, made the mistress laugh, and two not very healthy pink spots appeared on her cheeks.

"But why did you add to the name of your ancestor this nickname 'Zhysh'?"

"It's an old story," she answered, becoming gloomy again. "It seems it happened during a hunt. An aurochs charged the somewhat deaf king behind his back and the only one who saw it was Roman. He shouted: 'Zhysh'! This in our local dialect means 'Beware'. And the King turned about, but running aside, fell. Then Roman shot, at the risk of killing the King, and the bullet struck the aurochs in the eye. The aurochs fell down almost beside the King. After that a harquebus was added to our coat-of-arms and the nickname 'Zhysh' to our surname."

"Such incidents could have occurred in those days," I confirmed. "Forgive me, but I know nothing that concerns heraldry. The Yanovskys, it seems to me, go back to the 12th century?"

"To the 13th," she said. "And better if they didn't. These laws concerning one's origin are pure foolishness, but you cannot fight them. These fireplaces, this necessity for one of the heirs to live in this house, the ban on selling it... Whereas we are actually beggars. And this house, this awful house... It is as if some curse has been put upon us. We were twice deprived of our family coat-of-arms, were persecuted. Almost none of our ancestors died a natural death. This one here in the red cloak was still alive when the church performed the funeral service over his body. This woman here with an unpleasant face, a distant relative of ours, by the way, also a distant ancestor of the writer Dostoyevsky, killed her husband and attempted the same with her step-son. She was condemned to death.

It cannot be helped, all this must be paid for by descendants, and with me the Yanovsky family ends. But sometimes I ache so to lie in the warm sun, in the shade of real trees, trees that do not grow here. At times I dream of them – young, very large, airy as a green cloud. And spas, such bright, such full spas that take your breath away, that make your heart stop with happiness. But here this ugly, loathsome quagmire and gloom, these firs..."

The flames in the fireplace had brought a slight flush to her face. Behind the windows the dark night had already fallen and a heavy shower seemed to have begun.

"Oh Mr. Belaretsky! I am so happy that you are here, that a living person is sitting at my side. Usually I sing aloud on such evenings, though I don't really know any good songs, all are old ones from the manuscripts gathered by my grandfather. They are full of horrors. A man leaves a bloody track on the dewy grass, a bell that was long ago drowned in the quagmire tolls at night, just tolls and tolls on and on..."

The days come and the days go,

she began her song, her voice deep and trembling.

The days come and the days go,
A shadow looms over the land.
Skazko and Kirdziay, the Rat,
Raging, fight day and night.
Blood everywhere flows,
Flames spread, steel rings.
Falls our Skazko and calls:
"Where are you, my friends?"
Unheard are his cries.
But Lubka Yurzheuna hears.
Gathers her brethren.

Mighty and brave
Far and wide
They stormily rude
To the distant red marshes.

"The rest is bad, I don't wish to sing it. Only the last lines are good:"

And they loved each other
And in concord they lived
While over the land
Sunshine did reign
Till into the ground
Together were laid.

I was touched, to the very depths of my soul. Such a feeling can arise in a person only when he deeply believes what he is singing about. And what a wonderful song of olden times!

But she suddenly buried her face in her hands and began to sob. Upon my word of honour, my heart bled. I couldn't help it – I have an inexcusable and deep compassion for people.

Today I don't remember the exact words I found then to comfort her. I must say, dear reader, that up to this point in my story, I have been a severe realist. You must know that I do not very much like novels in the spirit of Madam Radcliffe, and would be the first to disbelieve, were anybody to tell me the things that took place later on. And therefore the tone of my story is going to change significantly.

Believe me, were this a product of my imagination, I'd have invented something entirely different. I sure hope to have a good taste, but not a single novelist with even a slightest amount of self-respect would dare to offer serious people anything like what I am about to tell you.

Mind you, I am relating the simple truth, as I mustn't lie. The subject concerns me personally, so important it is for me. Therefore I shall tell everything just as it happened.

We were sitting silent for some time; the fire was dying out and darkness had settled in the corners of the enormous room when I looked at her and was frightened: so wide were her eyes, so strangely bent her head. And her lips so pale, they were invisible.

"Don't you hear anything?"

I listened. My hearing is very good, but only after a minute did I indeed hear what she had heard. Somewhere in the hall, to our left, the parquet was creaking under someone's footsteps.

Someone was walking through the long, endless passages. The steps quieted down for a moment, then were heard again. Tap, tap, tap... went those stamping feet.

"Miss Nadzeya, what on Earth's the matter with you? What's happened?"

"Let me be! It's that Little Man! He's here again, coming after my soul!"

From all this I understood only that somebody was amusing himself with stupid jokes, that somebody was frightening a woman. I paid no attention when she seized me by the sleeve in an attempt to hold me back. I grabbed the poker from the fireplace and rushed off down the steps into the hall. This took only a moment and I opened the door with my foot.

Half of the tremendous hall was drowning in darkness, but I could very well see that no one was there. Nobody was there! Only the footsteps were there, they sounded as previously, somewhat uncertain, but quite loud. They were near me, but little by little they moved farther on to the other end of the hall.

What could I do? Fight an invisible person? I knew that would come to naught, but I thrust the poker straight into the space where I heard the steps. The poker cut the emptiness and with a loud ring fell to the floor.

Funny? At that moment, as you may guess, I was far from laughing. In answer to my vainglorious knight-ly thrust something groaned, followed by two, three steps – and vanished in silence.

Only at that moment did I remember that my hostess was alone in that tremendous, poorly-lit room, so I has-tened back to her.

I had expected to find her unconscious, gone mad with fright, to have died, anything except what I did see. Lady Yanovsky was standing at the fireplace, her face severe, gloomy, almost calm, with that same incomprehensible expression in her eyes.

"In vain you rushed off there," she said. "Of course, you saw nothing. I know, because only I see him and sometimes the housekeeper does, too. And Bierman has seen him."

"Who is 'he'?"

"The Little Man of Marsh Firs."

"But what is he, what does he want?"

"I don't know. He appears when somebody in Marsh Firs must die a sudden death. He may wander around a whole year, but in the end he'll get what he's after."

"It's possible," I joked unsuccessfully, "He'll keep wan-dering for yet another seventy years, before your great grandchildren bury you."

She threw back her head.

"I hate those who get married. And don't dare to jest on this subject. Eight of my ancestors perished in this way. They are the only ones about whom we have re-cords, and the Little Man is always mentioned there."

"Miss Yanovsky, don't worry, but our ancestors be-lieved, by the way, in witches, too. And there have always been people ready to swear they had seen them."

"And my father? My father? This was not notes, this I heard, this I saw myself. My father was an atheist, but he believed in the Little Man, even he believed until the very day when the Wild Hunt put an end to him. I hear him, you understand? Here you cannot convince me otherwise. These steps were heard in our castle almost every day before my father's death."

What could I do? Convince her that it had been auditory hallucinations? But I did not suffer from any hallucinations. I had distinctly heard steps and groans this time. To say that it was some cunning acoustic effect? I do not know whether that would have helped, although half the rumours about ghosts in old houses are based on just such tricks. For example, the famous ghost in the Luxemburg Palace in Dubrowna was finally discovered in the shape of a vessel filled with mercury and gold coins which some unknown joker had bricked up about a hundred years earlier in the flue on the sunny side. No sooner did the night's cold make way for the sun's warmth, than a wild howling and rustling arose in all the rooms on the second floor.

However, is it possible to make a foolish little girl change her mind? Therefore I asked her with an air of importance:

"But who is he, what is he like, this Little Man of Marsh Firs?"

"I saw him three times and each time from afar. Once it was just before the death of my father. The other two, not long ago. I've also heard him perhaps a hundred times. Nor was I ever frightened, except perhaps the last time... just a little, a very little. I went up to him, but he disappeared. It is really a very little man, he reaches up to my chest, skinny, and reminds one of a starved child. His eyes are sad, his hands are very long, and his head is unnaturally long. He is dressed as people used to dress

200 years ago, only in the western manner. His clothes are green. He usually hides from me around the corner of the hall and by the time I run up to him, he disappears, although the hall ends in a blank wall. There is only one room there, and it is bolted with long nails."

I felt sorry for her. An unfortunate creature, she was very likely going mad.

"And that is not all," she went on. "It's perhaps three hundred years since the Lady-in-Blue has been seen in this castle – you see that one there in the portrait. The family belief is that she has quenched her thirst for revenge, but I do not think so. She was not that kind of a person. When they dragged her in 1501 to her execution, she shouted to her husband: 'My bones shall find no peace until the last snake of your race has perished!' And then for almost a hundred years there was no escape from her. It was either a plague or a goblet of poison poured by some unknown person, or death caused by nightmares. She stopped taking revenge only on the great grandchildren... But now I know that she is keeping her word. Not long ago Bierman saw her on the balcony that is boarded up, and others saw her too. I alone have not seen her, but that is her habit – in the beginning she appears before others, but not to the person she is after. That she does only at the hour of his death... My family will end with me. I know that. Not long to wait for it. They shall be satisfied."

I took her hand and pressed it hard, desiring to bring the girl back to her senses, to somehow divert her thoughts from the horrors she was speaking about as if in her sleep.

"You mustn't worry. As far as that goes, I've also become interested in this. There's no place for apparitions in the Steam Age. I swear that the two weeks left for me to spend here, I shall devote to solving this mystery. The devil with it, such nonsense! But one thing, you mustn't be afraid."

She smiled faintly:

"Oh! Don't mind me... I'm accustomed to it. This kind of a parade goes on here every night."

And again the same expression on her face that had spoiled it so, and the one I couldn't understand. It was fright, chronic, horrible fright. Not the fright that makes one's hair stand on end for a moment, but the fright that finally becomes a habitual state impossible to get rid of even in one's sleep. This unfortunate girl would have been good looking, were it not for this constant, terrible fear.

And notwithstanding the fact that I was beside her, she moved up still closer to me to avoid seeing the darkness behind me.

"Oh! Mr. Belaretsky, it's dreadful. What am I guilty of, why must I answer for the sins of my forefathers? An excessive weight has been laid on the weak shoulders of mine. It's a clinging weight and a heavy one. If you could know how much blood, and dirt, how many murders, orphans' tears are on every coat-of-arms of the gentry! How many murdered or frightened to death, how many unfortunates! We haven't the right to exist, even the most honest of us, the very best of us. The blood in our veins is not blue, it's dirty blood. Don't you think that we are all up to the twelfth generation responsible for this and must answer for it, answering with suffering, poverty and death? We were indifferent to the people that suffered tortures side by side with us and from us, we considered the people cattle, we poured out wine, while they shed their blood. They had nothing but bad bread. Mr. Dubatowk, my neighbour, once came to my father and told him an anecdote about a peasant woman who took her son to the priest and the priest treated them to "kuldoons", those delicious baked potato pancakes stuffed with meat and cheese. The child asked what they were. The mother with that innate peasant delicacy pushed him with her foot under the table and whispered: "Hush!" The child ate up what was on his plate, then sighed and said quietly: "And I've eaten a dozen of these hushes." Everybody who heard this anecdote laughed, but I was ready to slap Dubatowk in the face. There's nothing funny in the fact that children have never seen "kuldoons", have never eaten any meat. Their hair is thin, their legs are crooked, at the age of fourteen they are still children, but at twenty-five they are ancient, their faces wrinkled and old. No matter how you feed them, they give birth to the same kind of children, if they do, at all, have any. They answered us with rebellions, savage rebellions, because they suffered unheard of wrongs. And then we had them executed. This one here on the wall, with a beaver collar, tortured his cousin to death because he had deserted to the detachment of Vasil Vashchyla, the leader of the 1740 rebellion.

His cousin's name was Aghei Hrynkievich–Yanovsky. How indifferent we were to everybody and everything. The same two-footed people as we are, they lived on grass, although our land is generous and bountiful. We bartered our land, sold it to greedy neighbours, to anybody who wanted it, while the peasants loved the land like their own mother, and starved for a lack of bread. And who will blame them when they take up their pitchforks and thrust them into our chests? It seems to me that even after a hundred years when we have all died out, if the descendants of these unfortunates accidentally find one of the gentry – they will have the right to kill him. The Earth is not for us."

I looked at her in astonishment. This vehement inspired outburst made her face look unusual. And I suddenly understood she was not at all ugly, not at all! Here before me was an unusual girl, surprisingly beautiful, with a mixture of madness and beauty. Gracious me, what beauty it was! In all probability such were our ancient "prophetesses" who fought in the detachments of Murashka and the Peasant Christ, the leaders of the rebellions around Miensk and in Prineman in the 17th century. It was an unearthly beauty, a tormented face with bitter lips and enormous dry eyes.

And suddenly it all disappeared. Again here in front of me was sitting the previous creature, puny and starved. Only now I knew her true worth.

"Even so, I do not want to die, not at all. How I wish to see the sun, the meadows, so different from those I know, and to hear childish laughter. My desire for life is great, although I haven't the right to live. It is only the dream of life that has given me the strength to endure the experiences of the last two years, even though there is no way out for me. These steps that we hear here at night, the Little Man, the Lady-in-Blue... I know that I shall die. And this is King Stakh's doing. If not for this Wild Hunt of his – we should probably yet live. The Hunt will kill us."

If previously I had been almost entirely indifferent to this emaciated child of the gentry, after her passionate outburst I understood that some miracle had occurred and changed her into a real person. I felt it necessary to help her.

And thus, lying with my eyes open in the darkness of the night, I thought almost till the very morning, that if yet yesterday I had decided to leave this abominable place and this high-born hostess of mine within two days, I should now remain here a week, two weeks, a month, as long as it takes to find the answer to all these secrets and return to this lady the peace she deserves.

CHAPTER THREE

The first thing that I did the following day was to break down the board from the door that was fastened with nails and in which the Little Man, if he were a being of flesh and blood, could have hidden himself. The nails were rusty, panels on the door were whole and a layer of dust three fingers deep covered the room. No one could have hidden himself there and I nailed the door up again. Then I examined all rooms in the other wing and was convinced that no one could have hidden himself there either. Above the hall where I had heard steps, there was an attic in which there were no traces of any footsteps either. To the right there was a door into my room and the room of the mistress of the house, behind which there was a blank wall and behind that the park.

My head was spinning from this all. Could it possibly be that something supernatural really existed in the world? I, a confirmed atheist, could never accept that.

I decided to go to the library and find out at last whatever this Wild Hunt was, about which it was inconvenient for me to question the mistress of the house. Incidentally, I had hopes of finding some old plan of the house there, and to be able afterwards to begin making a methodical search. I knew sometimes special mechanisms were built into the walls of old castles, so-called "listeners-in", that is, secret gaps. In them "voices" – specially shaped pitchers – were usually bricked up to amplify sounds. Thanks to them, the master of the house being at one end of the house could distinctly hear what his guests or servants were saying at the other end.

Perhaps something of the kind was to be found here, too. Some servant or other walked about at night on the ground floor, and his steps resounded up above. It was a faint hope, but truth is sometimes stranger than fiction.

With that in mind, I made my way to the library which was between the ground and first floors in a separate wing.

Seldom had I seen such neglected rooms. The parquet was broken here and there, the enormous windows were covered with dust, the chandeliers, hanging from the ceilings, were in dusty covers. This was, perhaps, the most ancient part of the house, around which the rest of the castle was later built. This thought struck me when I saw a strange room just in front of the library. And here, too, I found a fireplace, but such an enormous one, that an aurochs could have been roasted in it, and nests for the spits even remained in its walls. The windows were small, made of stained glass, the walls were crudely plastered, and the ceiling was crossed by heavy, square, carved beams all covered with smoke. On the walls hung crude old weapons.

In a word, this was a room of "the good old times" when the masters of the house, being the Polish landowners, together with their serfs gathered in one room and sat beside the fire. The women of the household and the servants would be spinning yarn while the master would be playing dice or another game "Twelve Fingers" with the boys. Those idyllic old times!

Forgive me, my dear readers, that I cannot omit describing even a single room. It can't be helped, in his old age a man becomes garrulous. And in addition, you have never seen and never will see anything the like of this, and perhaps it will be interesting to somebody.

The library was in the same style as the entrance hall. High arches, columned windows, armchairs covered with leather that now turned brown with age, enormous closets of moraine oak and books, books, and more books.

Well, how can I pass them by without saying at least a few words! My heart stops beating at these memories. Ancient parchment books, books made of the porous paper, first of its kind, books in which the paper had become yellow with time, paper smooth and glossy. Books of the 17th century which you can immediately recognize by their leather bindings. The red leather of the bindings of the 18th century; the wooden boards, bound with thin black leather, that covered the books of the 16th century.

And the titles, my God, what titles: *The Royal Roussian Catechism*, *An Authentic Chronicle of the Life of Yan Zbarowski*, *Varlaam the Indian*, *A Parable about Fame*, old *Six-Day* manuscripts telling of the creation of the world, collections of ancient legends, *Gesta Romanorum* consisting of two hundred stories, *Trishchan and Izota*, the Belarusian variant of *Bova*, *Apephegma*, *Speech of Mialeshka*. Full house! And there were newer books written in a mannered style, with long titles, such as *Cupid Contrives, or One Thousand Ways and Means an Adoring Lover Can Apply to Make His Beloved Consent to Love's Greed*. Enough already, for otherwise I risk never finishing my narration. I was so carried away by the books that I did not immediately notice another person in the room with me. The man, in the meantime, got up from his armchair and was expectantly looking at me with a pleasant smile on his lips, his eyes smiling too. With one hand on his belly he was timidly holding together the sides of his house coat. We introduced ourselves:

"Andrey Belaretsky."

"Ihnash Bierman–Hatsevich, the estate manager," his voice was quiet, affable.

We seated ourselves. I looked at this man with great interest. What was it that held him in this awful place, this Marsh Firs? Money? But there wasn't any. And he, as if anxious to answer my thoughts, said:

"Look at all these books. They are the ones I am living here for. I am a book lover."

The book-lover was a small badly built man. His face, soft, gentle, too gentle for a man of mid thirties, looked so lifeless, so much like a porcelain doll. In all respects he was too "doll-like". Large grey eyes, long eyelashes, a straight little nose, pleasantly-formed lips. Like a little shepherd on a snuff-box... And his beard hardly grew, as was the case with many Belarusians living in the unhealthy marshland.

"You are from the northern parts of Greater Miensk, aren't you?" I asked.

"Oh, the gentleman is not mistaken, yes," he answered. "Previously I lived in a provincial city, but now here."

Were I asked which trait stood out most of all in this little man, I should say "old fashioned gallantry". He was extremely well bred, this little doll-like man, bred in the spirit of that provincial gallantry of the gentry, a gallantry that makes us laugh. When you look at such people, it seems that the children of their families, while playing hide-and-seek hid themselves under their grannies' woollen, six-pieced skirts, while grannies – not skirts – busied themselves knitting stockings or darning new socks so that they should not wear through too quickly.

This impression, however, soon vanished. Something of cruelty and puritanical standoffishness was in his eyes, in his pursed lips. But the man that he was, that could not be taken away from him. He was a real connoisseur of books. That I understood in about twenty minutes. And moreover, I became convinced that this self-taught man knew ancient literature no worse than I did, being a man with a university education.

Therefore I directed our conversation towards the subject of the "Wild Hunt".

"Why does this subject interest you?"

"I am an ethnographer."

"Oh, then, of course. However, I doubt whether my modest person can tell you about that in a way required by so lofty a guest. Perhaps better to allow the yellowed pages of the books to do that. The gentleman understands the literary language of the 17th century, doesn't he?"

With an artistic movement of his thin, twice as long as normal fingers he opened one of the bookcases.

And there on my knees was an enormous volume written in a calligraphic hand in small letters turned brown with age: "The year one thousand six hundred and one knew no peace on this land. Judge Balvanovich has only just now investigated the murder – the ferocious murder – of His Worship Yanuk Babayed, committed by his serfs. And in other places, too, there was no peace. The cudgel came to the city of Vitsiebsk, to Krychaw and Mstsislaw, and here too the serfs brought death and murder and savagery. Fourteen landowners were killed, and it was said that three more were beaten so hard that it was uncertain whether they would live."

But it is probably too long winded to copy this in full. Therefore I shall relate the contents of this legend in a simple way.

In those days it was not only the serfs who rebelled. The ancient Belarusian gentry, deeply offended by the new order, also rebelled. In the vicinity of Marsh Firs the situation was particularly restless. Here, in the Chadanowsky virgin forest, sat the lame Father Yarash Shtamet who supported the high-born Belarusian landowner Stakh Horsky, a relative through his ancestors of the Vilnia Prince Alexander. This proud young man had but one aim: to achieve independence. He had everything on his side: the royal blood which flowed in his veins and was very important at the time, the support of the Greek Orthodox Church believers and the "Forest Brethren", the talent of a warrior, and what was most important – the awful poverty, the hopeless situation of the peasantry. The young leader was already called King throughout the entire region.

He gathered his forces in the meantime, and with great diplomacy clouded the heads of the representatives of the State Power. According to the manuscript his forces already consisted of eight thousand horsemen who were hiding partly in the virgin forest, and partly in his castle.

In the late autumn of 1602 all was finally ready. In the surrounding churches the peasants took the oath of allegiance to King Stakh, and with an unexpected stroke he seized the strongest castle in the district. They were only awaiting Yarash Shtamet with his followers, and since the army was strong, and the King decisive and resolute, a bright new page might have been written in the history of Belarus.

Roman Yanovsky, a powerful magnate, the owner of Marsh Firs, was the only one who was not enthusiastic about King Stakh. The King suspected that Roman had entered into reprehensible relations with the Lithuanian hetman who was a sort of a defense minister in Great Duchy of Lithuania and the Belarusian state during the Middle Ages, and even with the Roman Catholic Church. He warned Yanovsky that that would end badly for him. Yanovsky assured him of his respect and devotion and King Stakh believed him. He mixed his blood and Roman's in a goblet, and then both parties drank it. Stakh presented Roman with a silver dish.

It is unknown what had compelled Roman to decide on the following move. We know, however, that he was a friend of the lawful King. He invited King Stakh to go hunting with him, and the King came to him with his hunters, a group of twenty men. Shtamet was to appear at the castle the following day and there was plenty of time. The King decided to make a short delay as the object of their hunt was a very tempting animal – the marsh lynx which reminded one in size and colour of a tiger, and which at that time was already rare in our virgin forests, and afterwards entirely disappeared.

What Roman had planned was black treachery. Wouldn't God have blessed King Stakh's reign if he had seized the throne of his ancestors, even though he was a muzhyk king, even though he had rebelled against the lording sovereigns?

King Stakh arrived at Marsh Firs, and in his honour the castle was decorated with lights and feasting began. And he drank and made merry with the landowner, Roman, and the other landowners, and of these gentlemen there were, perhaps, a hundred and thirty. And at night they rode off on the hunt, since the nights were bright, and on such nights the marsh lynx leaves its bushy haunts and walks about the plain from Marsh Firs to the Kurhany and Pniuchi groves and catches not only cattle but also solitary wayfarers.

And that is why everybody hates the marsh lynx and kills it. The wolf would pass by, and the forest lynx would more often turn away, while the marsh lynx would not – he was a man-eater.

And so all the guests left, and Roman left to hunt the marsh lynx together with the King's hunt and his faithful old friend, his beater Alachno Varona, and with Dubatowk of the petty Polish gentry. And the night turned out to be one in which the moon barely shone and hardly anything was visible, and although it was autumn, blue marsh lights were skipping about in the swamps.

And people extinguished the lights in their dwellings, and, perhaps, even God moved by his indescribable wisdom, extinguished the lights in some human souls, too. And Roman and King Stakh lagged behind their beaters.

They had hardly taken a look around, when a marsh lynx sprang out from the bushes, knocked down Roman's horse, and tore out a piece of the horse's stomach together with his intestines, for such was this animal's habit. And Roman fell, and he felt mortal terror, for the animal, that was wider and longer than the man, looked at him with fiery eyes.

At this moment Stakh jumped down from his daredevil horse straight onto the animal's back, grabbed it by the ear, tore its snout from Roman, who was lying on the ground, and with his short sword slashed at its throat. The lynx shook Stakh off with its paw and pounced hard on him, but at this moment Roman jumped down and broke the skull of the man-eater with his fighting calk. And so the three of them lay there, and Roman helped the King to stand up, and said:

"We are quits, my friend. You saved my life, and I your heart."

When the other hunters met them, they all decided to spend the night in the forest and drink again and make merry, for their souls and their hearts had not yet had enough food and drink after the struggle with the lynx, and they asked for more wine. They made a camp-fire in the forest and began to drink. It was so dark when the moon disappeared, that on making a step from the fire you could not see the fingers on your hand. They took the barrel of wine that Roman had brought and they drank and celebrated. Nobody knew that the wine was poisoned, except Roman, Varona and Dubatowk, who had beforehand accustomed themselves to this poison.

Everybody drank, only King Stakh drank little.

Just a moment, Roman. What are you doing, Roman? This man wanted to give up his life for his country. Do you then wish to exchange God's plans for your own? You regret your supremacy, but have you thought that the will of your people is being trampled on, that their language and faith and their souls are being trampled on? You are not thinking of this, your heart is filled with envy and pride.

And they continued drinking until King Stakh's hunters could hardly keep their eyes open. But the King kept on talking, saying how happy he would make everybody when he took his seat on the throne of his forefathers.

And then the Polish landowner, Roman, took his lunge, holding it by the handle with both hands, come up to King Stakh from behind, threw the lunge over his head, and lowered the lunge with its sharp end onto the back of King Stakh's head. The drowsy King lifted his head, looked into Roman's eyes, and his face running with blood was like a terrible wail to God for vengeance.

"But what have you done? We are brothers, aren't we?" And attempting to rise, he shouted:

"Why have you sold your people, apostate? You have deprived many people of their happiness now."

Roman struck him with his sword a second time and Stakh fell, but he had not yet lost the gift of speech:

"Now beware, you traitor! My curse on you and your evil kin! May the bread in your mouth turn to stone, may your women remain childless, and may their husbands choke in their own blood!"

And then, his voice weakening, he said cruelly:

"You've betrayed your land, my former brother! But we shall not die. We'll yet come to you and to your children, and to their heirs, my hunters and I. Unto the twelfth generation will we take revenge ruthlessly, nor shall you hide from us. You hear? Unto the twelfth generation! And each generation shall tremble with greater pain and more terribly than I now at your feet."

And he dropped his head. And his hunters dumb until now, at last came to, and snatched up their knives. And they fought twenty against three, and the battle was a fearful one. But the three conquered the twenty and killed them.

And afterwards they strapped the corpses and the wounded, who were pitifully groaning, to their saddles and drove off the horses, and the horses hastened off in a straight line to the Giant's Gap.

But nobody had noticed that there was a spark of life yet in King Stakh's body. The horses flew on into the night, and a faint moon lit up their long manes, and somewhere ahead of them blue lights skipped about among the mounds.

And from this wild herd came King Stakh's voice:

"To the devil with my soul, if God doesn't help. Wait, Roman! Our horsemen are coming at a gallop to you! Tremble, Roman, and shiver, our eternal enemy. We shall come! We shall avenge!"

And nobody knew that these words were true words; that King Stakh had become a weapon in the hands of the devil for revenge and punishment. No murder whatever deserves such vengeance as fratricide.

Their days were numbered... The beater, Varona, was the first to see the ghosts of Stakh and his followers within two weeks. The Wild Hunt raced on heedlessly; onward it flew across the most terrible quagmire, across the forest, across the rivers.

No tinkling of bits, no ringing of swords. Silent were the horsemen on their horses. Ahead of the phantom King Stakh's Wild Hunt were the swamp lights skipping across the quagmire.

Varona went mad. And Dubatowk perished afterwards. The Lithuanian hetman dispersed peasant armies who were left without a leader; Yarash Shtamet was killed in battle. But Roman Yanovsky was alive and laughed.

Once after hunting, Yanovsky was returning home alone through the heather wasteland, the moon hardly lighting the way for him. Suddenly from somewhere behind him the marsh lights came skipping, the sound of bugles reached him, and the stamping of hoofs was heard but faintly. A moment later, vague apparitions of horsemen outlined themselves against the moonlight. The horses' manes waved with the wind, an unleashed cheetah ran ahead of the phantom Wild Hunt. Noiseless was their flight across the heather and the quagmire. Silent were the horsemen, while the hunting sounds came flying from somewhere on the other side. Ahead of all, dimly lit by the moon's silver, galloped the enormous King Stakh. Brightly burned the eyes of their horses, the riders and the cheetah.

Roman raced on, and they silently and quickly flew after him; the horses sometimes pawed the ground in their flight, and the wild heather sang, and the moon looked down at the chase with indifference.

Roman shouted three times: "The Wild Hunt!" So loud was his voice that he was heard by people even in distant huts. And then the Wild Hunt caught up with him, and his heart failed him. That is how Roman perished.

From that time on many people saw King Stackh's Wild Hunt in the peat-bogs, and although this Wild Hunt penalized not everybody, there were few people whose hearts did not fail them when they saw the dark shadows of the horsemen in the swamps.

In this way Roman's son and the son of his son perished, after whose death I am writing about this for the sake of science and to frighten his descendants who, perhaps, by doing good deeds could deprive the ancient curse of its power over them.

People, beware of the quagmire, beware of the swamps at night, when the blue lights gather and begin dancing in the worst places. There you will see twenty horsemen, their chief racing ahead of all of them, the brim of his hat pulled down over his eyes. No clanging of swords, no neighing of horses.

From somewhere, and only rarely, can be heard the song of a huntsman's bugle. Manes are flying, marsh lights are twinkling under the horses' hoofs.

Across the heather, across the fatal quagmire rides the Wild Hunt, it will ride as long as the world lasts. It is our land, a land we do not love, a terrible land. May God forgive us.

...I tore myself away from the papers and shook my head, desiring to rid myself of the wild images. Bierman looked at me biding his time.

"Well, I beg your pardon, but what does the gentleman think of this?"

"What an awful, a beautiful and fantastic legend!" I exclaimed. "It just begs for the brush of a great artist. There is nothing one's imagination cannot invent!"

"Oh! If this were, I beg your pardon, but a legend... You must know I am a free-thinker, an atheist, as is every person who lives in the spirit of our highly-educated age. But I believe in King Stakh's Wild Hunt. And, indeed, it would be strange not to believe in it. It is due to the Wild Hunt that Roman's descendants have perished and the Yanovsky family has almost become extinct."

"Listen," I said, "I have already said this to one person, and now I shall say it to you. I can be carried away by an old legend, but what can make me believe it? Roman's descendants were killed by The Hunt two hundred years ago. In those days the Mahilow Chronicle seriously claimed that before the war bloody imprints left by the palms of hands appeared on the Mahilow stone walls which a man cannot climb."

"Yes, I remember that," the book lover answered. "And a number of other examples might be given, but they ...m-m... are somewhat frivolous. Our ancestors were such crude people."

"So you see," I said reproachfully. "And you believe in this Hunt."

The doll-like man, it seemed to me, hesitated somewhat.

"Well, and what would you say, Honourable Sir, were I to declare that I had seen it?"

"A fable," I cut him off harshly, "and aren't you ashamed of yourself to frighten a woman with such reports?"

"They are not fables," Bierman turned pink, "This is serious. Not everyone can be a hero, and I, honestly speaking, am afraid. Now I do not even eat at the same table with the mistress, because King Stakh's anger falls also on such as she. You remember, don't you? In the manuscripts?"

"And how did you see the Wild Hunt?"

"As it is described here in the book. I was at Dubatowk's, a neighbour of the Yanovskys, and was returning home from his house. By the way, a descendant of that very Dubatowk. I was walking along the heather wasteland just past the enormous pile of boulders. And the night was rather bright. I didn't hear them appear! They rushed past me directly across the quagmire. Oh! It was frightening!"

A turbid look of confusion flashed in his eyes. And I thought that in this house, and probably, in the entire plain there was something wrong with the brains of the people.

"Isn't there at least one normal person here? Or all of them are insane?" I thought.

"Most important was that they tore along noiselessly. The horses, you must know, of such an ancient breed, they are nowhere to be found today for love or money – they are extinct now. Genuine Palessie's "drygants" with their tendons cut at the tails. The manes waved with the wind, their cloaks were clasped at the right shoulder so that they did not interfere with the hand holding the sword."

"Those caped cloaks were worn only over a coat of mail," I told him disrespectfully. "But what coat of mail could there be when on the hunt?"

"That I know," simply and very frankly did this doll-like man agree with me, fixing his big fawning eyes on me, eyes as tender as a deer's. "Believe me, if I had wished to lie, I could have invented something much better."

"Then I beg your pardon."

"These capes are blown about by the wind behind the riders' backs. Their lances extend upwards in the air, and they race, race like an invasion."

"Again I must beg your pardon. But tell me, perhaps at supper at your neighbour's you had been treated to some mead?"

"I don't drink," Bierman–Hatsevich compressed his lips with dignity. "And I can tell you, they didn't even leave any imprints, and the horses' hoofs were hidden by the fog. The King's face was calm, lifelessly dull, dry if you wish, and quite grey, like a fog. Most importantly, they arrived at the Yanovskys' castle that night. When I returned home I was told that at midnight the ring on the door thundered and a voice cried: "Roman of the twelfth generation, come out!""

"Why Roman?"

"Because Nadzeya, the last of Roman's descendants, is exactly the twelfth generation."

"I do not believe it." I said again, resisting to the very end at seeing Bierman's really pale face. "Give me the Yanovsky family register."

Bierman readily dragged out and unrolled the parchment manuscript with the family tree. And indeed, eleven generations appeared in the list. From the time of Roman the Old. Below the eleventh generation, again Roman, a handwritten entry was made in small letters: "October 26th, 1870 my daughter, Nadzeya, was born. She is the last one, our twelfth generation, and my only child. Cruel fate, remove your curse from us, let only the eleventh generation perish. Have pity on this tiny bundle. Take me, if that is necessary, but let her live. She is the last of the Yanovskys, I set my hopes on you."

"This was written by her father?" I asked, deeply moved, and I thought that I was eight years old when this little girl was born.

"Yes, by him. You see, he had a presentiment about it... His fate is a proof of the truth of the legend about King Stakh. He knew it, they all knew it, for the curse hung over these unfortunate people like an axe. One will go mad, the other will be killed for his brother's money, and another will perish while hunting. He knew and he made preparations for it. He provided the girl with an income, though a miserly one, it's still an income. He found guardians in good time, drew up his will. By the way, I am afraid of this autumn, many of the Yanovskys did not live to see their coming of age. Her birthday will be in two days, and the Wild Hunt has already appeared twice at the walls of the castle. Roman never left the house at night. But two years ago Nadzeya went to visit Kulsha's wife, a relative on her mother's side. The girl stayed there till late. Roman was very nervous when she didn't come home. The Kulsha's house stood near the Giant's Gap. He saddled his horse and rode off. The little girl returned home with Ryhor, the Kulsha's watchman. But the master hadn't come. He was searched for. It was autumn, however, the time when King Stakh's Wild Hunt appeared particularly often. We followed in the tracks of the master's horse, me being Ryhor and I. I was afraid, but Ryhor – not a bit. The tracks led along the road, then turned and began to make loops across the meadow. And Ryhor found other tracks on the side.

He is a good hunter, this Ryhor. How horrible, sir! Those tracks were made by twenty horsemen! And the horseshoes were old ones, with tridents resembling forks. Their like has not been forged here since forever. At times the track disappeared, then within twenty or thirty steps they appeared again, as if the horses had flown across the air. Then we found a wad from the master's gun, I'd have recognized it among hundreds. Ryhor recalled that when he was carrying the little girl home, someone had fired a shot near the Gap. We drove the horses faster, for about five hours had passed; the night had grown dark before the dawn. Soon we heard a horse neighing somewhere. We came out onto a large glade overgrown with heather. Here we noticed that the horses of the Wild Hunt had begun to gallop faster. But the master's horse had stumbled several times, apparently tired."

Bierman's voice became wild, and broke off. "And at the end of the glade just where the Gap begins, we saw the horse still alive. He was lying with a broken leg, screaming as terribly as if he were a man. Ryhor said that the master had to be somewhere nearby. We found his footprints, they stretched from the quagmire. I moved on in their tracks which led to the horse and disappeared right at it. Here, in the damp ground were dents as if a person had fallen there. And nothing more. No footprints nearby. The Hunt had turned about two metres or so from this pace. Either Roman had risen or else King Stakh's horses had reached him by air and taken him away with them. We waited about half an hour, and in the darkness preceding the dawn Ryhor clapped on his forehead and ordered me to gather heather. I, a man of the gentry, obeyed this serf. At that time he had such authority over me as if he were a baron. When we had lit the heather he bent down over the footprints. "Well, what can you say, sir?" he said with an air of apparent superiority. "I don't know why he had to go away from the quagmire, how he got there," I answered, perplexed. Then that boor burst out laughing... "He didn't even think of going away from the quagmire. He, Honourable Sir, he went towards it. And his feet weren't at all turned backwards forward, as you are probably thinking. He retreated to the quagmire, from something fearful. You see, right here he hit against the ground. The horse broke his leg, and Roman flew over its head. He sprained an ankle. You see the print of his right foot is bigger and deeper, that means that he sprained his left foot. He moved backwards towards the quagmire. Let's go there, there we shall probably see the end."

And really, we did see the end. With his torch Ryhor lit the way for us to a precipice in the quagmire, and he said, "You see, here he slipped." I held him by the belt, and he bent over the edge of the precipice and then called to me: "Look!" And here I saw Roman's head sticking out from the brown, oily, dung water of the Gap and I saw his twisted hand with which he had managed to catch at some rotten tree. We dragged him out with great difficulty, but we dragged out a dead man. You see, in these marshes there are often springs in the depths of the pools, and he simply froze there. Besides that, his heart had failed him, the doctor told us afterwards. My God! The fear on his face was so terrible, a fear it was impossible to endure and remain alive! There was a kind of a bite on his hand, his collar was torn off. We tied the corpse to my saddle and rode off. Hardly had we ridden thirty paces than we saw through an opening in the forest vague shadows of floating horses. Surprisingly, there were no sounds of hoofs. And then a horn began to blow somewhere from quite another direction, and so stifled, as if coming through cotton wool. We rode on with the corpse, greatly depressed, the horses were nervous, – they sensed the dead body. And the night was, oh! What a night! And somewhere there blew the horn of the Wild Hunt. Afterwards it appeared only from time to time. Now it's back again... The hour of vengeance has come."

He stopped talking, burying his face in his hands, his white, artistic fingers about twice as long as the fingers of an ordinary person. I kept quiet, but suddenly I lost all patience:

"You should be ashamed of yourself. Men, grown up men, you are unable to defend your mistress? Were it even the devil himself – you should fight, damn it! And why doesn't this Hunt appear all the time? Why hasn't it been here since I've come?"

"Often though they appear, they don't ever come on the eve of holy days or on Wednesdays and Fridays."

"Right... Strange ghosts. How about Sundays?" The desire to give this inert, weak-willed, porcelain fellow a good slap on the face was growing ever stronger within me, for such men as him are unable to perform any kind of deed, be it good or evil. They are not people, but grass-lice that choke the flower-beds. "On St. Philip's Day, on St. Peter's Day they do appear if they are such holy saints, don't they!?"

"God allows them to on Sundays, for, if you re-member, it was on Sunday that Stakh was killed," he answered quite seriously.

"So what then is He, this God of yours?" I barked at him. "Has He then bumped into the devil? You mean to say that He takes the lives of innocent girls in whose blood there is perhaps but one drop of the forefather Roman's blood?"

Bierman was silent.

"A four thousand and ninety-sixth part of Roman's blood flows in her veins," I counted up. "So what is He good for, anyway, this God of yours?"

"Don't blaspheme!" He groaned, frightened. "Whose part are you taking?"

"Too much devilry is going on here, even for such a house..." I didn't give in. "The Little Man, the Lady-in-Blue, and here, in addition, the Wild Hunt of King Stakh. The house has been surrounded from without and within. May it burn, this house!"

"M-m, to be frank with you, Honourable Sir, I don't believe in the Little Man or the Lady."

"Everybody has seen them."

"I haven't seen them, I've heard them. And the nature of the sound is unknown to us. And add to that the fact that I am a nervous person."

"The mistress has seen him."

Bierman lowered his eyes modestly. He hesitated and said quietly:

"I cannot believe everything she says... She... well, in a word, it seems to me that her poor head hasn't been able to cope with all these horrors. She... m–m... she's peculiar in her psychic condition, if not to say anything more."

The same had previously occurred to me, therefore I kept silent.

"But I, too, heard steps."

"Wild fancy. Simply an acoustic illusion. Hallucinations, Honourable Sir."

We sat in silence. I felt that I myself was beginning to lose my sanity with that entire hullabaloo going on here.

In my dream that night King Stakh's Wild Hunt silently raced on. The horses neighed, their hoofs landed, and their engraved bridles rocked. Beneath their feet was the cold heather, bending forward, the grey shadows dashed on, marsh lights glittering on the horses' foreheads. Above them a lonely star was burning, a star as sharp as a needle.

Whenever I awoke that night I heard steps in the hall made by the Little Man, and at times his quiet pitiful moaning and groaning. On with the black abyss of the heavy sleep again; the Wild Hunt, as swift as an arrow, galloped across the heather and the quagmire.

CHAPTER FOUR

The inhabitants of the Giant's Gap were, evidently, not very fond of attending large balls, because it is a rare occurrence in such a corner for someone to inherit a large estate on coming of age. Nevertheless, within two days no less than forty persons arrived at Marsh Firs. I, too, was invited, although I agreed with great reluctance. I did not like the provincial gentry, and in addition, had done almost no work these days. I had made almost no new notes, and most important of all, had not advanced in unravelling the secret of this devilish den. An old 17th century plan of the castle didn't contain any air vents for listening, while steps and moaning sounded with an enviable regularity each night.

I wracked my brains over the entire devilry, but could not think of anything.

So thus, for the first time, perhaps, in the last twenty years, the castle was meeting guests. The lampions above the entrance were lit, the covers on the chandeliers were removed, the watchman became the doorman for the occasion, three servants were taken from the surrounding farmsteads. The castle reminded one of an old Granny who had decided to attend a ball for the last time, and got herself all dressed up to recall her youth and then to lie down in her grave.

I do not know whether this gathering of the gentry is worth describing. You will find a good and quite a correct description of something of the like in the poetic works of Phelka from Rukshanitzy, an unreasonably forgotten poet. My God, what carriages there were! Their leather warped by age, springs altogether lacking, wheels two metres high, but by all means at the back they had a footman whose hands were black from the soil they had worked on. And their horses! Rocinant beside them would have seemed Bucephalo. Their lower lips hanging down like a pan, their teeth eaten away. The harnesses almost entirely of ropes, but to make up for that here and there shone golden plates with numbers on them, plates that had been passed on from harnesses of the "Golden Age".

"Goodness gracious! What is going on in this world? Long ago one gentleman rode on six horses, while now six gentlemen on one horse." The entire process of the ruin of the gentry was put into a nut shell in this mocking popular saying.

Behind my back Bierman–Hatsevich was making polite but caustic remarks about the arriving guests.

"Just look, what a fury – in the Belarusian of the 16th century a jade was called a fury. Most likely one of the Sas' rode on her: a merited fighting horse... And this little Miss, you see how dressed up she is, as if for St. Anthony's holiday. And here, look at them, the gypsies."

It was really an unusual company that he called "gypsies". A most ordinary cart had rolled up to the entrance with the strangest company I had ever seen. There were both ladies and gentlemen, about ten of them, dressed gaudily and poorly. They were seated in the cart, crowded like gypsies. And curtains were stretched on four sticks as on gypsy carts. Only the dogs running under the cart were lacking. This was the poor Hrytskievich family, roaming from one ball to another, feeding themselves mainly in this way. They were distant relatives of the Yanovskys. And these were the descendants of the "crimson lord"! My God, what you punish people for!?

Then arrived some middle aged lady in a very rich antique and rather shabby velvet dress. She was accompanied by a young man, as thin as a whip and clearly fawning upon her. This "whip" of a fellow gently pressed her elbow.

The perfume the lady used was so bad that Bierman began to sneeze as soon as she entered the hall. And it seemed to me that, together with her, someone had brought into the room a large sack of hoopoes and left it there for the people to enjoy. The lady spoke with a real French accent, an accent, as is known, that has remained in the world in two places only: in the Paris salons and in the backwaters of Kabylany near Vorsha.

And the other guests were also very curious people. Faces either wrinkled or too smooth, eyes full of pleading, worried, devouring eyes, eyes with a touch of madness. One dandy had extremely large, bulging eyes like those of the salamanders in subterranean lakes. From behind the door I watched the ceremony of introductions. Some of these close neighbours had never seen one another, and probably never would again in the future. The decaying palace, perhaps once in the recent eighteen years, saw such a storm of eager visitors.

Sounds reached me badly, for in the hall the orchestra was already piping away, an orchestra that consisted of eight veterans of the Battle of Poltava. I saw oily faces that gallantly smiled, saw lips that reached the mistress' hand. When they bent down, the light fell on them from the top, and their noses seemed surprisingly long while their mouths seemed to have vanished. They shuffled their feet without a sound and bowed, spoke noiselessly, then smiled and floated off, and new ones came floating over to take their place. This was like a bad dream.

They grinned and it was as if they were apparitions from the graves, they kissed her hand and it seemed to me that they were sucking the blood out of her. Then they noiselessly floated on. She was so pure in her low-necked dress, but her back reddened when some newly arrived Don Juan in close-fitting trousers showed too great an ardour as he pressed her hand. These kisses, it seemed to me, smeared her hand with something sticky and filthy.

And only now did I realize how solitary she was, not only in her own house, but also amidst of this crowd.

"What does this remind me of?" I thought. "Aha, Pushkin's Tatyana among the monsters in the hut. Enclosed, poor girl, as a doe during a hunt."

Almost no pure looks to be seen here, but to make up for it what names! It seemed as if I was in an archive reading ancient documents of some Court of Acts and Pleas.

"Mr. Sava Matfieyevich Stakhowsky and sons," the lackey announced.

"Mrs. Ahata Yuryewna Falendysh–Chobalev with her husband and friends."

"Mr. Yakub Barbare–Haraburda."

"Mr. Maciej Mustafavich Asanovich."

"Mrs. Hanna Awramovich–Basyatskaya and daughter."

And Bierman, standing behind me, was passing remarks.

For the first time in these days I liked him, for so much malice was there in his utterances, with what blazing eyes he met each newly arrived guest, and especially the young ones.

Suddenly an unfamiliar flash in his eyes took me aback. I involuntarily looked in the same direction he was looking in, and my eyes nearly popped out of my skull, such a strange sight opened to me. A person came rolling down the steps into the hall. That's right, rolling; no other word to describe what he was doing. The man was over two metres, approximately at my own height, but three Andreys Belaretskys would have fitted into his clothes. A tremendous abdomen, the lower legs like the thighs, as if they were hams, an incredibly broad chest, and palms like tubs. Few such giants had ever come my way, but this was not the most surprising thing about him. The clothes he was wearing can be seen today only in a museum. Red high-heeled horseshoed boots that our ancestors called "kabtsy", tight-fitting trousers made of a thin cloth. He sported a caftan made of cherry coloured gold cloth that was ready to split on his chest and abdomen. Over the caftan this giant had pulled over a "chuga", an ancient Belarusian coat. The chuga hung loosely in pretty folds and shiny designs on it were green, gold and black. A bright Turkish shawl was tied around it almost up to the man's armpits.

On top of all this magnitude sat a surprisingly small head that didn't seem to belong on such a body. His cheeks were puffed as if the man was about to burst out laughing. His long grey hair gave certain roundness to his head, his grey eyes were very small, and his long dark whiskers – they had very few grey hairs in them – reached down to his chest. The appearance of this man was a most peaceful one, if not for a "karbach", a thick, short lash with a silver wire at its end that hung from his left hand.

In a word, he was a dogman, a provincial bear, a merry fellow and a drunkard – this was immediately apparent.

While yet at the door he did burst into a robust, merry laughter, with his bass voice making me smile involuntarily. As he walked, people stepped aside to make way for him, answering him with smiles. Such smiles could have appeared on these sour faces of these people of a nearly extinct caste only because they, evidently, loved him. "At last, at least one representative of the good old century," I thought. "Not a degenerate, not a madman who might as well commit a crime just as easily as he would a heroic deed. Just a kind and simple titan. And how rich his Belarusian was, and how beautifully he spoke it!"

Don't let this last observation take you by surprise. Although Belarusian was spoken among the petty gentry at this time, the gentry of that stratum of society that this gentleman apparently belonged to did not know the language. Among the guests no more than a dozen spoke the language of Martsinkevich and Karatynsky, the language of the rest was a wondrous mixture of Polish, Russian and Belarusian.

But out of the mouth of this one, while he was walking from the door to the hall on the upper floor, poured apt little words, jokes, and sayings as out of the mouth of any village matchmaker. I must confess that he captured me at first sight. Such a colourful person he was that I did not immediately notice his companion, although he also deserved attention. Imagine for yourself a young man, tall, very well-built, and what was rare in this remote corner, dressed according to the latest fashion. He would have been handsome were it not for his excessive paleness, sunken cheeks, and an inexplicable expression of animosity that lay on his compressed lips. His large eyes with their watery lustre deserved most of the attention on his fine though bilious face. They were so lifeless that it made me shiver. Lazarus, when he was risen from the dead, probably had just the eyes.

In the meantime the giant had come up to an old lackey who was somewhat blind and deaf, and suddenly jerked him by the shoulder.

The lackey had been napping on his feet, but he immediately pulled himself together, and taking in who the new guests were, smiled broadly and shouted:

"The most honourable gentleman, Hryn Dubatowk! Mr. Ales Varona!"

"A very good evening to you, gentlemen," Dubatowk roared. "Why so sad, like mice under a hat? No matter, we'll make you merry in a jiffy. Varona, pay attention to little ladies! I was definitely born too early. Such beauties-cuties!"

He walked through the crowd. Varona had stopped near a young lady, as Dubatowk approached Nadzeya Yanovsky. His eyes narrowed and began to sparkle with laughter.

"A good day to you and good evening, my dear!" He gave her a smacking kiss on her forehead and he stepped back. "And how slender, how graceful and beautiful you've become! All Belarus will lie at your feet! And may Lucifer carry tar on my back in the next world, if I, an old sinner, won't be drinking a toast to you from the little slipper in a month from now at your wedding. Only your little eyes are somewhat sad. But no matter, I'll make you merry right away."

And with the fascinating grace of a bear, he turned round on his heels.

"Anton, you devil! Hryshka and Pyatrush! Has the cholera got you, or what?"

And there appeared Anton, Hryshka and Pyatrush, bending under the weight of some enormous bundles.

"Well, you louts and lubbards, place everything at the feet of the mistress. Unroll it! You rascals! Your hands, where do they grow from? Not your back by any chance? Take it, daughter!"

On the floor in front of Lady Yanovsky lay an enormous fluffy carpet.

"Keep it, my dear. It was your grandfather's, but it hasn't been used at all. You'll put it in your bedroom. The wind comes in here, you, the Yanovskys, have always had feeble feet. Too bad you, Nadzeyka, did not come to live with me two years ago. I begged you to, but you wouldn't agree. Well, be that as it may, too late now, you are all grown up. Easier for me now. To the devil with this guardianship."

"Forgive me, dear uncle," Yanovsky said quietly, touched by her guardian's attention. "You know that I wanted to be where my father was... my father..."

"Well – well – well," Dubatowk said, embarrassed. "Let it be. I myself hardly ever came to see you, knowing that you would be upset. We were friends with Roman. But no matter, my dear, we are, of course, worldly people. We suffer from overeating and too much drinking; however, God must look into people's souls. And if he does, then Roman, although he was wont to pass the church by but not the tavern, has already long been listening to the angels in heaven, and is looking into the eyes of his poor wife, my third cousin. God – He's nobody's fool. The main thing is one's conscience, whereas that hole in one's mouth that asks for a glass of vodka is a vile thing. And they look at you from heaven and your mother does not regret that she gave life to you at the price of her own: such a queen have you become. And you'll soon be getting married. From the hands of your guardian into the fond and strong hands of a husband. Well, what do you think?"

"I hadn't thought of it before, and, now I don't know," Yanovsky suddenly said.

"Well, well," becoming serious, said Dubatowk. "But... the man should be a good one. Don't be in a hurry. And now another present... It is an old costume of our country, a real one. Not some kind of an imitation. Afterwards go and change your dress before the dances. There's no point in wearing all this modern stuff."

"It will hardly suit her, and will only spoil her appearance," a foxy young miss of the petty gentry put in a word, trying to be flattering.

"And you keep quiet, love. I know what I am doing," Dubatowk growled back at her. "Well, Nadzeyka, now to the very last thing. I thought long and hard about whether to give this to you, but I am not accustomed to keeping what does not belong to me. This is yours. Among your portraits one is missing. The line of ancestors must not be broken. You know that yourself, because you belong to the most ancient of all the families in the whole province."

On the floor, freed of the white cloth covering it, stood a very old, unusual portrait, the work, apparently, of an Italian painter, a portrait which you can hardly find in the Belarusian iconography of the 17th century. There was no flat wall in the background, no coat-of-arms hung on it. There was a window opening into the evening marsh, there was a gloomy day overhead, and there was a man sitting with his back to all this. An indefinite greyish blue light shone on his thin face, on the fingers of his hands, on his black and golden clothes.

The face of this man was more alive than that of any living man, and it was so surprisingly dismal and hard that it was frightening. Shadows lay in the eye sockets and a nerve even seemed to quiver in the eyelids. And there was a family likeness between his face and that of the mistress, but all that was pleasant and nice in Yanovsky, was repulsive and terrible in the man on the portrait. Treachery, cunning symptoms of madness, an obdurate imperiousness, an impatient fanaticism, a sadistic cruelty could be read in this face. I stepped aside. The large eyes that seemed to read the very depths of my soul turned and again looked me in the face. Someone in the crowd sighed.

"Roman the Old," Dubatowk said in a muffled voice, but it had already occurred to me who it was, so correctly had I imagined him from the words of the legend. I had guessed this was the one who was guilty of the curse, because the face of our mistress had become pale and she swayed back slightly.

I don't know how this deathly still scene would have ended, but someone silently and disrespectfully pushed me in the chest. Involuntarily I recoiled. It was Varona making his way through the crowd, and in making his way to Yanovsky, he had pushed me aside. Calmly he continued walking without begging my pardon, he didn't even turn around, as if an inanimate object were standing in my place.

I was born in a family of ordinary intellectuals, the intelligentsia who from generation to generation had served the Polish gentry, who were themselves learned men, nevertheless plebeians, from the point of view of this arrogant aristocrat, a man whose forefather was the whipper-in of a wealthy magnate, a murderer. I had often had to defend my dignity against such, and now all my "plebeian" pride bristled.

"Sir," I said loudly. "You can consider it worthy of a true aristocrat to push a person aside without begging his pardon?"

He turned around.

"You are addressing me?"

"You," I calmly answered. "A true aristocrat is a gentleman."

He came up to me and began scrutinizing me with curiosity.

"H-m," he said. "Who is going to teach a gentleman the rules of good behaviour?"

"I don't know," I answered, just as calmly and as bitingly. "Whoever that might be, it is not you. An uneducated priest must not teach others Latin – nothing will come of it."

I saw, over his shoulder, Nadzeya Yanovsky's face, and was happy to notice that our quarrel had diverted her attention from the portrait. The blood had returned to her face, but in her eyes there flashed something resembling alarm and fear.

"Choose your expressions carefully," Varona said in a strained voice.

"Why? And most importantly, for whom? A well-bred man knows that in the company of polite people one should be polite, while in the company of rude fellows, the greatest degree of politeness is to repay in the same coin."

Varona was apparently unaccustomed to being repulsed. I knew such arrogant turkey-cocks. He was surprised, but then glanced at the hostess, turned towards me again, and a turbid fury flashed in his eyes.

"But do you know with whom you are talking?"

"With whom? Not with God Himself?"

I saw Dubatowk appear at the side of the hostess. His face showed that he had become interested. Varona's blood was boiling.

"You are speaking with me, with a man who is in the habit of pulling parvenus by the ear."

"But hasn't it occurred to you that certain parvenus are themselves capable of pulling your ears? And don't come up closer, otherwise, I warn you, not a single gentleman will receive such an insult, as you from me."

"A caddish fist fight!" he exploded.

"Can't be helped!" I said coldly. "I have met noblemen on whom nothing else had any effect. They weren't cads, their ancestors were long-serving hound-keepers, whippers-in, ladies' men for the widows of magnates."

I intercepted his hand and held it as with a nipper.

"Well..."

"Damn you!" he hissed.

"Gentlemen, gentlemen, calm yourselves," Lady Yanovsky exclaimed, alarmed beyond expression. "Mr. Belaretsky, don't, don't! Mr. Varona, for shame!"

Evidently, Dubatowk also understood it was time to interfere. He came up, stood between us, and put a heavy hand on Varona's shoulder. His face was red.

"You pup!" He shouted. "And this is a Belarusian, an aristocrat? To insult a guest in such a way! A disgrace to my grey hair. Don't you see whom you are picking a fight with? He is not one of our chicken-hearted fools. This is not a chick, this is a man. And he will quickly tear off your moustache for you. You are a nobleman, sir?"

"A nobleman."

"So you see, the gentleman is an aristocrat. If you must have a talk together you can find a common language. This man is an aristocrat and a good one, too; his forefathers and ours may have been friends. Do not compare him to the modern snivellers. Ask your hostess to forgive you. You hear me?"

Varona was as if a changed man. He muttered some words and walked aside with Dubatowk. I remained with Yanovsky.

"My God, Mr. Andrey, I was so frightened for you. You're too good a person to have anything to do with him."

I raised my eyes. Dubatowk stood nearby and curiously looked at me and then at Miss Yanovsky.

"Miss Nadzeya," I said with a warmth I hadn't myself expected. "I am very grateful to you, you are a kind and sincere person, and your concern for me, your goodwill, I shall long remember. It can't be helped, but my pride – the only thing I have – I never allow anybody to tread on."

"So you see," she lowered her eyes. "You are not at all like them. Many of these highborn people would have given in. Evidently, you are the real gentleman here, while they only pretend to be gentlemen... But remember, I have great fear for you. This man is dangerous, he's a man with a dreadful reputation."

"I know that," I answered jokingly. "The local 'aurochs'..."

"Don't joke about it. He is a well-known brawler among us and a rabid duellist. He has killed seven men in

ULADZIMIR KARATKEVICH

duels. And it is perhaps worse for you that I am standing beside you. You understand me?"

I did not at all like this feminine dwarf with her large sad eyes. Her relations with Varona held no interest for me whatsoever, whether he was a sweetheart or a rejected admirer. However, one good deed deserves another. So sweet was she in her care for me, that I took her hand and carried it to my lips.

"My thanks, mademoiselle." She did not remove her hand, and her transparent gentle little fingers slightly trembled under my lips. In a word, all this sounds too much like a sentimental and somewhat cheap novel about life in high society.

The veteran orchestra began to play the waltz "Mignon" and the illusion of "high society" immediately disappeared. In conformity with the orchestra were the clothes, in conformity with the clothes were the dances. Cymbals, pipes, something resembling tambourines, an old whistle, and violins. Among the violinists were a gypsy and a Jew, the latter's violin trying all the time to play something very sad instead of the well-known melodies, but when it fell into a merry vein it played something resembling "Seven on a Violin". And dances that had long gone out of fashion: "Chaqu'un", "pas-de-deux", even the Belarusian mannered parody on "Minuet" – "Labedzik". And luckily I could dance all of these, for I liked national dances.

"Miss Nadzeya, may I invite you for the waltz?"

She hesitated a moment, shyly raising her fluffy eyebrows.

"I was taught it some time ago, and have probably forgotten."

She put her hand somewhat awkwardly under my shoulder. At first I thought we would be a laughing stock for everybody in the ball room, but was soon set at ease.

I had never met such a light dancer as this girl. She did not dance, she flew about in the air, and I almost carried her along on the floor. And that was easy to do, since she was as light as a feather. Approximately in the middle of the dance I noticed her face that had been concentrated and uncertain, becoming suddenly simple and very sweet. Her eyes sparkled, her lower lip somewhat protruding.

Then we danced some more. She became surprisingly lively, her cheeks turned rosy, and in this intoxication such youth sparkled in her face, that warmth filled my heart.

"This is me," her soul seemed to be saying in her eyes, in her big, black and shining eyes, "This is me. You thought me far away, but I am here, here I am. In this one short evening I have shown you myself, and you are surprised. You didn't consider me a living being, found me pale and bloodless, as the sprout of a dahlia in a dungeon, but you have taken me out into the world. I'm so grateful to you, you are so kind. You see live verdure has appeared in my stem, and soon if the sun warms me, I'll show the world my wonderful scarlet flower. But there's one thing that you must not do, you mustn't carry me back into the cellar."

It was strange to see in her eyes a reflection of the joy that she felt on sensing her own full value. I, too, was carried away by this, and my eyes, probably, began to shine with only my side vision tracking my surroundings now. Suddenly the squirrel whisked back into its hollow, the joy disappeared from the eyes, and the former horror settled behind her eyelashes: Varona was giving orders to lackeys who were hanging the portrait of Roman the Old above the fireplace.

The music stopped. Dubatowk came up to us, red in the face and merry.

"Nadzeya, my beauty, allow this old fool your little paw."

He lowered himself heavily on a knee and, laughing, kissed her hand.

In a minute he spoke in an altogether different tone:

"According to the law a guardian must make his report immediately upon his ward's reaching the age of eighteen."

He withdrew from his pocket an enormous bulbous enamelled silver watch and, becoming official, declared:

"It is seven o'clock. We are going to make known our report. I shall speak; then, for the second guardian, Mr. Kalatecha–Kazlowsky, who lives in town and due to illness could not come, an arrangement has been made that Sava Stakhowsky and Mr. Ales Varona will speak in his stead. And an independent witness is necessary." His eyes rested on me searchingly. "You're just the man. You are a young man yet, and will live long yet. You will be able then to bear witness to the fact that everything was carried out here according to the old customs and to the dictates of conscience. Miss Yanovsky, please come together with us."

Our conference did not last long. At first an inventory of the property was read – the real estate and the personal property – that was left, according to the last will and testament of her father. It turned out that it consisted mainly of the castle and the park, the entailed estate, from which not a single thing might vanish and which had to be kept up in such a way as to maintain the greatness of the family and its honour.

"A fine honour!" I thought. "The honour of dying of hunger in a wealthy house."

Dubatowk proved that the real estate property had been well looked after and retained intact.

Next was the question of profits. Dubatowk announced that the money invested by Roman Yanovsky – 24,000 roubles – in two banking offices, at 8 % without the right to touch the basic capital, returned from 150 to 170 roubles monthly. This profit, due to the efforts of the guardian, even increased. Moreover, the basic capital had increased by a sum which, if it were so wished, could be added to the dowry of the heiress. All the people there shook their heads. The profits were scanty, especially if the necessity of running the house and keeping it in order were taken into consideration.

"And how are the servants paid?" I asked.

"A part of the inheritance is allotted for that in the will, as they are an inseparable part of the entailed estate."

"I would ask Mr. Dubatowk to explain to me how things stand with the leased land belonging to the Marsh Firs estate," said Sava Stakhowsky, a small thin man with such sharp knees it seemed they were on the point of cutting through his little trousers. He evidently always exchanged caustic remarks with Dubatowk and now asked him this venomous question. Dubatowk, however, wasn't taken aback, he pulled out large silver spectacles, a kerchief which he spread out on his knees, then a key and only after that a scrap of paper. His spectacles, however, he did not put on, and began to read:

"Miss Yanovsky's great-grandfather had 10,000 hectares of good arable land, not including the forest. Miss Yanovsky, as you probably know, most respected Mr. Stakhowsky, has fifty hectares of arable land, considerably impoverished. She has also the park which doesn't give any returns, and the virgin forest, which is also effectively an entailed estate, as it is a Forest Reservation. Frankly speaking, this rule could be waived. However, firstly, access for the woodcutter to the virgin forest is impossible because of the quagmire. And secondly, would it be wise? Nadzeya may have children. What could they do with fifty hectares of poor land? Then the family will come to a complete downfall. Of course, the young lady is now grown up, she can decide for herself..."

"I quite agree with you, Uncle," Lady Yanovsky said, blushing and almost in tears. "Let the virgin forest stand. I'm glad that one can get to it only by small paths, and at that only in dry weather. A pity to destroy such a dense forest. Virgin forests are God's gardens."

"That's right," continued her guardian, "Besides, almost the entire Yanovsky region is but a quagmire, a peat-bog and waste land on which nothing besides heather can grow. No one has ever lived on this land, as long as man can remember. And that means that we take only the fifty hectares which are rented out for half the crop. The land isn't fertilized, only rye is planted on it, and each hectare gives thirty, at the most forty measurements, which means that at a price of fifty kopeck per measurement a hectare gives an income of ten roubles a year, and thus, from all the land, 500 roubles annually. And that is all. This money is not withheld, you can believe me, Mr. Stakhowsky."

I shook my head. The landlady of a large estate had a monthly income of a little over 200 roubles. While an average official received 125 roubles. Nadezhda Yanovsky had a place to live in and food to eat, nevertheless hers was an undisguised need, a need without a ray of hope. I, a learned man and a journalist, the author of four books, received 400 roubles monthly. And I didn't have to put it all into this hole – the castle, to make presents to the servants, to keep the park in relative order. I was Croesus in comparison with her.

I felt sorry for her, this child, on whose shoulders such an overwhelming load had fallen.

"You are rather poor," Dubatowk said sadly. "As a matter of fact, after all the necessary expenses, you have only kopecks left on hand."

At this he glanced in my direction very expressively and meaningfully, but my face, I dare say, expressed nothing. Indeed, how could it concern me in any way?

The papers were handed over to the new owner. Dubatowk promised to give his personal orders to Bierman, then he kissed Yanovsky on her forehead, and left the room. The rest of us also returned to the dancing hall where the guests had by now had time enough to tire of dancing.

Dubatowk again called forth an outburst of merriment and excitement.

There was some kind of a local dance that I did not know, and therefore Varona immediately carried off Nadzeya. Then she disappeared somewhere. I was watching the dancing, when suddenly I felt someone looking at me. Not far from me stood a thin but evidently strong young man with a frank face, modestly dressed, although the accentuated stress laid on its tidiness was quite apparent.

I had not seen him appear, but I liked him at first sight. I even liked the soft ascetism of his large mouth and clever brown hazel eyes. I smiled at him and he, as if that was what he had been waiting for, stepping lightly, walked over in my direction with an outstretched hand.

"I beg your pardon for this informality, Andrey Svetsilovich. It's been an old wish of mine to make your acquaintance. I'm a former student of the Kiev University. I was expelled for my participation in student disturbances."

I, too, introduced myself. He smiled a broad Belarusian smile, such a kind and frank smile that his face immediately became beautiful.

"You know, I've read your collections. Don't consider it a compliment. I'm in general not fond of that, but after reading them I felt inexplicably drawn to you. You are doing something useful and necessary, and you understand your tasks. I judge that from your prefaces."

A conversation between us got under way and we walked over to a window in a far corner of the room.

I asked him how he happened to be in Marsh Firs. He began to laugh:

"I'm a distant relative of Nadzeya Yanovsky. A very distant one. As a matter of fact, we two, she and I, are the only ones left now, and I am from a female line of the family. It seems that some drop of blood of the former Deinowsky princes still flows in the veins of Haraburda, but his kinship, as well as that of the Hryckieviches, not a single expert in heraldry could prove. It is simply a family tradition. In any case Nadzeya is the only real Yanovsky."

His face softened, became thoughtful.

"And anyway, this is all foolishness. All these heraldic entanglements, the small princes, the entailed estates of magnates. Were it up to me I would empty my veins of all this magnate blood. It only causes my conscience to suffer deeply. I think Nadzeya feels the same way."

"But I was told that Miss Nadzeya is the only one of the Yanovskys."

"That's really so, yes. I am a very distant relative, and also, I was thought to be dead. It's been five years since I've visited Marsh Firs, and now I'm 23. My father sent me away because at the age of eighteen I was dying of love for a thirteen year old girl. As a matter of fact that was unimportant, we'd have had to wait only two years, but my father believed in the power of the ancient curse."

"Well, did the banishment help you?" I asked.

"Not a bit. Moreover, two meetings were sufficient for me to understand that the former adoration had grown into love."

"And how does Nadzeya Yanovsky feel?" I asked.

He blushed so that tears even welled up in his eyes.

"You've guessed! I beg you to keep silent about that. The thing is that I don't know yet what she thinks about it. That is not so important. Believe me... It's simply that I feel so well in her presence, and even should she be indifferent – believe me – life would still be a good and happy thing, she will still be living on this land, won't she? She is an unusual person. She is an extraordinary being. She is surrounded by such a dirty world of pigs, by such undisguised slavery, while she is so pure and kind."

This youth with his clear and kind face awakened such an unexpected tender emotion within me that I smiled, but he, apparently, took my smile for a sneer.

"So you, too, are laughing at me as did my deceased father, as did Uncle Dubatowk..."

"I don't think they were laughing at you, Andrey. On the contrary, it is pleasant for me to hear these words from you. You are a decent and kind person. Only perhaps you shouldn't tell anybody else about this. Now you've mentioned the name of Dubatowk..."

"I am grateful to you for your kind words. However, you didn't really think, did you, that I could've spoken about it with anybody else? You guessed it yourself. And Uncle Dubatowk – he too, did, though I don't know why."

"It's well that it was Dubatowk who guessed it, not Ales Varona," I said. "It would otherwise have ended badly for one of you. Dubatowk is the guardian, interested in Nadzeya's finding a good husband. And it seems to me that he will not tell anybody else, and neither will I. But, in general, you should not mention it to anybody."

"That's true," he answered guiltily. "I hadn't thought that even the slightest hint might harm Miss Nadzeya. And you are right – what a good man Dubatowk is and how sincere! People like him. A fine swordsman, simple and patriarchal! And so frank and merry! How he loves people and doesn't interfere with anybody's life. And his language! When I first heard it, it was as if a warm hand were stroking my heart."

His eyes even became moist, so well did he love Dubatowk.

"Now you know, Mr. Belaretsky, but no one else will. And I will never compromise her. I shall be dumb. Look, you have been dancing with her, and it makes me happy. She is talking with someone – it makes me happy, if only it makes her happy. But to tell you the truth, to be frank with you..." His voice became stronger, his face showing determination like the young David's coming out to fight Goliath. "Were I at the other end of the world and my heart felt that someone intended to hurt her, I'd come flying over, and were it God Himself, I would break His head for Him, I would bite Him, would fight to my last breath, and then I would crawl up to her feet and breathe my last. Believe me. And even when I am far away I am always with her."

Looking at his face, I understood why the powers that be fear such slender, pure and honest young men. They have, of course, wide eyes, a childish smile, a youngster's weak hands, a proud and shapely neck as if made of marble, as if it were especially created for the hangman's pole axe, but in addition to all this, they are uncompromising, conscientious even unto trifles. They are unable to accept the superiority of crude strength, and their faith in the truth is fanatic. They are inexperienced in life, are trusting children right into their old age, in serving the truth they are bitter, ironic, faithful to the end, wise and unbending. Mean people fear them even when they haven't yet begun to act, and governed by their inherent instincts, always poison them. This base trash knows that they, these young men, are the greatest threat to their existence.

I understood that were a gun put into the hands of such a man, he would with that sincere smile of white teeth, come up to the tyrant, put a bullet into him and then calmly say to death: "Come here!" He will undergo the greatest suffering and if he doesn't die in prison of his thirst for freedom, he will come up calmly to the scaffold.

So boundless was the faith which this man called forth in me, that our hands met in a strong handshake and my smile was a friendly one.

"Why were you expelled?"

"Oh, some nonsense. It began when we decided to honour the memory of Shevchenko. We were threatened that the police would be brought into the university." He even began to blush. "Well, we rebelled. And I shouted that if they only dared to do that with our sacred walls, we would wash that shame off them with our blood, and the first bullet would strike the man who had given that order. Then it became noisy and I was grabbed. And in the police station, when I was asked my nationality, I answered: "Write – Ukrainian.""

"Well said."

"I know it was very imprudent for those who had taken up the struggle."

"No, that was good for them, too. One such answer is worth dozens of bullets. And it signifies that everybody is fighting a common enemy. There is no difference between the Belarusian and the Ukrainian if the lash is held over them."

We looked at the dancers silently until Svetsilovich winced.

"Dancing. The devil knows what it's like. A waxworks show of some kind... antediluvian pangolins. In profile not faces but ugly mugs. Brains the size of a thimble, and paws like a dinosaur's with 700 teeth. And their dresses with trains. And the frightening faces of these curs... We are after all an unfortunate people, Mr. Belaretsky."

"Why?"

"We have never had any really great thinkers among us."

"Perhaps it's better so," I said.

"And nevertheless we are a people without a land to settle on. This infamous trade of one's country over a period of seven centuries. In the beginning it was sold to Lithuania, then, before the people had hardly become assimilated, to the Poles, to everybody and anybody, regardless of honour and conscience."

The dancers began to cast glances at us.

"You see, they are looking at us. When a person's soul is screaming, they don't like it. They all belong to one gang here. They trample on the little ones, they repudiate honour, sell their young daughters to old men. You see that one over there – Sava Stakhowsky? I would not put a horse into the same stable with him, for the horse's morals would be endangered. And this Chobaleva, a provincial Messalina. And this one, Asanovich, drove a serf's daughter into her grave. Now he can't do that, hasn't got the right to, but all the same he continues to lead a dissolute life. Unfortunate Belarus! A kind, complaisant, romantic people in the hands of rascals. And so it will always be while this nation allows itself to be made a fool of. It gives up its heroes to the rack and itself sits in a cage over a bowl of potatoes or turnips, looking blank, and understanding nothing. Much would I pay the man who at last shook off from his people's neck this decaying gentry, these stupid parvenus, these conceited upstarts and corrupt journalists, and made the people become masters of their own fate. For that I would give all my blood."

Apparently my senses had become very sharp. All the time I felt somebody's look on my back. When Svetsilovich had finished, I turned around and was stupefied. Standing behind us was Nadzeya Yanovsky, and she had heard everything. But it was not she, it was a dream, a forest sprite, a being out of a fairy tale. Her dress was like that worn by women in the Middle Ages. No less than fifty lengths of Vorsha golden satin had gone into its making. And this dress had over it another, a white one, with free designs in blue that seemed as if of silver as the colours played in the numerous cuts hanging from the sleeves and the hem of the dress. Her tightly tied waist was bound by a thin golden cord falling almost to the floor in two tassels. On her shoulders was a thin "robok" made of a white and silver tinted cloth. Her hair was gathered in a net, an ancient head dress reminding one somehow of a little ship woven from silver threads. From both horn lets of this little ship a thin white veil hung down to the very floor.

This was a Swan Queen, the mistress of an amber palace, in another word, the devil alone knows what, but only not the previous ugly duckling. I saw Dubatowk's eyes popping out of his head, his jaws sagging. He, too, had evidently not expected such a transformation. The violin screamed. Silence fell.

This attire was quite uncomfortable and it usually fetters the movement of a woman unaccustomed to it, makes her heavy and baggy, but this girl was like a queen in it, as if she had all her life worn only such clothing, her head proudly thrown back, she floated dignified and womanly. From under her veil her large eyes smiled archly and proudly, stirred by a feeling of her own beauty.

Dubatowk grunted even, so surprised was he, and he came up to her with quickening steps. With an incomprehensible expression of pain in his eyes, he took her face in the palms of his hands and kissed her on the forehead, muttering something like "such beauty".

And then his lips again broke out into a smile.

"A Queen! My Beauty! I have lived to see this, holy martyrs! Yanovsky to her very finger tips! Allow me, dear daughter, your little foot."

And this enormous bear, grunting, spread himself out on the floor and put his lips to the tip of her tiny slipper. Then he arose and began to laugh:

"Well, my little daughter, with such capital you should sit as quiet as a mouse, otherwise somebody will steal you."

And he suddenly winked:

"And why not recall the old days, the clays of your childhood when we used to dance together? Give this old beaver one dance, and then let death come upon me."

The white queen held out her hand to him.

"Come on, my swans, my beauties!" Dubatowk shouted to the veterans. "In the beginning give us our 'Light Breeze' – two circles, and then from my place – you know which one, don't you? – change to a mazurka!"

And in a whisper he turned to me:

"Our dances are good in all respects, but there just isn't such a fiery one as the Polish mazurka. Only 'Lavonicha' might dispute it, but to dance that there must be several pairs, and can these hags and snivellers dance it? For this you need ballet legs... like mine here."

And he burst out laughing. But I looked in fright at his legs that were like hams and thought: "What he will make of this good dance with those?"

In the meantime everybody moved aside to clear the space for them. I heard a voice:

"He, Dubatowk... will dance!"

I did not leave this profanation, because I wished to see this forgotten dance about which I had heard more than once, and which, people said, had been widespread some eighty years ago.

The enormous bulk that was Dubatowk straightened up, and took Yanovsky by the limpid transparent wrist of her left hand.

From the first notes of "Light Breeze" he kicked his heels, made a three step with the right and then with the left foot. This huge man moved with an unexpected ease, at first kicking his heels after every three steps, and then simply on the tips of his toes. And at his side she floated, simply floated in the air, a golden, white and blue being, as if she were a bird of paradise, her veil soaring in the air.

Then they whirled, floated, sometimes drawing together, sometimes drawing apart, sometimes crossing each other's path. No, this was not a profanation, just as the dance of an old man, once a great dancer, but now grown heavy, is not a profanation. It was in the full sense of a light breeze changing gradually into a storm, and the veil was circling in the air, the feet flashing by... And suddenly the musicians started a mazurka. As a matter of fact it was not a mazurka but some kind of an ancient local variation of its theme, including in itself elements of the "Light Breeze".

And here the huge bulk rushed ahead, thundered with his heels, then began rising smoothly into the air, striking one foot against the other. And at his side she floated, light, and smiling and sublimely majestic.

This was indeed a real miracle: two people dressed as in olden times, creating a fairy tale before our very eyes.

Having circled about, Dubatowk led Yanovsky up to me. He was red as a lobster.

"She has tired me out..."

"But, Uncle, you are like a young man."

"Young, young! No, words won't help... The horse's riding days are over. Soon I'll be sent off to drink my beer with our forefather Abraham. For you, young ones, life's ahead! Sing your songs and dance your dances! Dance, young fellow!"

The dancing was resumed. Svetsilovich did not like to dance. Varona sulked and he, too, did not come over, and I was left to dance with Miss Yanovsky till supper time. How she danced! Involuntarily I became lost in contemplation of this childish face, which had suddenly become so alive and pleasantly cunning. We danced and danced, and it was all not enough, we whirled about the hall, the walls circled in front of us, and it was impossible to see anything on them. She probably felt as I did, but my feeling can be compared only with the dreams which sometimes come to us in our youth. In your dream you are dancing and a mysterious happiness envelops your heart. I could see only her pink face and her head thrown back, as it lightly turned about in time with the music.

We went to have supper. While leading her into the dining room, it seemed to me I heard some hissing in a corner of the hall. I looked there and in the semi darkness saw someone's eyes – some old ladies were sitting there – and I walked on. And I distinctly heard somebody's dry voice squeaking:

"Making merry as if death were facing them! They have sinned, have angered God and can yet make merry... A cursed family... It does not matter, soon the Wild Hunt will come... Just look at her, shameless one, all evening with this stranger, this atheist. She has found herself a friend, she has. Never mind! I swear that King Stakh will rise against her, too. The dark nights are beginning."

These vile, icy words filled me with alarm. Now that I came to think of it, I would leave and perhaps deprive the girl of the possibility of getting married. Why am I spending the entire evening with her? What am I doing? I am not at all in love with her, and never will be, because I know my own heart. And I firmly decided not to dance with her any more or sit beside her at the table. And anyway, I had to leave that place. Enough of the idyll of an aristocratic gentleman. Must be off as soon as possible to common people, back to work. I seated her and stood aside, intending to find Svetsilovich and seat him with her. However, all my intentions went up in smoke. On entering the hall,

Svetsilovich immediately took a seat at the end of the table. And Dubatowk sat down beside the mistress at the right and growled at me:

"Why are you standing? Sit down, my boy."

"A fine Polish gentleman you would have made some hundred years ago. Strong hands, eyes like steel. A handsome fellow. But I'm curious to know whether you are a serious person. Not a featherbrain, are you?"

I had to sit next to the mistress, look after her, touching her hand with mine, at times touching her knee with mine. And it was a good feeling, but also I was very angry with Dubatowk. He was sitting there, as gloomy as a dragon, looking at me searchingly, inquisitively. Could he be measuring me as the future husband of his ward? Very soon everybody became quite merry. The people ate a lot and drank even more. Their faces became red, witty jokes came thick and fast.

And Dubatowk drank and ate more than anybody else, cracking jokes that made everybody hold themselves by their bellies.

Gradually my anger subsided. I was even grateful to Dubatowk that he had detained me here.

Then there was dancing again, and only at about five o'clock in the morning did the guests begin to leave. Dubatowk was one of the last to leave. Passing by us, he came up closer and said in a hoarse voice:

"Look here, young man, I invite you to come the day after tomorrow to a bachelor's party. And how about you, daughter? Perhaps you, too, will come to us and spend some time with my step daughter?"

"No, thank you, Uncle dear. I'll remain at home."

Her guardian sighed:

"You're ruining yourself, daughter. Well, all right."

And turning towards me, he continued:

"I shall be waiting for you. Look at my hut. I don't have any of these outlandish foreign things, your visit should be interesting for you."

He left, and I parted heartily with Svetsilovich.

The house became empty, the steps quieted down, again everything there became silent, probably for the next eighteen years. The servants walked about putting out the candles. The mistress disappeared, but when I entered the hall I saw her in her fairy tale attire at the blazing fireplace. The corners of the hall were again in darkness, though music and laughter still seemed to be resounding there. The house was again living its usual life, a dark, dismal and depressing one.

I came up closer to her and suddenly saw a pale face in which the last traces of joy had died out. The wind was howling in the chimney.

"Mr. Belaretsky," she said. "How quiet it is. I've lost the habit for all this. Come, let's have one more waltz, before forever..."

Her voice broke off. I put my hand on her waist, and we floated along the floor in time with the music that was still ringing in our ears. The shuffling of our feet sounded hollow beneath the ceiling. For some reason or other I felt terrible, as if I were present at a funeral, but she was experiencing all over again the events of the entire evening. Her veil flew round and about, the flames of the blazing fireplace falling on us were reflected in her dress, its colour changing to the sky blue when we moved away from the fireplace. This attire of olden times, this veil touching my face from time to time, this waist in my hand and these thoughtful eyes, I shall probably never forget.

And suddenly, for one instant, her forehead touched my shoulder.

"That's all. I cannot continue, not anymore. Enough! Thank you... for everything!"

And that was really all. She went to her room, and I stood watching the little figure in its attire of olden times walking down the hall, becoming lost in the darkness, her ancestors looking down from the walls.

I forgot that night to put out the candle on the little table at the window; as I lay in bed, a bed as large as a field, and was almost asleep, footsteps along the hall broke into my drowsiness. Knowing that were I to look out, I should again see nobody, I lay calmly. I felt drowsy again, but suddenly started.

Through the window pane the face of a human being was looking at me. He was very small. I could see him almost down to his belt, dressed in a caftan with a waist girdle round it, and with a wide collar. It was a man, but something inhuman was about him. His little head was compressed at the sides and unnaturally drawn out in length, his hair was long and thinned and was hanging down. But the most surprising thing about this Little Man was his face. It was as green as his clothes, his mouth big and toothless, his nose small, while the lower eyelids were excessively large, like a frog's. I compared him to a monkey, but he looked more like a real frog. And his eyes, wide and dark, looked at me in stupid anger. Then an unnaturally long green hand appeared. The being groaned a hollow groan, and that saved me from freezing with fear. I rushed to the window, stared through the window, but there was no Little Man there. He had disappeared.

I thrust the window open noisily – the cold air flew into the room. I put my head out and looked from all sides – not a soul in sight. As if he had evaporated into space. He could not have jumped down, in this place there was yet a third storey, the house stood partly on a slope, the windows to the right and left were shut, and the ledge was such a narrow one that even a mouse could not have run along it. I shut the window and fell to thinking, for the first time doubting whether I was in my right mind.

What could it have been? I believe neither in God nor in ghosts. However, this creature could not have been a living being. And moreover, from where could it have appeared, where had it disappeared to? Where could it exist? There was something mysterious in this house. But what? Is it possible that it really was a ghost? My entire upbringing rebelled against that. But perhaps I was drunk? No, I had drunk almost nothing. But where had the steps come from, those steps that are even now echoing down the hall? Did they sound then or didn't they when I saw the face of that monster in the window?

My curiosity reached the limits of feasibility. No, I would not leave this place the next day, as I had thought. I had to unravel all this. The girl, who had today given me yet another fine memory to keep, will go mad with fright. Something not in accordance with the laws of nature was going on there and I wouldn't leave till this is resolved. But who would help me in my search? Who? And I recalled Svetsilovich's words: "I would crawl up to her feet and breathe my last." Yes, it was with him that I had to meet. We would catch this abominable thing, and if not – I would begin to believe in the existence of green ghosts and God's angels.

CHAPTER FIVE

Two days later I was approaching Dubatowk's house. I did not want to go there, but my hostess had said: "You must go! It's my order. I won't be afraid here."

I was to follow a grass covered lane in a south-west direction from the house. A park stood along both sides of this path, as gloomy as a forest. The lane led to a fence where at one place an iron rod was missing and I could creep through it - this was Yanovsky's secret which she had confided to me. Therefore I didn't have to go north along the lane I had arrived on and walk around the whole territory to reach the road that led to Dubatowk's house. I crept through the hole and came out onto level land. To the left and straight ahead of me there was boundless heather waste land with sparse groups of trees. To the right some undergrowth, and behind it a full little river like an eye, then a swampy forest, and farther on, again hopeless quagmire. Somewhere very far from the heather waste land, trees of probably Dubatowk's estate could be seen.

I walked slowly through the waste land, only from time to time guessing where my path lay. The autumn field was gloomy and uninviting, but even though an enormous raven twice flew overhead, after Marsh Firs the field was rather pleasant. Everything around me was familiar. The moss on the marsh mounds among the dry heather, a tiny mouse dragging white down from a tall thistle to the nest it was preparing for winter.

I reached Dubatowk's estate only towards dusk, when the windows of his house were already brightly lit. It was a most ordinary house, the usual thing among the gentry. An old low building with small windows, it was shingle-roofed, freshly whitewashed, had a porch with four columns. The provincial architect had very likely been unaware of the well-known secret and therefore the columns seemed to bulge in the middle and looked like little barrels. The house with a large orchard behind it was surrounded by old, enormous, almost leafless lindens that separated the mansion from a vast piece of ploughed land.

I was late, apparently, for noisy voices were already thundering throughout the house. I was met warmly, even ardently.

"Goodness gracious! Holy Martyrs!" Dubatowk shouted. "You've come after all, the prodigal son has come! Come to the table! Antos, you lout, where are you? Have you got two left paws, or what? A welcoming drink for my guest! Missed meeting him, you devils, didn't salute him, didn't give him a drink at the door! Oh! You blockheads!"

About ten people were sitting at the table, all men. Among them I knew only Svetsilovich, Ales Varona and Stakhowsky. Almost all of them were already quite drunk, but for some reason they examined me with increased interest. The table was bursting with viands: Dubatowk was, evidently, of the well-to-do local gentry. His wealth, however, was relative. Of food and drink there was plenty, yet the rooms through which I went showed no such splendour. The walls were whitewashed, the shutters were covered with fretwork and brightly painted, the furniture was not very beautiful, but as if to make up for that, very heavy. Filled with the persistent spirit of antiquity, strangely enough the dining room had nothing else to boast with but a wide oak table, stools covered with a green, silky linen, two Dantzig armchairs covered with golden Morocca, and a triple mirror in a brown frame, depicting a city with church domes. The gaudily dressed guests examined me with curiosity.

"Why are you staring?" Dubatowk shouted. "Have you never seen a man from the capital city, you bears? Move, make the guest at home, share with him whatever food you fancy."

The hairy jaws began to smile, the paws indeed began to move. Soon an enormous goose landed on my plate, accompanied by cranberry jam and the leg of a turkey served with apples, pickled mushrooms and a dozen kuldoons. From all sides came:

"And here are doughnuts and mushrooms with garlic... here is a piece of ham from a wild boar, strongly peppered, burns like fire. I swear to it by the memory of my mother... take it. Try this, this is wonderful. And this here is something exceptional..."

"This is how we, Belarusians, treat our guests," the host exclaimed at seeing my confusion and laughed boisterously.

Food was piled high in front of me. I tried to protest, but that called forth such an outburst of indignation, and one of the guests even began to shed tears. Truth be told, he was in a blue haze, and I yielded.

The lout Antos brought me a glass of vodka on a tray, for a start. I am not intimidated by intoxicating liquors, but seeing it I got scared. There was no less than a bottle of some yellow transparent liquid in the glass.

"I couldn't!"

"What do you mean you couldn't? Only a virgin wench can't, but even she quickly agrees."

"It's too much, Mr. Dubatowk."

"When there are three wives in a hut, that's too much, though even that may not be so for everyone... Oh! Boys, we aren't respected. Ask the dear guest to..."

"Don't offend us... drink..." The guests roared like bears. I was forced to drink. The liquid burned my insides, fiery circles swam before my eyes, but I kept steady, didn't even make a wry face.

"Now that's my man!" Dubatowk praised me.

"What was that?" I asked referring to the drink as I swallowed down a big piece of ham.

"Oho! You know Starka, the old Polish vodka, you know the Ukrainian vodka Spatykach, but our Tris Deviniris you do not know? In Lithuanian, brother, it is "Thrice Nine", vodka infused with extracts of twenty seven herbs. This secret we wormed out of the Lithuanians hundreds of years ago. Now the Lithuanians themselves have forgotten it, but we still remember. Drink to your heart's content, then I'll treat you to some mead."

"And what's this?" I wanted to know, sticking my fork into something suspiciously dark on my plate.

"My dearly beloved, these are moose's lips in sweetened vinegar. Eat, brother, refill yourself. This is food for giants. Our forefathers, may they rest in peace, were no fools. Eat, don't procrastinate, just eat!"

And within a minute, having forgotten that he had recommended me the lips, he shouted:

"No, brother, you won't leave me without having tasted cold pasties stuffed with 'foie gras'. Antos!..."

Antos came over with the pasties. I tried to refuse.

"Go down on your knees at the feet of our guest. Beat your foolish head against the floor, beg him, because as a guest he is offending us."

Soon I, too, reached everyone's condition. While other guests were cheering and singing, I continued investigating the food. Dubatowk was hanging on to my shoulder, mumbling something, but I paid no attention. The room was beginning to swing.

"Let's have a drink, then another," someone howled. And suddenly I recalled that house far away in the fir park, the trees under a thick layer of moss, the fireplace, the melancholic figure near it. "I'm a drunken swine," feeling sick at heart, I kept beating myself up, "Indulging like that when someone else is in trouble..." So deep was my pity for her that I found myself on the verge of breaking into tears... and that immediately sobered me up.

The guests were beginning to leave the table.

"Gentlemen," Dubatowk said, "Take a little walk, the table has to be refreshed."

Good Lord, this was only the beginning! And everyone was already as wasted as wasted could be given the amount of liquor they took in. It was eight o'clock in the evening. Exact time was of little importance, it was still early. I was certain, after having instantly become sober, that I wouldn't get drunk again tonight. Still, I decided to drink with caution to avoid getting stuck in the quagmire which in itself would be hell to pay.

We rested, talked. Dubatowk showed us a fine collection of weapons. He praised an old sabre very highly; the one he had begged Roman Yanovsky to give him. He said that the Russian damask steel sword could cut through a plate, the Polish "Zygmuntowka" through quite a thick nail, but this one, ours, was a secret that the Tartars had brought with them in the time of Vitawt. The sabre was filled with mercury, providing for the blow of such a strength that it could cleave not only a thin copper plate, but a thick block. Nobody believed Dubatowk and he ordered Antos to bring a block. Antos brought in a short block, the thickness of three human necks, and placed it on the floor.

The room grew quiet. Dubatowk aimed at his target, grinned, baring his teeth, and suddenly the sabre described an almost invisible half circle in the air.

Dubatowk let out a deep guttural sound, drew the sabre towards him and split the block obliquely. He waved his wrist in the air. Everybody kept silent.

"That's the way to do it!" He shouted at us.

I managed at this time to get Svetsilovich out onto the porch and tell him of all that had occurred at Marsh Firs.

He became very excited, said that he had previously heard something about it, but had not quite believed it.

"And now do you believe it?"

"I believe you," he said simply. "And I promise that while I am alive, not a single hair shall fall off her head. Be he the devil or ghost or whatever else, I'll stand in his way."

We arranged to investigate things together, that he would come to see me in a couple of days and tell me all that he had learned in the vicinity of the village – finally various rumours and gossips might be of definite use. We decided not to get Dubatowk involved in this affair as yet; the old man could get very excited and act as was his habit in his devil-may-care way.

Supper continued. We were again treated to food, offered drink. I noticed that Dubatowk was filling our wine glasses, both his and mine, equally, and as he drank he kept sizing me up. Whenever I drank a glass of wine, a look of satisfaction appeared on his face. He was in a way egging me on into a competition. And during intervals he would offer either pancakes with a sauce made of flour, meat, fat, smoked ham and ribs, or else those unusual "shtoniki" – meat dumplings swimming in ghee, so good as saints had never eaten" as he called them. He was evidently studying me from every angle. I drank but did not get drunk.

The rest of Dubatowk's visitors, excluding Svetsilovich, were already in the sort of state when nobody listens to anybody, when one drinks, another tells some love story, a third is doing all he can to make somebody pay attention to some colourful fact in his biography, and a fourth is recalling what a good woman his mother had been, while he, such a drunkard, such a scoundrel, is profaning her memory, living such a dissolute life.

The singing went on:

In the hut's my wife,
At a drinking spree am I.
At the tavern my bullock's tied,
In the devil's keep my lost soul.
Another man drawled his song:
Tell me, my good people,
Where my beloved sleeps.
If in a distant land
Please, God, help him
But if in a widow's bed
Oh! God! Punish him!
But if in a widow's bed...

Someone raised his head from the table and sang his own version of the last line:

Please, God, help him too!

Everybody burst out laughing.

In the meantime Dubatowk shook his head as if to chase off his stupor, got up and announced:

"At last I've found a real man among the young aristocrats. He has drunk more than I have, I've become tipsy, but he's fresh, as fresh as a bush in the rain. None of you here would have taken in half as much. Nine of you would have fallen flat on your faces, while the tenth would have mooed like a calf. This is a man! Him and only him, would I gladly have accepted for a friend in my youth."

Cries came from everybody "Glory! Glory!" Varona alone looked at me with acid and gloom in his eyes. They drank to my health, to the gentry – the salt of the Earth, to my future wife.

When the enthusiasm had abated somewhat, Dubatowk looked me in the eyes and asked confidentially:

"Getting married?"

I shook my head uncertainly, although I understood very well what he was driving at. He was certain about it, evidently, whereas I had no wish to convince him of the reverse. I liked the old man, he was drunk and might be offended if I openly told him that I hadn't ever thought about it and did not even wish to think about it.

"She's beautiful," Dubatowk continued and sighed, looking at me sadly.

"Who?" I asked.

"My ward."

Things had gone too far, and to pretend any further was impossible, for otherwise it would have turned out that I was compromising the girl.

"I haven't thought about it," I said. "But even if I had thought about it, it doesn't depend on me alone. First of all it is necessary to ask her."

"You are avoiding an answer," Varona suddenly hissed through his teeth. I hadn't suspected that he could be listening to our quiet conversation. "You do not want to speak frankly and directly with serious people. You don't want to say that you are after money and a wife of noble birth."

I turned pale. Trying to keep calm, I answered:

"I have no intention of getting married. And I consider speaking about a girl in a drunken company of bachelors no honour to a true gentleman. Stop talking, Varona,

don't attract the attention of drunken people to an innocent girl, don't taint her reputation, and I, although it is
a terrible insult, forgive you."

"Ha, ha!" exclaimed Varona. "He forgives me. This pig,
this cad."

"Stop it!" I shouted. "Be quiet! Just think how you are
insulting her with each one of your words!"

"Gentlemen! Gentlemen!" Dubatowk tried to calm us.
"Varona, you are drunk."

"Think for yourself. I once allowed an offence of yours
to pass by unnoticed, but in future I won't!"

"You scoundrel!"

"Me?"

"Yes, you!" I shouted so loudly that even those who were
sleeping raised their heads from the table. "I'll force you to
shut up!"

A knife from the table whisked through the air and fell
flat on my hand. I jumped up from my seat, grabbed Varona
by the chest and shook him. At the same moment Dubatowk grabbed us by the shoulders and separated us, shoving
Varona aside.

"Shame on you, Ales!" Dubatowk thundered. "You pup...
Make up with him immediately!"

"No, wait a moment, Dubatowk. This is serious. It's too
late. My honour has been insulted," Varona roared.

"What about *my* honour as host? Who will now come to
visit me? Everyone will say that Dubatowk treats his guests
to duels instead of good vodka."

"Go to hell," Varona shouted, baring his teeth.

Without uttering a word, Dubatowk slapped him in the
face.

"Now you will first fight me with a sabre, for he only
took hold of you by the chest," he hissed so loudly that many
started. "I shall do what has to be done for my guest to leave
here safe and sound."

"You're mistaken," Varona retorted calmly. "He who first offended is first in line. And then I'll fight with you, kill me if you will."

"Ales," Dubatowk almost begged him, "Don't bring shame on my house."

"He shall fight with me," Varona said firmly.

"Oh well, then," our host unexpectedly agreed. "It does not matter, Mr. Belaretsky. Be courageous. This pig is so drunk that he can't hold a pistol. I think I'll stand beside you, and that will be the safest place."

"Don't worry," I said, placing my hand on his shoulder. "It's unnecessary. I'm not afraid. You be brave, too."

Varona stared at me with his deadly black eyes.

"I haven't yet finished. We shan't shoot in the garden, for otherwise this dandy will escape. And not tomorrow, for otherwise he will leave. We shall shoot here and now, in the empty room near the shed. And three bullets each. In the dark."

Dubatowk made a protesting gesture, but a reckless cold fury had already crept into my heart. It was all the same to me now. I hated this man, forgot Yanovsky, my work, even myself.

"I submit to your will," I answered caustically. "But won't you use the darkness to run away from me? However, as you like."

"You lion cub!" I heard Dubatowk's broken voice.

I glanced at him and was shocked to see a pitiful old man. His bitter distorted face, his eyes expressing an inhuman fear and shame, such shame that death would be better. He was almost in tears. He did not even look at me, just turned around and waved his hand.

The shed was attached to the house. It was an enormous chamber with grey moss in the grooves of its walls. Spider webs, resembling an entangled delivery of linen, hung down from the straw roof and shook at our steps.

Two young gentlemen carried candles and accompanied us into a room near the shed, a room entirely empty, with grey, wet plastering and without any windows. It smelled of mice and of abominable desolation.

To be quite honest, I was afraid, very much afraid. My situation could be compared with that of a bull in the slaughterhouse or of a man in the dentist's chair. It was nasty and vile, but impossible to run away.

"Well, what'll happen if he shoots me in the stomach? Oh! That'll be awful! If I could only hide somewhere!"

I don't know why, but I was terribly afraid of being wounded in the stomach. After such a wonderful meal, I suppose.

I was so depressed and disgusted that I could hardly keep from bellowing, but I gathered myself just in time and glanced at Varona. He was standing with his seconds against the opposite wall, holding his left hand in the pocket of his black dress coat, and in his right hand, held downward, was the gun for the duel. Two other guns were put in his pockets. His dry yellow face expressed disgust, but was calm. I don't know whether I could have said the same of myself.

My two seconds - one of them was Dubatowk - handed me a pistol too and pushed two others into my pockets. I noticed nothing of their manipulations. I was looking only at the face of the man I had to kill, for otherwise he would kill me. I looked at him with an inexplicable avidity, as if wishing to comprehend why he wanted to kill me, why he hated me.

"And why should I kill him?" I thought, as if only I were holding a pistol. "No, I must not kill him. But that is not the point. The point is that human neck, such a thin and very weak neck, is easy to wring." I also had no wish to die and therefore decided that Varona should shoot three times and that should be the end of the duel.

The seconds left, leaving us alone in the room and closed the door. We found ourselves in pitch darkness. Soon the voice of one of Varona's seconds announced:

"Begin!"

With my left foot I made two "steps" to the side, and then carefully put my foot back into its former place. To my surprise, all my excitement had passed, I acted as if automatically, but so wisely and quickly as I could never have done had my brain been controlling my actions. Not with my hearing, but rather with my skin did I feel Varona's presence in the room.

We kept silent. Now all depended on our self control.

A flash lit up the room. Varona's nerves had failed him. The bullet whizzed past somewhere to the left of me and rattled against the wall. I could have fired at this very moment, for during the flash I saw where Varona was. But I did not shoot. I only felt the place where the bullet had struck. I don't know why I did that. And I remained standing in the very same place.

Varona, evidently, could not even have supposed that I'd twice act in the same way. I could hear his excited hoarse breathing.

Varona's second shot resounded. And again I did not shoot. However, I no longer had the will power to stand motionless, all the more so because I heard Varona beginning to steal along the wall in my direction.

My nerves gave way. I also began to move carefully. The darkness looked at me with the barrels of a thousand pistols. There might be a barrel at any step, I could stumble on it with my belly, all the more so that I had lost the whereabouts of my enemy and couldn't say where the door was and where was the wall.

I stood still and listened. At this moment something forced me to throw myself down side wards on the floor.

A shot rang right over my head, it even seemed that the hair on my head had been moved by it.

But I still had three bullets. For a moment a wild feeling of gladness overwhelmed me, but I remembered the fragile human neck and lowered my pistol.

"What's going on there with you?" a voice sounded behind the door. "Only one of you fired. Has anyone been killed or not? Fire quickly, stop messing about."

This was when I raised my hand with the pistol, moved it away from the place where Varona had been at the time of the third shot and pressed the trigger. I had to fire at least once. I had to use up at least one bullet. In response, entirely unexpectedly, I heard a faint groan and the sound of a body falling.

"Quick, over here!" I shouted. "Quick! To my aid! It seems I've killed him!"

A blinding yellow stream of light fell on the floor. When people came into the room, I saw Varona lying stretched out motionless on the floor, his face turned upward. I ran up to him, raised his head. My hands touched something warm and sticky. Varona's face became even yellower.

"Varona! Varona! Wake up! Wake up!"

Dubatowk, gloomy and severe, came floating from somewhere, as if from out of a fog. He began fussing over the body lying there, then looked into my eyes and burst out laughing. It seemed to me I had gone mad. I got up and, almost unconscious, took out the second gun from my pocket. The thought crossed my mind that it was very simple to aim it at my temple and...

"No more! I can't take any more!"

"Well, but why? What's wrong, young man?" I heard Dubatowk's voice. "It wasn't you who insulted him. He wanted to bring disgrace on both you and me. You have two more shots yet. Just look how upset you are!

It's all because you're not used to it, because your hands are clean, because you have a conscientious heart. Well, well... but you haven't killed him, not at all. He's been deafened, that's all, like a bull at the slaughter. Look how cleverly you've done him. Shot off a piece of his ear and also ripped off a piece of the skin on his head. No matter, a week or so in bed and he'll be better."

"I don't need your two shots! I don't want them!" I screamed like a baby, and almost stamped my feet. "I give them to him as a gift!"

My second and some other gentleman whose entire face consisted of an enormous turned up nose and un-shaven chin carried him off somewhere.

"He can have these two shots for himself!"

Only now did I understand what an awful thing it is to kill a person. Better, probably, just to kick the bucket yourself. Not that I was such a saint. Quite another thing if it's a skirmish, in a battle, in a burst of fury. Not in a dark room where a man is hiding from you as a rat from a fox terrier. I fired both pistols right at the wall, threw them down on the ground and left.

Some time had passed before I entered the room in which the quarrel had taken place. There I found the company sitting at a table again.

Varona had been put to bed in one of the distant rooms under the care of Dubatowk's relatives. I wanted to go home immediately, but they would not let me. Duba-towk seated me at his side and said: "It's alright, young man. It's only nerves that are to blame. He's alive. He'll get well. What else do you need? And now he'll know how to behave when he meets real people. Here – drink this... One thing I must say to you, you are a man worthy of the gentry. To be so devilishly cunning, and to wait so courageously for all the three shots – not everyone is able to do that. And it is well that you are so noble – you could have killed him with the two remaining bullets, but you didn't do that. Now my house to its very last cross is grateful to you."

"But nevertheless it's bad," said one of the gentlemen. "Such self control is simply not human."

Dubatowk shook his head.

"Varona's to blame, the pig. He picked the quarrel himself, the drunken fool. Who else, besides him, would have thought of screaming about money? You must have heard that he proposed to Nadzeya, and got a refusal for an answer. I'm sure that Mr. Andrey is better provided for than the Yanovskys are. He has a head on his shoulders, has work and hands, while the last of their family, a woman, has an entailed estate where one can sit like a dog in the manger and die of hunger sitting on a trunk full of money."

And he turned to everybody:

"Gentlemen, I depend upon your honour. It seems to me that we should keep silent about what's happened. It does no credit to Varona – to the devil with him, he deserves penal servitude, but neither does it do any credit to you or the girl whose name this fool allowed himself to utter in drunken prattle... Well, and the more so to me. The only one who behaved like a man is Mr. Belaretsky, and he, as a true gentleman, will not talk indiscreetly."

Everybody agreed. The guests, apparently, could hold their tongues, for nobody in the district uttered a word about this incident ever since.

When I was leaving, Dubatowk detained me on the porch:

"Shall I give you a horse, Andrey?"

I was a good horseman, but now I wanted to take a walk and come to myself somewhat after all the events that had taken place. Therefore I refused.

"Well, as you like..."

I took my way home through the heather waste land. It was already the dead of night, the moon was hidden behind the clouds and a kind of sickly grey light flooded the waste land. Gusts of wind sometimes rustled the dry heather and then fell complete silence. Enormous stones stood here and there along the road. A gloomy road it was. The shadows cast by the stones covered the ground. Everything all around was dark and depressing. Sleep was stealing on me and the thought of going round the park on a long road past the Giant's Gap frightened me. Perhaps better to take the short cut again across the waste land and look for the secret hole in the fence?

I turned off the road and almost immediately fell into deep mud; I was covered with dirt, got out onto a dry place, and then again got into dirt and finally came up against a long and narrow bog. Cursing myself for having taken this roundabout way, I turned to the left to the undergrowth on the river bank knowing that dry land had to be there, because a river usually dries the soil along its banks. I soon came out again onto the same path along which I had walked on my way to Dubatowk's place, and finding myself half a mile away from his house, walked off along the undergrowth in the direction of Marsh Firs. Ahead, about a mile and a half away, the park was already visible, when some incomprehensible presentiment forced me to stop. Maybe it was my nerves strung to such a high pitch this evening by all the drinking and the danger, or perhaps it was some sixth sense that prompted me that I was not alone in the plain.

I didn't know what it was, but I was certain that it was yet far away. I hastened my steps and soon rounded the tongue of the bog into which I had just a while ago crept and which blocked the way. It turned out that directly in front of me, less than a mile away, was the Marsh Firs Park. The marsh hollow, about ten metres wide, separated me from the place where I had been about forty minutes ago and where I had fallen into the mud. Behind the hollow lay the waste land, equally lit by the same flickering light, and behind that – the road. Turning around, I saw far to the right a twinkling light in Dubatowk's house, peaceful and rosy; and to the left, also far away, behind the waste land the wall of the Yanovsky Forest Reserve was visible. It was at a great distance, bordering the waste land and the swamp.

I stood and listened, although an uneasy feeling prompted me that whatever that was, was now nearer. But I did not want to believe this presentiment. There had to be some real reason for such an emotional state. I saw nothing suspicious, heard nothing. What could this signal have been, where had it come from? I lay down, pressed my ear to the ground and felt an even vibration. I cannot say that I am a very bold person. It may as well be that my instinct of self-preservation is more advanced than in others, but I have always been very inquisitive. I decided to wait and was soon rewarded. From the side of the forest some dark mass came moving very swiftly through the waste land. At first I could not guess what it was. Then I heard a gentle and smooth clatter of horses' hoofs. The heather rustled. Then everything disappeared, the mass had perhaps gone down into some hollow, and when it reappeared – the clattering was lost. The mass raced on noiselessly, as if floating in the air, coming nearer and nearer all the time. Yet another instant and my whole body moved ahead. Among the waves of the hardly transparent fog, horsemen's silhouettes could be seen galloping at a mad pace, the horses' manes whirling in the wind. I began to count them and counted up to twenty. At their head galloped the twenty-first. I still had my doubts, but here the wind brought somewhere from afar the sound of a hunting horn. A cold, dry frost ran down my spine giving me the shivers.

The horsemen's faint shadows ran obliquely from the road to the swampy hollow. Their capes were swirling in the wind, the horsemen were sitting straight as dolls in their saddles, yet not a sound reached my ears. The silence was creating this horror that enveloped me. In the fog bright spots were dancing. And racing on ahead was sitting the twenty-first, motionless in his saddle. A hat with a feather in it was lowered to cover his eyes. His face was pale and gloomy, his lips were compressed.

The wild heather sang beneath the horses' hoofs.

I looked attentively at the sharp noses that stuck out from under their hats, at the thin and shaggy legs of the horses that were of an unknown species.

Bending forward, grey, transparent horsemen raced on, silently they raced, no one other than King Stakh's Wild Hunt.

I didn't immediately grasp the fact that roaming in the marsh they had fallen on my track and were now following after me. They stopped, just as noiselessly, near the place where I had fallen into the swamp. They were no more than twenty metres away from me across the swamp, I could even see that their horses, misty horses, were of a black and varicoloured coat, but I did not hear a single sound, only at times somewhere near the dense forest the horn sang in a muffled tone. I saw that one of them had bent down in his saddle, looked at the tracks and straightened up again. The leader waved his hand in the direction I had gone, rounding the hollow, and the Hunt raced on. A cold anger boiled within my heart. *Well, no, be you apparitions or whatever else, but I shall meet you in a fitting manner!* A revolver and six bullets – and we shall see. I thrust my hand in my pocket, and a cold sweat covered my forehead – I could find no revolver.

Only now did I recollect that I had left it at home in the table's drawer.

"This is the end," I thought.

But to await the end with folded arms was not among my rules. They will be here within fifteen minutes. The country here is rugged. Here and there are hillocks that I can run across, while horsemen are afraid to get stuck in the mud on their horses. In this way I can confuse the tracks. Although, if they are apparitions, they can fly across the dangerous places through the air.

I removed my boots so that the noise of my steps should not attract the attention of the Hunt. At first I went stealthily, and then, when the bushes concealed the hollow, I jumped about more quickly in loops, running across the heather, wetting my feet in the dew.

At first I went along the hollow, then made a sharp turn in the bushes towards Marsh Firs. I rushed through water and dirt – how could I now pay attention to such trifles? I was soon again on a path and on turning about I saw the Wild Hunt already on the other side of the swamp. It was moving in my tracks with a dull stubbornness. The Hunt raced on, the manes and capes swirling in the air.

Since the bushes hid me and the path was downhill, my running was of a class that I had never shown before and most likely never did afterward. I tore down at such a speed that the wind whistled in my ears, burnt my lungs, and perspiration ate my eyes. And the chase behind my back was slowly but surely coming closer. Soon it seemed to me I was about to fall and would be unable to get up - I had in fact stumbled twice - but I ran and ran, on and on. Slowly, very slowly, the dark park was coming nearer, but the clatter of the horses' hoofs sounded ever closer.

Luckily, as people would say today, I got my second wind. I ran straight through holes and ravines, skirting hills on which I might be noticed. The horses' hoofs sounded now nearer, now farther, now to the left, now to the right. No time to look round, but nevertheless I looked through the bushes. The riders of the Wild Hunt were flying after me in a milky, low fog.

Their horses stretched out in the air, the horsemen sat motionless, the heather rang beneath their hoofs. Above them, in a strip of clear sky, burnt a lonely sharp star.

I rolled down a hill, crossed a wide path, jumped into a ditch and ran along its bottom. The ditch was not far from the fence. I crept out from it and with one leap reached the fence. They were about forty metres away from me, but they lingered a little, having lost my scent and it enabled me to creep through a hardly noticeable hole and hide in the lilac. The park was in complete darkness and therefore when they raced past me along the path I couldn't get a good look at them. But I distinctly heard the leader groan:

"To the Gap!"

On raced the Wild Hunt, and I sat down on the ground. My heart was beating like a lamb's tail, but I jumped up quickly, knowing that I must not sit after this race. I understood very well that I had only a minute's respite. They could reach the house in a roundabout way more quickly than I in a straight line. And again I ran on. My feet were bleeding. Several times I caught my feet on roots, and fell down, pine needles lashed against my face. The large castle grew up in front of me entirely unexpectedly, and simultaneously I heard the clattering of the horses' hoofs somewhere ahead of me. They sounded again, they thundered so often that my skin sensed their incredibly fast gallop.

I decided to put everything at stake. I could hide in the park, but in the castle was a girl who was now most likely dying of fright. I had to be there. Besides, that was where I had left my weapon.

A few jumps and I landed on the porch. I began beating on the door.

"Nadzeya! Miss Nadzeya! Open the door!"

She might fall unconscious on hearing my screaming. But the hoofs were already beating near the castle. Again I began to thunder.

The doors opened unexpectedly. I jumped into the house, locked the doors and was about to rush off for my weapon, but through the eye in the door I saw the misty horses racing past and disappearing behind the turn in the lane.

I glanced at first at Yanovsky and then in the mirror. She was evidently shocked at my appearance, in rags, all in scratches, blood on my hands, my hair dishevelled. I looked at Yanovsky again. Her pale face had grown stiff with fright, she shut her eyes and asked:

"Now you believe in King Stakh's Wild Hunt?"

"Now I believe," I answered darkly. "And weren't you afraid to open the door at such a moment?! Such a courageous little heart!"

In answer she burst into tears:

"Mr. Belaretsky... Mr. Andrey... Andrey. I was so afraid, I had such fear for you. My God... my God! Let only me be taken!"

I clenched my fists.

"Miss Nadzeya, I don't know whether they are apparitions or not. Apparitions couldn't be so real, and people couldn't be so transparent or blaze with such malice and rage. But I swear to you: for this fright of yours, for your tears, they shall pay, shall pay a high price. This I swear to you."

Somewhere in the distance the fast clattering of horses' hoofs was fading away.

CHAPTER SIX

If my story has formerly been somewhat slow in its development, it will now, very likely be too swift. But that cannot be helped, the events which followed that dreadful night came so thick and fast that my head was in a whirl. The following morning Yanovsky went with me to the village where I wrote down some legends. All along the way I was trying to convince her that she needn't be in such fear of the Wild Hunt, told her how I had outwitted the hunters the day before, but one thought wracked my brain: "But what was it? What was it?"

Though my hostess became somewhat merrier, she was, nevertheless, still depressed. I hadn't seen her previously in such a mood. When I returned to the castle with Yanovsky remaining behind at one of the wings with the watchman, I noticed a dirty piece of paper stuck with a thorn onto the bark of a fir tree in a conspicuous place. I tore it off:

"What's fated must die. You, a tramp, a newcomer, get out of the way. You are a stranger here, these cursed generations are no business of yours. King Stakh's Hunt comes at midnight. Await it."

I only shrugged my shoulders. After the apocalyptic fright I had experienced the night before, this threat seemed to me a bad melodrama, a thoughtless move, and it convinced me that the devilry was of Earthly origin.

I hid the note. And at night two events occurred simultaneously. I slept very badly now, nightmares tortured me. At midnight I was awakened by steps, but this time, a kind of incomprehensible certainty that they were not merely sounds, forced me to get up. I threw on my dressing gown, carefully opened the door and went out into the hall. The steps sounded at the far end and I saw the housekeeper with a candle in her hand. I followed her carefully, doing my best to stay in the dark. She entered one of the rooms. I was about to follow her, but she looked out of the door and I only just managed to press myself against the wall. And when I came up to the room I saw nothing in it except an old desk and a fretted closet. On the window sill stood a candle. I entered the room, looked into the wardrobe carefully – it was empty. The room, too, was empty. To my regret, to remain in it was impossible or I might spoil everything. Therefore I returned very quietly to the turning in the hall and stood there. My dressing gown didn't keep me warm at all, my feet were freezing, but I remained standing there. Perhaps about an hour had passed, when suddenly I was startled by another apparition. The figure of a woman in blue came moving along the hall at its far end. I moved towards her, but stopped dead, startled even more. This woman's face was a copy of Nadzeya Yanovsky's, only surprisingly changed. It was majestic, calm and significantly older. Where had I seen this face? I had already guessed, but I didn't believe my own eyes. Of course, the portrait of the executed lady. The Lady-in-Blue!

I forgot about the housekeeper, about the cold, about everything. I had to unravel this secret immediately. But she kept on floating, floating away from me, and only now I noticed that a large window in the hall was half open. She stepped onto the low window sill and disappeared. I ran over to the window, looked out and saw nothing, as if someone had played a trick on me. The corner of the house, truth be told, was not at all far away, but the ledge was just as narrow as the one under the window of my room. I pinched my hand – no, I wasn't asleep.

So amazed was I by this last event that I almost missed the housekeeper's return. She was walking with a candle, holding some kind of a sheet of paper in her hand. I pressed myself into the niche in the door, she passed me by, stopped at the window, shook her head, muttering something, and shut it.

Then she began to go down the stairs to the first floor. *What had she been looking for, here at the top?* I was about to go into my room, but suddenly stopped and quietly knocked at Yanovsky's door. You never can tell, maybe it was she who had been in the hall? I whispered:

"Miss Nadzeya, are you asleep?"

In answer I heard a sleepy muttering.

I returned to my room and without lighting a candle, sat on my bed. I was shivering with cold and wracking my brain trying to find an answer to all these contradictory thoughts.

CHAPTER SEVEN

When Miss Yanovsky and I were taking a walk in the tree alley the following day, I told her about what had occurred the previous night. Perhaps I should not have done that, I don't know, but I could not rid myself of the thought that there was something suspicious about the housekeeper. She was not surprised, looked at me with her large, meek eyes and slowly answered:

"You see, I was so worried about you that I couldn't fall asleep for a long time. And later I was so exhausted that I heard nothing. You shouldn't get up at night, Mr. Belaretsky. If anything should happen to you, I'd never forgive myself. You're mistaken about the housekeeper. As a matter of fact she can go about anywhere and everywhere. I don't keep to the old rules that a housekeeper must come up to the second floor only when she is called upon. She is not the worst thing here – you have yet to see the Lady-in-Blue. She has appeared again. Something bad will occur most assuredly."

And with austere courage she added:

"It will be a death most likely. And I have every reason to believe that it is I who is to die."

We were sitting in the old, abandoned summer house. Time had covered the stones with moss that after the rain was freshly green again. In the middle of the summer house was a girl in marble with an ear missing, and a snail was creeping over her face. Miss Yanovsky looked at the statue and sadly smiled.

"There, and that's how it's with us, the abominable desolation of our lives. You said that you didn't quite believe it might have been a ghost. I don't agree with you. But even if it were so – what difference does it make? Isn't it all the same what you are suffering from, if suffer you must to atone for sins?"

"You have atoned for them these two years…" I began. However she paid no attention.

"People fight as spiders do in a jar… The gentry is becoming extinct. We were, formerly, as strong as stone, whereas now… You know, were we to chop off a piece of stone from this old building, slugs would be found there. Who knows what it is they feed on there? Should you strike something against this stone, it will fall to pieces. The same with us. Well, let them strike – the sooner the better."

"And you will not regret the loss of such beauty?" I said pointing to the house and everything around.

"No. My only wish is that the sooner it should come the better. I've long been ready to disappear together with this dump. I'd have no regrets, either for it or for myself. But I've begun to notice lately that I'm slightly worried about life, that I should regret its loss, life is probably not so bad after all, so it seems to me. There may be some sense in believing in the sun, in friends, in the budding of the trees, in bravery, and in faithfulness."

"It's a good thing that you have begun to think so."

"No, it's very bad. It's a hundred times more difficult to die loving life than to die believing it to be what I had formerly supposed it was. Previously, my soul was habitually in a state of fright. Now it is changing into something that I have no name for, something that I have no wish for. And all because I have begun to believe a little in people. This belief is unnecessary. Unnecessary is this hope. It was better and calmer the way things were previously."

We kept silent for a while. She bent down to a branch half fallen down from a maple tree and ran a hand over it.

"People don't always lie. I'm very grateful to you, Mr. Belaretsky. You must forgive me for having listened to your conversation with Svetsilovich. Such a kind and pure soul, the only real person in this district besides yourself, and yes, perhaps my dear uncle. I'm thankful that not everywhere do people have more nerve than brains."

"By the way, about Dubatowk. What, in your opinion, must I do? Shall I tell him everything and then together we could begin to expose all the abominations?"

Her eyelashes quivered.

"No, don't! He is a very good man. He has a hundred times proved his devotion and faithfulness to our family. He didn't let Haraburda bring an action against us for a promissory note when my father was still alive, and the means he used were not quite proper. He called out Haraburda to fight a duel and said that all his relatives would call out Haraburda as long as he lived. And that's why I'd not wish to have Dubatowk interfere. He's too hot-tempered, this dear uncle of mine."

Her eyes were thoughtful and sad, but suddenly brightened.

"Mr. Belaretsky, I've long wished to say this to you. After our talk last night, when you swore your oath, I realized there was no time to be lost. You must leave Marsh Firs, leave it today! At the latest – tomorrow, and return to the city. Enough's enough! The violins have played their song, the fineries have been put away. Death has its own laws. There is nothing you can do here. Leave us, leave this house that the centuries have been covering with filth, leave these despicable people and their crimes to what best fits them – the night and the rain. You are too much alive for all this. And you are a stranger."

"Miss Nadzeya!" I exclaimed. "What are you saying? I've already been reproached here, have already been called an outsider. Could I have expected to hear this cruel word from you, too? What have I done to deserve it?"

"Nothing," she answered dryly. "But it's too late. Everything comes too late in the world. You are too much alive. Go to your people, to those who are alive, who go hungry and can laugh. Go and conquer. And leave the graves to the dead..."

"But aren't *you* my people?" I exploded. "And these people, frightened and hungry, aren't *they* my people? And Svetsilovich, whom I shall have to betray, isn't he of my people? And their godforsaken swamps where abominable things occur, aren't these swamps my land? And the children crying at night when they hear the hoofs of the Wild Hunt, trembling with fright all their lives, aren't they my brethren's children? How can you even dare suggest such a thing to me?"

She wrung her hands.

"Mr. Belaretsky, don't you understand it's too late to awaken this land, and me, too? We are tired of hoping. Don't awaken new hopes in us. It's too late. Too late! Don't you understand that you are alone, that you cannot do anything, that your death would be an inconsolable misfortune? I should never forgive myself. Oh! If only you knew what frightful apparitions they are, how they thirst for blood, the blood of other people!"

"Miss Yanovsky," I said coldly, "Your house is a fortress. If you drive me out, I shall go to a less dependable one, but I will not leave these parts. One of two things is necessary now... to die or to conquer. To die – if they are spectres. To conquer – if they are people. I shall not leave this place, not for anything in the world. If I bother you, that's another matter. But if your request is due to your fear for my safety, because you don't wish me to risk my skin – I shall remain. When all's said and done, it's my own skin. And I have the full right to dispose of it to my liking. You understand that, don't you?"

She looked at me taken aback, with tears in her eyes.

"How could you, even for a moment, have thought that I don't wish to see you in this house? How could you have thought that? You are a courageous man. With you I feel safe. Finally, I feel safe with you, even when you are as rude as you have just been. An aristocrat would not have put it that way. The gentry are such gallant men, refined, subtle, are able to hide their thoughts. I'm sick to death of all that. I wish to see you as you were yesterday, or..."

"Or killed," I finished. "Don't worry. You shall never see me like that again. My weapon is with me. And now, it is not I who will flee from them, it is they who shall flee from me, if there is a drop of blood in their incorporeal veins."

She arose and left the summer house. At the very exit she stood a moment, turned around and, looking down at her feet, said:

"I didn't want you to risk your life. My wish was very great. Though after hearing your answer, my opinion of you is a hundred times better. But be careful. Don't forget to carry a weapon with you at all times. I... am glad that you do not want to take my advice and have decided to remain. And I agree with you that one must help the people. The danger threatening me is a trifle in comparison with the peace of mind of the people. They perhaps are more deserving of happiness than those living in the sunny valleys, because they have suffered more in anticipation of it. And I agree with you – someone must help them."

She left, while I remained sitting for some time yet, thinking about her. To meet with such nobility and spiritual beauty in this remote corner was a startling experience.

You know how it uplifts a person and strengthens him to feel that he is being depended upon as on a stone wall. But evidently, I knew myself badly, for the memory of the following night is one of the most awful and unpleasant ones in my life. Ten years later, recalling it, I groaned with shame, and my wife asked me what was wrong. But I never, to this very day, have ever told anybody about that night or what I thought then.

Perhaps I shouldn't reveal it even to you, but I think that shameful thoughts are certainly not so important in themselves as is the question whether a person can conquer them, whether they recurred to him or not. And I have decided to share them with you for the sake of science.

Towards evening Svetsilovich came to see me. Our hostess had a headache, and she locked herself up in her room before his appearance. We talked together, the two of us, sitting near the fireplace, and I related the events of the previous night.

His face expressed amazement and I asked him what had so startled him.

"Nothing," he answered. "The housekeeper – that's rubbish. She, perhaps, simply steals from her mistress's miserly income, or perhaps it's something else entirely. I've known this woman a long time; she's rather stingy and foolish, foolish as a pall. Her brains are overgrown with fat and she is incapable of crime, though it's not a bad idea to keep your eye on her. The Lady–in–Blue is also nonsense. The next time you see her, shoot in her direction. I'm not afraid of women ghosts. But better make a guess why I was so surprised on hearing of the Wild Hunt."

"I – I don't know."

"Well then, tell me, don't you suspect Varona? Let's say that Varona is courting Yanovsky, asks her to marry him, receives a refusal, and then to take revenge, he begins to play tricks with the Wild Hunt. You haven't heard anything about this courtship, have you? Yes, yes, it was two years ago, when Roman was still alive, that Varona offered Nadzeya, who was still a child then, his hand and heart... That's the reason why he is angry with you, that's why he picked a quarrel with you, but when nothing came of it, he decided to remove you from his path. Though I had thought it would take place somewhat later." Hearing this made me think.

"I must confess that such thoughts did enter my mind. It's possible I would even have gone on thinking them if I hadn't known that Varona was lying wounded."

"That's just nonsense. Almost immediately after you left, he appeared at the table, green and dismal, but sober. Bloodletting helped. His bandaged head looked like a cabbage, only his nose and eyes were visible. Dubatowk said to him: 'Well, young man, shame on you – got as drunk as a pig, picked a duel with me, but ran up against a man who gave you a dressing down.' Varona attempted to smile, but he staggered, so weak he was: 'I myself see, Uncle, what a fool I am. And Belaretsky has taught me such a lesson that I'll never again pick a quarrel with people.' Dubatowk only shook his head. 'That's what vodka, with God's will, does to blockheads.' And Varona said to him: 'I think that I should ask his pardon. It turned out that we invited him to be our guest, but we tried to finish him off.' Then he changed his mind, and went on: 'No, I shan't ask to be forgiven, I am angry. And after all, he received satisfaction.' But I can tell you that he sat together with us, and we drank till the very dawn. Dubatowk got so drunk that he recalled being a Christian during Nero's reign and all the time was trying to put his hands in the bowl of hot punch. He drank it hot, blowing out the flames as he drank. Your second in the duel, a blockhead of about forty, was weeping all the time and shouting, 'Mother dear! Come and cuddle me, stroke my head. Your little son is being treated badly. They won't give him any more vodka.' About three people fell asleep under the table. Not a single one of them left for even a minute, so neither Varona nor Dubatowk are in any way connected with the Wild Hunt."

"And do you mean to say that you suspected Dubatowk, too?"

"Why not him?" Svetsilovich said sternly. "I trust nobody now. The question concerns Miss Nadzeya. Then why should Dubatowk be excluded from among the suspects? What reason can there be for that? That he is kind? Well, a person can pretend kindness! I myself... during the duel didn't approach you, fearing that they might suspect something if they are the criminals. And in future I shall conceal our friendship. I suspected even you. What if... but I caught myself in time. A well known ethnographer joins a band! Ha! In the same way Dubatowk might pretend being a little lamb. What displeased me most of all was that gift of his, the portrait of Roman the Old. As if he had a definite purpose in view to unsettle the girl..."

"And why not?" I started. "That's really suspicious. Now she's even afraid to sit at the fireplace."

"That's just it," gloomily confirmed Svetsilovich. "That means that he is not King Stakh. This gift is the very thing that speaks in his favour. And the events at his house."

"Listen," I said. "And why not suppose that you yourself are King Stakh? You left later than I did yesterday. You are jealous of me without any reason. Perhaps you are throwing dust in my eyes, while in fact, no sooner do I leave than you say: 'To your horses, men!'"

I did not think so, not for an instant, but I didn't like this young man being so suspicious today, a young man usually so trusting and sincere.

Svetsilovich looked at me as if he had gone out of his mind, understanding nothing, then he suddenly burst out laughing, and immediately he was his good old self again.

"That's it," I answered in the same tone. "It's wrong to sin against such old men as Dubatowk, so don't. It doesn't take long to slander a person."

"Alright, now I no longer suspect him," he answered still laughing. "I said that they were with me, didn't I? At daybreak Varona began to feel very ill, his wound began to bleed again, he began to rave. An old quack doctor was sent for, then even a proper doctor was brought over. They weren't too lazy to ride off to the district centre for a doctor whose verdict was Varona must stay in bed a whole week. The doctor was told it was an accident."

"So, who else could it have been?"

We turned over in our minds names of everybody in the entire region, but couldn't settle on anybody. We even thought of Bierman and although we understood that he is a lamb, decided to write a letter to a friend of Svetsilovich's in the province, to learn how Bierman had lived there formerly and what kind of a man he is. That was necessary, for he was the only one among the people of the Yanovsky district about whom we knew absolutely nothing. We made all kinds of guesses, but could think of nothing.

"Who is the wealthiest person living in the environs of Marsh Firs?" I asked.

Svetsilovich thought awhile:

"Lady Yanovsky, it seems... Although her wealth is dead capital. Then there is Harovich who doesn't live here, then Mr. Haraburda – by the way he is Yanovsky's principal heir should she die now. Then there is, certainly, Dubatowk. He has little land; his belongings and his house, you see for yourself, are poor, but he must have money hidden somewhere, for he is always entertaining guests in his house, always plenty of eating and drinking there. The rest are unimportant, small fry."

"You say that Haraburda is Yanovsky's heir. Why he and not you, while you are a relative of hers?"

"But I've already told you that my father relinquished his rights to any heritage. It's dangerous, the estate has no income, and according to rumours, some promissory notes are attached to it."

"And don't you think that Haraburda..."

"Him? No, I don't. What has he to gain in earning by crime what will belong to him anyway? Let's say that Yanovsky gets married – he has the promissory notes, if it isn't a fable. In addition he's a coward, not many like him."

"So," I meditated, "Then let's look at things from a different angle. We must learn who had called out Roman from his house that evening. What do we know? That his daughter was visiting some Kulsha. But perhaps it wasn't even to them that Roman went. We have only Bierman's word for it. We'll have to ask Kulsha. And you will make inquiries concerning Bierman's life in the province."

I saw him off to the roadway and was going home through the lane. Dusk had already fallen. My feelings were unpleasant. The lane, as a matter of fact, was now but a narrow path, and in one place an enormous lilac bush crossed it, a bush that had grown into a tree. Its wet leaves, resembling hearts, were still green and shone dully, transparent drops falling off from them. The bush was weeping...

I passed round it and had already taken about ten steps, when suddenly I hear a dry crack behind me. I felt a burning pain in my shoulder.

It is shameful to confess, but I was quaking with fear. "This is it," I thought, "He'll shoot again and that'll be the end of me." I should have shot straight into the bush or simply run away – anything would have been wiser than what I did. Terribly frightened, I rushed off into the bush, my breast open to the bullet. And here I heard something cracking in the bush. I chased after him like a madman, only wondering why he didn't shoot. While he, evidently, also acted according to instinct – he took to his heels at full speed. And so quickly did he run, I couldn't even see him, let alone catch up with him.

I turned around and went home. I walked on almost crying with mortification. In my room I examined the wound. A trifle – a muscle of the upper shoulder blade was scratched. *But why? Why?* It's too late locking the stable door after the horse has bolted. The excitement had probably brought on a nervous shock, for I lay in bed about two hours literally writhing with fright. I should never have thought that a person could be such a booby.

I recalled the warnings, the steps in the hall, the frightful face in the window, the Lady-in-Blue, the chase along the heather waste, this shot in my back.

They are out to kill me, they will certainly kill me. It seemed to me that the darkness was looking at me with invisible eyes of some monster, that somebody would immediately come creeping over and grab me. It is shameful to confess, but I pulled my blanket over my head as if it could defend me. And involuntarily a mean little thought arose: "I must run away. It's easy for them to put their hopes on me. Let them make sense of these abominations and this Wild Hunt by themselves. I'll go mad if I remain here one more week..."

No moral criteria could help. I trembled like an aspen leaf and fell asleep entirely weakened by fear. If the steps of the Little Man were heard that evening, I'd in all probability have hidden under the bed, but luckily that did not happen.

The morning brought me courage. I was calm.

I decided to go to Bierman that day, all the more so that our mistress was still ill. Behind the house grew enormous burdock. It was already taller than a man and drying up. I made my way through it, reached the porch and knocked at the door. Nobody answered. I pulled at the door and it opened. The small anteroom was empty, only Bierman's coat was hanging there. I coughed. There was a rustling of something in the room. I knocked – Bierman spoke in a broken voice:

"Who, who's there? Come in!"

I entered. Bierman got up from behind the table, wrapped his dressing gown tighter about him. His face was pale.

"Good afternoon, Mr. Bierman."

"S-sit down, sit down, please," he began fussing about to such an extent it made me feel uncomfortable. *Why have I come dragging myself here? A person likes his solitude. Just look how alarmed he is...*

But Bierman had already taken himself in hand.

"Take a seat, Honourable Sir. Be seated, please."

I looked at the armchair and saw a plate on it. Some unfinished food in it and a spoon. Bierman quickly removed everything.

"I beg your pardon, I had decided, how shall I put it? To satisfy my appetite."

"But, please, go on eating," I said.

"Oh! Unthinkable! To eat in the presence of a highly respected gentleman. I just... could not."

The lips of this porcelain doll pleasantly rounded out.

"Have you never noticed what an unpleasant sight is a person eating? Oh! It's awful! He chews dully, and reminds one of cattle. There is a striking resemblance in all people to some kind of animal. This one guzzles like a lion. That one champs, I beg your pardon, like the animal the prodigal son pastured. No, my dear sir, I never eat in the presence of anybody."

I took a seat. The room was furnished very modestly. An iron bed, reminding a guillotine, a dinner table, two chairs, another table with books and papers piled on it. Only the table cloth on the first table was unusual, a very heavy one, blue and golden, hanging down to the very floor.

"You are surprised, aren't you? Oh! Honourable Sir, it's the only thing that has remained from former times."

"Mr. Bierman..."

"I'm listening to you, sir."

He sat down, bent his doll-like head, opened wide his large grey eyes and raised his eyebrows.

"I want to ask you whether you haven't any other plans of this house."

"Not exactly, no. There is one more, made about thirty years ago, but it's plainly stated there that it is a copy of the one that I gave you, and only some new partitions are indicated. This is it. Take it, please."

I examined the paper. Bierman was right. "But tell me, isn't there any hidden room on the second floor near the room with an empty closet?"

Bierman thought awhile. "I don't know, Respected Sir, I don't know, Sir. There must be a personal secret archive of the Yanovskys somewhere, but where it is, I do not know."

His fingers were moving quickly across the table cloth, knocking out some kind of a march that I could not understand.

I stood up, thanked him and left.

"What had frightened him so?" I thought. "His fingers beating away, his pale face... This devil of a bachelor has begun to fear people..."

And, however, an obtrusive thought continued to drill my brain.

"Why? Why? There's some dirty business going on here. And why does the word 'hands' keeps whirling in my brain? Hands, hands. What is connected here with hands? There must be something hidden in this word, if it so persistently repeats itself in my subconscious".

I left him firmly convinced it was necessary to be very watchful. I didn't like this doll-like man and especially his fingers, which were twice as long as normal ones and wriggled on the table like snakes.

CHAPTER EIGHT

The day was grey and gloomy, such an indifferent grey day, that I wanted to cry on my way to the estate belonging to the Kulshas. Low grey clouds were creeping over the peat bogs. The landscape lay before me looking like a monotonous barrack. Grey spots were moving about here and there on the smooth brown surface of the plain: a shepherd was grazing sheep there. I walked along the edge of the Giant's Gap, and there was no place, literally, for the eye to rest on. Something dark lay in the grass. I came up closer. It was an enormous stone cross about three metres long. It was knocked down long ago, for the hole in which it had stood was almost levelled with the ground and was covered with undergrowth. The letters on the cross were hardly visible:

"God's slave, Roman, died a quick death here. Passers-by, pray for his soul, so that someone should pray for yours, because it is your prayers that are especially to God's liking."

I stood long near it. So this is where Roman the Old perished!

"Sir, kind sir," I heard a voice behind my back.

I turned around. A woman in fantastic rags was standing behind me with a hand outstretched. Young she was and quite pretty, but her face with its yellow skin was so frightful that I lowered my eyes. In her arms lay a child.

I gave her some money.

"Perhaps the gentleman has at least a tiny piece of bread? I'm afraid I won't be able to reach my place. And baby Yasik is dying..."

"But what's wrong with him?"

"I don't know," she answered tonelessly.

I found a sweet in my pocket and gave it to the woman, but the baby remained indifferent to it.

"Then what shall I do with you, my poor one?"

A peasant was riding along the road in a cart driven by a bull. I called to him, took out a rouble and asked him to take the woman to Marsh Firs, she should be fed there and given shelter.

"May God give you health, sir," the woman whispered, in tears. "Nobody anywhere has given us anything to eat. May God punish those who drive people from the land!"

"And who drove you off?"

"A gentleman."

"What gentleman?"

"The gentleman, Antos. Such a skinny one he is..."

"But what's his surname? Where's your village?"

"I don't know his surname, but the village is here, behind the forest. A good village. We had some money even, five roubles. But they drove us away."

Her eyes expressed wonder. Why didn't the owner take the five roubles, why did he drive them away?

"And where is your husband?"

"They killed him."

"Who killed him?"

"We screamed, wept, didn't want to go away. Yazep also screamed. Then they shot him. And at night came the Wild Hunt and drowned those who screamed the loudest. They disappeared... Nobody screamed anymore."

I hastened to send them off, and myself walked on, desperate beyond description. God, what darkness! What oppression! How to move the mountain? At Dubatowk's we had guzzled so much it would have been sufficient to save the lives of forty Yasiks. The hungry man is not given any bread; his bread is given to the soldier who'll shoot at him since he is hungry. State wisdom! And these unfortunates keep silent! For what sins are you, my people, being chastised, why, on your own native land, are you stormily driven here and there like autumn foliage? What forbidden apple did the first Adam of my tribe eat?

Some guzzled more food than they could possibly eat, others died of hunger under their windows. This torn down cross is here over the one who lived on the fat of the land, and here is a child dying of hunger.

This gap between the one and the other has existed for ages, and this is the end, a logical completion, a running wild; throughout the entire state there is gloom, dull fright, hunger, madness. And all Belarus – a common battlefield for the dead over which the wind howls, dung under the hoofs of contented fat cattle.

Wanderers will not pray for you, Roman the Old. Every man shall spit on your fallen cross. And may God give me strength to save the last one of your kin, she who is innocent of any crime against the inexorable truth of our stepmother, our Belarus.

Is my people really such a forgotten, such a dead nation?

I spent about forty minutes making my way through the damp forest behind the Giant's Gap and reached the narrow path covered with brushwood. Indulging the season, aspens along both sides of the road were already losing their leaves. Birches stood out in the midst of this crimson mass. Birches had already turned yellow, while oaks were yet quite green. A small path led down into a ravine with a murmuring brook, its water the colour of strong tea. Sinking in soft green moss, the banks of the brook were connected by green bridges made of the trees that had been broken down by storms. Along these tree trunks – on some of which the moss was stripped off – people used to cross the brook.

It was silent and solitary. Not a living soul around. A tiny bird was chirping somewhere inside a tree crown, and hanging down from the cobwebs among the trees were lonely leaves that had gotten caught falling down from the branches. Floating about in the brook were tiny red and yellow, sad leaf boats, but in one place there was a small pool in which they whirled about as if they were being cooked there by a water sprite for its supper. In order to cross the brook I had to break down a rather thick, but quite dry aspen to support me, and I broke it down with one kick of my foot.

Behind the ravine the forest became dense. The path disappeared in an impassable thicket, literally jungles of raspberry canes, dry stinging nettle, wild blackberries and other weeds. Hops climbed the trees like green flames, twined about them, hung down from them in sheaves that caught onto my head. There soon appeared the first signs of human life. Bushes of wild lilac, squares of fertilized soil where flower beds once used to sit, and man's fellow companion – tall burdock. The lilac thickets were so dense that I could hardly get out of them and onto a small clearing in which a house stood safely hidden. It was built on a high stone foundation with a wing made of bricks. The wooden columns there had most likely been painted white in the lifetime of their grandfathers; the building leaned over on one side, as if a fatally wounded man about to fall. Twisted plat bands, torn down boarding and glass, grown opalescent with age. Burdock, marigold, oleander in between the steps of the front wing almost blocking the way to the door. And on the way to the back door a puddle filled with bricks. The roof green, and thick with fat, fluffy moss. I sneak-peeked into the house through a little grey window. The inside of the house seemed gloomier and even more neglected. In a word it was a cottage standing on its last legs. Only the witch Baba Yaga was missing, she who should have been lying on the ninth brick, saying, "Fie! I smell the blood of a man!"

Speaking of the devil – through the window a woman's face was looking at me, a face so dry it was merely a skull tightly enveloped in thin yellow parchment. Grey plaits fell on her shoulders. Then a hand, resembling a hen's claw, beckoned me with a wrinkled finger.

I stood in the yard not knowing whom this gesture was meant for.

The door opened a little and that very same hand pushed itself through the slit.

"Here, come in, kind sir, Mr. Hryhor," the head pronounced, "You came to the right address - here unfortunate victims get murdered."

I cannot say that after such a consoling piece of information I had a great desire to enter the house, but the old woman walked down to the last step of the porch and reached out her hand to me across the puddle.

"I've long been awaiting you, our courageous deliverer. The thing is that my slave Ryhor has turned out to be a man who stifles people as did Bluebeard. You remember our reading together about Zhila the Bluebeard, such a gallant cavalier? I'd have forgiven Ryhor everything if he'd done his murdering just as gallantly, but he's a serf. So what can one do?"

I followed after her. In the anteroom was a sheepskin coat on the floor, next to it a saddle, on the wall a whip and a few hardened fox-skins. Besides that, a three-legged stool and the portrait of a man lying on its side, a portrait dirty and torn through and through. The room itself was in such a mess as if a branch of the Grunwald

Battle had been located there 400 years ago, and since that time nothing in the room had ever been dusted, nor had the windows been washed. A crooked table with legs the shape of antique hermae and next to it an armchair resembling war veterans without legs and hardly breathing. At the wall a closet leaning over and threatening to fall down on the first person who would come up to it. On the floor near the door stood a large bust of Voltaire bearing a resemblance to the mistress of the house. He looked at me coquettishly from under the rags which crowned his head instead of laurels. A cheval glass was squeezed into one corner and something resembling bird droppings covered its surface. Its upper half was covered with a thick layer of dust. To make up for that, its lower half was carefully wiped clean. Fragments of dishes, bread crumbs, fish bones were scattered just about everywhere, just like in a kingfisher's nest, where the bottom is covered with fish scales. And the mistress herself reminded one of a kingfisher, that gloomy and strange bird that prefers solitude.

She turned towards me, and again I saw her face, saw a nose hanging down to her very chin, and enormous teeth.

"My Knight, wouldn't it be nice if you wiped off the dust from the upper half of the cheval glass? I'd like to see myself in my full height... In all my beauty..."

I shifted from one foot to the other, hesitating, not knowing how to fulfill her request, but she said suddenly:

"You see, you greatly resemble my deceased husband. What a man he was! He was taken alive into heaven, the first among men after the prophet Elijah. But Roman fell alive into the nether regions. All due to the evil genius of the Yanovsky region – King Stakh's Wild Hunt. From the day my husband died, I stopped cleaning the house as a sign of mourning. Beautiful, isn't it? And so romantic!"

She smiled a coquettish smile and began making eyes at me according to the unwritten rules at aristocratic girls' boarding schools: "Keep your eyes on the person talking with you, then to the side with a slight bending of the head, again at the person you are talking to, then at the upper corner of the room and down at the ground."

This was a malicious parody on human feelings. It was all the same as if a monkey had unexpectedly begun performing Ophelia's song in its English original.

"It is beautiful here. Only frightening. Oh! How frightening!"

Suddenly she threw herself on the floor away from me and buried her head in a pile of some old rags.

"Away! Away with you! You are King Stakh!"

The woman beat herself hysterically and shouted loudly. Horrified, I thought that such a fate probably awaited all the people in this region if the black wing of incomprehensible fear were to remain hanging over this land.

I was standing at a loss, when somebody's hand was laid on my shoulder and a man's rough voice said:

"Why are you here? Don't you see that she is a bit – not in her right mind? A wonder, isn't she?"

The fellow went to the anteroom, brought a portrait full of holes from there, and put it on the table. A middle aged man was depicted in the portrait in a dress coat and with the Order of St. Vladimir in a button hole.

Then he dragged the woman out from among the rags, seated her in front of the portrait.

"Mrs. Kulsha, this is not King Stakh, not at all. Mr. Fieldmarshal has come to take a look at our well known local beauty. And King Stakh – this one here in the portrait – is dead and cannot kill anybody."

The woman looked at the portrait and fell silent. The man took out a piece of bread from his bosom, bread as black as earth. The old woman started laughing happily. She began to pinch off bits of bread and put them in her mouth, but kept her eyes on the portrait.

"King Stakh! My dear husband. Why are you turning your face away?"

She either scratched the portrait or happily whispered something to him, continuing to eat her bread. I had a good view of the unknown man and used the occasion to examine him. He was about thirty years old, in a peasant's cloth coat and in leather sandals. Tall as he was, well built, his chest powerful and bulging. Whiskers made his face look severe and somewhat harsh. This impression was strengthened by two little wrinkles between the eyebrows and widely set burning eyes. A white felt hat was lowered down on his forehead. Something about him breathed of freedom, of the forest.

"You are Ryhor, aren't you? Kulsha's watchman?"

"Yes," He answered with a hint of irony in his voice. "And you, apparently, are Miss Yanovsky's guest. You're a well known bird around here now, seems you sing well."

"And are you always like that with her?" I showed at the old woman who was spitting on the portrait with great concentration.

"Always. She's been this way for two years already."

"But why don't you take her to the district centre for treatment?"

"I pity her. Guests would come when she was in good health, but now not a single dog. The gentry! Our young ladies, to the devil with them..."

"But isn't it difficult for you?"

"No, not at all. Zosya looks after her when I am hunting. She's no trouble most of the time, has scarce needs. Only eats a lot of bread, lots of it. She wants nothing else."

He took out an apple from his pocket and offered it to the old woman.

"Highly respected lady, take this."

"Don't want it," eating her bread with gusto. "Poison, everything is poison, bread alone is pure, godly."

"You see," Ryhor said gloomily. "Once a day we force her to eat a hot meal. Sometimes she bites my fingers. When we give her food – she always tries to grab me... But she wasn't bad when young. Even if she were bad, we couldn't leave her to herself, the God's child as she is now."

And he smiled such a guilty, childish smile that I was surprised.

"But why is she like that?"

"Got frightened after Roman's death. They all live in fear, and I can tell you, for most of them it's what they deserve."

"Yanovsky as well?"

"It would be evil to speak badly about her. A kind woman. I'm sorry for her."

I became bolder now, for I understood – this man was not a traitor.

"Listen, Ryhor, I came here to ask you about something."

"Ask away," he said, changing the tone of his voice and sounding more fraternal now, which I liked.

"I have decided to unravel this Wild Hunt of King Stakh's. You know? I've never seen a ghost, want to feel it with my own hands."

"Ghosts... spooks," he grumbled. "Fine ghosts they are, if their horses leave very real excrement along the road! However, sir, why do you want to do that? What reasons have you?"

Now I did not like the way he addressed me.

"Don't call me 'sir!' I'm no more a 'sir' than you. While as to my reason why... well... it is interesting, that's all. And I feel sorry for the lady and many other people."

"We understand such things. Like Zosya is for me...
But why don't you say that you are angry with them,
that you want to take revenge? You see, I know how you
escaped from the Wild Hunt near the river." I was as-
tonished.

"You know about that, do you? How?"

"Every person has eyes, and every person leaves footprints in the Earth. You ran away like a sensible man.
What's bad is that I always lose their footprints. And they
begin and end on the highway."

I told him about everything from the very beginning.
Ryhor listened, sitting motionless, his large rough hands
on his knees.

"I've listened attentively," he said, when I had finished.
"I like you, sir. From the peasantry, aren't you? From
muzhyks, I think; yes, and if not from muzhyks, you're
not far from them. I, too, have long wanted to get at
these spooks, crush them, burn their wings, but I've had
no comrade. If you're not joking, then let's get together.
However, I see that this idea to turn to me has only just
now come to you. So, why now, so suddenly? And what
did you have in mind before?"

"I don't know, why I decided to. People speak well of
you. When Miss Yanovsky became an orphan, you took
pity on her. She told me that you even wanted to come
to Marsh Firs to work as watchman, but something interfered. Well, and then I like your being independent,
and that you take care of the sick woman, and pity her.
But previously I simply wanted to ask you how it had
come about that Yanovsky was delayed at the Kulsha's
that evening when Roman was killed."

"Why she was delayed I, myself, don't know. That day
a number of girls had gathered from neighbouring estates
at the house of my mistress. They were having a good
time there. And why Miss Yanovsky was invited – that,

too, I don't know. She hadn't been there, you see, many years before that event. And you see for yourself what this woman is like now, she won't tell..."

"Why won't she tell?" the old woman suddenly smiled almost quite sensibly. "I will tell. I'm not mad, it's simply more convenient this way and safer. It was Haraburda who asked that poor Nadzeya should be invited. And his niece was in my house then. You are such a gentleman, Mr. Fieldmarshal, that I shall tell you everything. Yes, yes, it was Haraburda who advised us then to take the child. Our people are all very kind. Mr. Dubatowk had our promissory notes – he didn't begin proceedings against us for their recovery. That's so to speak, a guarantee that you will come to visit me more often and drink wine. Now I can force you to drink even vodka. Yes, everybody invited Nadzeya. Haraburda, and Fieldmarshal Kamiensky, and Dubatowk, and Roman... and King Stakh, this one here. But your poor little head, Nadzeya, and your golden braids, lie together with your father's bones!"

These lamentations for a living person were distasteful to me and made me wince.

"You see, you've learned something," Ryhor said gloomily.

When we left, the old woman's wailing quieted down.

"Well then," Ryhor said, "all right, let's look for them together. I want to see this surprising marvel. I'll try to find out something among the common people, while you'll look among papers and ask the gentry. And maybe we'll learn something..."

His eyes suddenly became bitter, the corners of his eyebrows meeting at the bridge of his nose. "Girls were invented by the devil. All of them should be strangled to death, and the boys fighting among themselves for the few remaining ones, will kill themselves out. But nothing can be done..." Unexpectedly he ended up with:

ULADZIMIR KARATKEVICH

"Take me, for instance. Although my forest freedom is dear to me, still I sometimes think about Zosya, who also lives here. Maybe I'll live alone all my life in the forest. That's why I believed you, because I sometimes begin to go mad for those devilish female eyes..." I didn't think so at all, but didn't consider it necessary to convince this bear that he was wrong. Ryhor continued, "But, my friend, remember this well. If you have come to stir me up and then to betray me – there are many who have a grudge against me here – so know this – your stay will not be long on this Earth. Ryhor is not afraid of anybody. Quite the opposite, everybody is afraid of Ryhor. And Ryhor has friends. It's impossible to live here otherwise. And his hand shoots accurately. In a word, you must know this, I'll kill!"

I looked at him reproachfully, and he, glancing at my eyes, burst out laughing loudly, and his tone, as he ended up, was quite a different one:

"And anyway, I've been waiting for you a long time. For some reason or other it seemed to me that you wouldn't leave things alone, and if you took to clearing them up, you wouldn't pass me by. So well then, why not help each other?"

We parted at the edge of the forest near the Giant's Gap, arranging to meet in the near future. I went home straight through the park.

When I returned to Marsh Firs, twilight had already descended on the park, the woman and her child were sleeping in one of the rooms on the first floor, but the mistress was not in the house. I waited for about an hour, and when it was quite dark, I could not bear it any longer and went out in search of her. I hadn't walked far along the dark lane when I saw a white figure moving towards me in fright.

"Miss Nadzeya!"

"Oh! Oh, it's you? Thank God! I was so worried! You came straight here?"

Bashfully she looked down at the ground. When we came up to the castle, I said to her quietly:

"Miss Nadzeya, never leave this house in the evening. Promise me that."

She promised, but only reluctantly.

CHAPTER NINE

This night gave me a clue to the solution of a question that interested me, a question that turned out to be an entirely uninteresting one, save perhaps only in that I once again became convinced of the fact that stupid people, otherwise generally kind-hearted souls, can be contemptible.

On hearing steps again in the night, I went out and saw the housekeeper with a candle in her hand. I followed her as she went into the room with the closet, but this time I decided not to retreat. The room was again empty, the closet also, but I tried all the boards of the back wall – the closet stood in a niche – then I tried to raise them and became convinced that they were removable. The old woman was probably deaf; otherwise she would have heard me. With great difficulty I managed to push myself through the cracks I had made, and I saw a vaulted passage that led sharply downstairs. The steps were damaged and slippery, and the passage so narrow that my shoulders rubbed against the walls. I went down the steps and saw a small room, also vaulted. There I found two closets, and along the walls of the room stood trunks, bound with iron. Everything was open and paper and leaves of parchment were scattered everywhere. A table stood in the middle, beside it on a roughly knocked together stool was sitting the housekeeper. She appeared to be examining a sheet, quite yellowed with time. The greedy expression on her face was shocking.

When I entered, she screamed with fright, made an attempt to hide the sheet. I managed to grab her hand.

"Miss housekeeper, give that to me. And be kind enough to tell me why you come here every night to this secret archive, what you are doing here, why you frighten people with your footsteps."

"Ugh! My God! How quick you are!" She exclaimed, collecting herself quickly. "Wants to know everything..."

Evidently, because she was on the first floor and did not consider it necessary to stand on ceremony with me, she began to speak with that expressive intonation of the common folk. "And teal and poppy you don't want? Just see what he needs! And he's taken the paper. May your children hide your bread from you in your old age as you have hidden this paper from me. Perhaps I have more right to be here than you. But he, just look, sits there, asking his questions.... May you be overtaken by ulcers the way you overtake me with your questions!"

This had become boring, and I said: "What is it you want? Prison time? Why are you here? Or perhaps it's you who sends signals to the Wild Hunt from here?"

The housekeeper was offended. Wrinkles gathered on her face.

"Shame on you, sir, what a sin!" she quietly muttered. "I'm an honest woman, I've come here to get what's mine. There it is, in your hand. It belongs to me." I looked at the piece of paper. It was an extract from a resolution passed by a smallholder claims committee:

"And although the above mentioned Zakrewsky declares to this very day that he and not Haraburda is heir to the Yanovskys, this case which has lasted over a period of twenty years, is now closed, as not having been proven, and Mr. Isidore Zarkevsky is deprived of his rights to aristocratic rank for the lack of proof."

"So what?" I asked.

"This is what, my dear fellow," the housekeeper came back bitingly, "I am Zakrewsky, that's what I am. And it was my father who went to court with the great and the powerful. I didn't know about it, but my thanks to some good people. They told me what to do. The district judge took ten little red ones, but he gave me good advice. Give me that paper."

"It won't help you," I said. "It isn't really a document. Here the court refuses your father his request, even his right to the gentry is not established. I know about this examination of the petty gentry very well. If your father had had papers to prove his right for substitution after the Yanovskys – that would be another matter. But he did not hand in any papers – and that means that he did not have them."

The housekeeper's face reflected a piteous attempt to understand these complicated things.

Then, not believing me, she asked:

"But perhaps the Yanovskys bribed them? These people who raise trifling objections, just you give them some money! I know. They took the papers away from my father and hid them here."

"And can you sue them twenty years running?" I asked. "Twenty more years?"

"My dear fellow, by that time I'll have gone to wash God's portals for him."

"Well, so you see. And you have no papers. You have searched everything here, haven't you?"

"Everything, young man, everything. But it's a shame to lose what's mine."

"But they are all only vague rumours."

"But the money – those red ones and the blue ones – mine."

"And it is very bad to rummage nights among papers not belonging to you."

"My dear fellow, the money is mine," she drawled dully.

"The court will not grant you it, even if there were any papers to prove it. This entailed estate has belonged to the Yanovskys over a period of 300 years or even longer."

"But it's mine, my dear fellow," almost in tears, and the greed on her face was loathsome to see. "I would have stuffed them, the dear ones, here, right here in my stockings. I would have eaten money, slept on money."

"There aren't just any papers," losing all patience. "There is a lawful heir."

And at this moment something awful occurred. The old woman stretched her neck, the neck became very long – and with her face close to mine, hissed:

"So perhaps... perhaps... she will die soon."

Her face even brightened at this hope.

"She will die, and that's all. She's weak, sleeps badly, almost no blood in her veins, coughs all the time. It won't cost her anything to die. The curse will be fulfilled. Why must Haraburda get this castle when I could live in it? It won't make any difference to her, her suffering will be over – and off with her to the holy spirits. While I here would..."

The expression on my face probably changed for something frightening, for I was furious and she suddenly pulled her head back into her shoulders.

"Hyena! Scavenging a corpse? Only she's no dead corpse, she is a living, breathing person. And such a person who is worth dozens of your kind, who has a greater right than you to walk this Earth, you foolish, empty thing."

"My dear fellow..." she whined.

"Shut up, you witch! And you wish to send her to her grave? You are all alike here, blood suckers! You are all ready to murder a person for the money. All of you – spi-

156   ULADZIMIR KARATKEVICH

ders. For the sake of those blue little papers... And do you know what life is, that it is so easy for you to speak of taking another person's life? I wouldn't scatter pearls at your feet, but hear me! You want her to exchange the sunlight, joy, good people, the long life awaiting her for the worms in the ground, is that what you want? So that *you* can sleep on money? The same money that the Wild Hunt is seeking here? Maybe it's you who lets the Lady-in-Blue in? Why did you open the window in the hall yesterday?"

"Oh, dear Lord! I didn't open it! It was so cold then. I was even surprised at it being open." She was almost wailing.

Her face expressed such fear that I could no longer keep silent. I lost all prudence.

"You want her death! You evil dog, you crow! Get out! She's a noble lady, your mistress. Perhaps she'll not drive you out, but I promise you, that if you do not leave this house that you have polluted with your stinking breath, I'll see that everyone of your kind here is put in prison."

She went over to the staircase crying bitterly. I followed. We went upstairs to the room where that closet was, and I stopped in surprise. Lady Yanovsky in a white dress with a candle in her hand was standing before us. Her face was sad, and she looked at the housekeeper with disgust.

"Mr. Belaretsky, I heard your talk accidentally, heard it from the very beginning. I had followed in your footsteps. At last I've learned the meaning of indignity and the depth of one's conscience. And you..." she turned to Zakrewsky, standing aside with head lowered, "You can remain here. I forgive you. With difficulty, but I forgive you. And you, Belaretsky, forgive her. Stupid people should sometimes be forgiven. Because... Where will she go from here? Nobody needs her, a foolish old woman."

A tear fell off her eyelashes. She turned around and left. I went after her. Lady Yanovsky stopped at the end of the hall and said quietly:

"For the sake of these papers people cripple their souls. If my ancestors hadn't forbidden it, how gladly I would have given this mouldy old house to somebody. This house, and also my name, are a torture for me. If only I could die soon. Then I'd leave it to this woman with a heart of stone and a stupid head. Let her be happy if she is able to creep on her belly for the sake of this junk."

In silence we went down into the room on the lower floor and over to the fireplace. We stood there looking at the fire, and its crimson reflections fell on Yanovsky's face. In the last few days she had changed noticeably, perhaps she had grown up, perhaps she was simply coming into womanhood. I hope no one besides myself had noticed this. I was the only one to see that life was warming up as yet unnoticeably in this pale sprout that had been growing underground all this time. Her look had become more meaningful and inquisitive, although her face was still just as badly disfigured by the mask of that same chronic fear. All together, she had become a little livelier. For some reason the pale sprout had come to life.

"It's good to stand like this, Miss Nadzeya," I said pensively. "A fire burning..."

"A fire... It's good to have it, to see it burn. It is good when people don't lie."

A wild cry, an inhuman cry, reached us from the yard – it seemed that a demon screamed and sobbed, not a human being. And immediately following this cry, we heard a steady, mighty thundering of hoofs near the porch. And the voice sobbed and screamed so terrifyingly that it could not have come from out of the breast of a human being.

"Roman of the last generation – come out! The revenge is here! The last revenge!"

And something else screamed, something nameless. I could have run out onto the porch, could have shot at these dirty, wild swine and laid down on the spot at least one of them, but in my arms was Nadzeya, and I felt the beating of her frightened little heart through her dress, felt how it was gradually dying out, beating perceptibly less and less often. Frightened for her life, I began to stroke her hair timidly. Slowly she regained consciousness and her eyelashes imperceptibly began to quiver at the touch of my hand on her head. In such a way a frightened puppy accepts the caress of a person who pats it for the first time; its eyebrows quiver, expecting a hit each time the hand is raised.

The thunder was already retreating and my entire being was ready to jump out on the porch together with her, shoot at those bats, and fall down on the steps together with her and die, feeling her at my side, all of her here at my side. In any case, to go on living like this was impossible.

And the voice was sobbing already from far away in the distance:

"Roman! Roman! Come out! Fall under the horses' hoofs! Not now, not yet! Later! Tomorrow! Later! Promise we will come! We'll come!"

And silence. She was in my arms. It seemed as if quiet music had begun playing somewhere, perhaps in my own soul. Quietly, so quietly, far, far away, gently. About sunshine, about raspberry-coloured meadows under glistening dew, about nightingales' merry songs in the crowns of far away lindens. Her face was calm, like that of a sleeping child. Here a sigh broke out, her eyes opened, she looked around in surprise, became severe.

"I beg your pardon, I'll leave."

And she made her way to the staircase leading to the second floor – a white little figure.

It was only now, trembling with excitement, that I understood how courageous, how strong was her soul, if after such nerve wracking experiences she had gone out to meet me and opened the doors twice. Once when I, a complete stranger, arrived here, and once when I ran up to her doors, alarmed by the thundering hoofs of the Wild Hunt under her very windows, chasing me. Most likely it was the Hunt and the dark autumn nights that had impelled her to do that, as does a trustful feeling compel a hare hunted down by dogs, to press itself against the feet of an accidental passerby. This girl had very good nerves if she had endured this life here for two years.

I sat down at the fireplace to watch the flames. Yes, the danger was a terrible one. Three persons against all those dark forces, against the unknown. But enough of sentimentality! They came into the park near the Giant's Gap. Tomorrow I am going on a stake out, to wait for them there. My hands were shaking and my nerves were strung to the utmost. In general my state was worse than a dog's.

"Perhaps I should leave this place?" Stirred a belated thought, an echo of that night of mine, that "night of frights", and it died under the pressure of despair, under an iron determination and the desire to fight.

Enough! Victory or the Giant's Gap – it's all the same. Leave? Certainly not!

I could not leave this loathsome, cold house because she lived here, she whom I had fallen in love with. Yes, fallen in love with. I wasn't afraid to acknowledge my feelings nor was I ashamed of them. Up till now, in my relations with women, there were equality and comradeship, sometimes there was an admixture of some incomprehensible aversion, as is the case with any man, morally

ULADZIMIR KARATKEVICH

uncorrupted, lacking excessive sensuality. That's how it is with many men, probably until the real thing comes. Now it came. *Go away?* Here I was at her side, big and strong – my inner hesitation did not concern her – she depended on me, she was sleeping peacefully now, probably for the first time in many nights.

The moment when I held her in my arms was a decisive one. It decided everything for me that had been accumulating in my heart ever since the time when she rose in defence of the poor, there on the upper floor, at the fireplace. With what joy would I take her away from here, take her somewhere far away, kiss these eyes which were red with weeping, these little hands, take her under my warm, dependable wing, forgive the world its roughness.

But what am I to her? No matter how bitter the thought, but she will never be mine. I have nothing to my name. She is also poor, but she belongs to one of the oldest families, she is blue blood, backed by that "proud glory of endless generations". *Proud glory?* I knew it now, this proud glory that had come to a wild end, but that did not make things any the easier for me. I am a plebeian. Yes, I'll keep silent about this. Nobody shall ever reproach me, nor ever say that I had for the sake of money married into an ancient family, for whom perhaps some antecedent of mine had died somewhere on the battlefield. Nor shall anybody say that I married her taking advantage of her helplessness. The only thing that I can do for her sake is to lie down in the grave, give up my soul for her sake and somehow, to some extent, repay for the radiance of the untold happiness that has brightened my soul on this gloomy evening at this large, unfriendly fireplace. I shall help her to escape – that's all.

I shall be true, forever be true, to this joy mixed with pain, to the bitter beauty of her eyes, and shall repay her with kindness for her thinking well of me. And then will be the end of it all. I shall leave this place forever, and the roads of my country shall be before me in an endless chain, and the sun shall rise in iridescent circles made by the tears quivering on her eyelashes.

CHAPTER TEN

The following day Svetsilovich and I were on our way to a rather small island near the Yanovsky Forest Reserve. Svetsilovich was in a very merry mood, talked at length about love in general and about his own in particular. And how pure and sincere the look in his eyes, so naive and childish his love, that I mentally promised myself never to stand in his way, never to interfere with him, but to clear the way for him to this girl whom I, too, loved.

We Belarusians can rarely be in love without sacrificing something, and I was no exception to this rule. We usually torment her whom we love and even to a greater degree ourselves, because of conflicting thoughts, questions and deeds, which others easily manage to bring to a common denomination.

Svetsilovich had received a letter from the city containing information about Bierman.

Oh, Bierman... Bierman. A fine bird he turned out to be. Comes of an old family, but now impoverished and estranged. The letter states that all of them had an irresistible inclination for solitude, were quite noxious and unsociable. His father was deprived of a fortune; he had embezzled an enormous sum of money, and managed to save himself by losing a large sum of money to the inspector. His mother lived behind curtained windows almost all the time, would go out for a walk at dusk only.

But the most surprising personality was Bierman himself. He was reputed as being an exceptionally fine authority on ancient wooden sculpture and glassware. Something unpleasant had occurred several years ago. He had been sent to Mnichavitsy by the Amateur Antiquity Society which was headed by Count Tyshkievich. The old Polish Roman Catholic Church was being shut down there and, according to rumours, the sculptures in it were of great artistic value. Tyshkievich had his own private museum and he wished to purchase these sculptures for it, for he was handing his museum over to the city as a gift. Bierman went to Mnichavitsy, sent Tyshkievich a statue of St. Christopher and a letter in which he wrote that the sculptures in the church were of no value whatsoever. He was taken at his word, but after some time had passed, it accidentally became known that Bierman had bought all the sculptures, all in all 107 figures, for a miserly sum of money and had sold them to another private collector for a large sum of money. Simultaneously a significant sum of money was found missing from the treasury of the Amateur Society. A search was begun for Bierman, but he had disappeared together with his mother and younger brother, who was being brought up at some private boarding school and had arrived in the city only the previous year. His brother, in addition, was noted for being unsociable, in spite of the fact that he had lived at a boarding school.

When their absence was noticed, it turned out that they had sold their house and had disappeared. The authorities became interested in them. And it became clear that these Biermans were in general not Biermans at all, but who they were in truth – nobody knew.

"Well, yes... A little we have learned," I said. "There is one interesting thing here – Bierman is a criminal. But he fooled a man who like himself was a thief, and it is not for me to judge him. He will receive his just deserts, but that will be later. What's curious here is something else. Firstly, where are his mother and brother? Secondly, who is he in reality? It's clear why he turned up here in the castle. He had to hide. But who he is, who his relatives are – that has yet to be cleared up. I shall without fail follow up this matter. But, Svetsilovich, I have almost no news, except what I learned, and that from the mouth of a mad woman, that on that fatal night Roman was lured from his house by Garaboorda somebody. But I don't even remember what his mug is like, even though I must have seen him at Yanovsky's party."

"That doesn't matter, we'll find out."

We came up to the grove and walked deep into it. It was the only grove in the district in which leaf bearing trees predominated. And there in a glade, not a very large one, we saw Ryhor leaning against an enormous upturned root, holding a long hand gun on his knees. Seeing us, he got up, looked sideways at us as a bear does and changed the position of the rifle stock to hold it more conveniently.

"Be on your guard when walking in the swamp, be on your guard in the park and especially at its southern and western, outskirts," he muttered instead of a greeting.

"Why?" I asked, having introduced him to Svetsilovich.

"This is why," he growled. "They are not phantoms. Too well do they know the secret paths across the Giant's Gap. It surprises you that they can race where no roads are, but they know only too well all the secret hide outs in the region and all the paths leading to them; they use very ancient horseshoes which are nailed onto the horses' hoofs with new calks. What's true is true. The horses step as bears do – at first with their left and then with their right feet, and their steps are wavy, much wider than those our horses make. And for phantoms they are too feeble. A phantom can pass through anything, while these only through the broken down fence at the Gap... And I have learned something else too. There were no more than ten of them the last time, because only half of the horses rode as a horse rides with a person on his back. On the rest there was something lighter on their backs. The one rushing at their head is very hot tempered; he tears at the lips with the bits. And what is more – one of them takes snuff. I found the dust of green tobacco at the place where they had stopped off before making their last race and had left many footprints, having trampled the ground there. It is the place where the large oak stands not far from the torn fence."

"Where can their meeting place be?" I asked

"I know where to look," Ryhor answered calmly. "It is somewhere in the Yanovsky Reserve. I determined that from the footprints. Look here." With a vine twig he began to draw on the ground. "Here is the virgin forest. At the time when Roman was killed, the footprints disappeared right here, almost at the bog surrounding the Reserve. When they were pursuing you after the evening at Dubatowk's, the footprints disappeared northwards, and after what took place near the Yanovsky castle, when they shouted, slightly farther northward. You see, the paths almost coincide."

"Really, that's so," I agreed. "And if they are prolonged they will come together at one point, somewhere in the bog."

"I've been there," Ryhor slightly snorted, as if about some most usual thing. "The swamp there in that place is considered fatal, but I've seen bristle grass growing there in some places. And wherever this grass grows, the horse belonging to a lousy fellow, can always put his foot, if that is what his lousy owner needs."

"Where is this darn place?" Svetsilovich demanded, suddenly growing pale.

"At the Cold Hollow where the stone called the Witch's Mortar lies."

Svetsilovich grew even paler. Something had alarmed him, but he managed to control himself.

"And what else?" I asked.

"This is what else." Ryhor gloomily muttered. "You are on a false track. Although it was Haraburda who lured Roman out of his house, he has no connection with the Wild Hunt. Those two nights when it appeared the last time, Haraburda was sitting in his lair as a rat in its hole. I know that because his place was well watched."

"But he is interested in Yanovsky's dying or going mad. That would benefit him. It was he who persuaded Kulsha to invite Yanovsky to his house that evening, it was he who sent his own daughter to the Kulsha's too, and then detained everybody there till night-time."

Ryhor became thoughtful. Then he muttered:

"Perhaps you are right. You are clever, and you must know. But Haraburda was not there, I bet my head on that. He rides a horse badly. He's a coward. And he keeps to his castle all the time. But he can talk others into doing dirty tricks."

And here Svetsilovich became even paler, staring into space, as if he were considering something extremely important. I did not disturb him. If he wanted to, he'd tell us himself. However, he didn't think long before opening up.

"Brothers, it seems I know this person. You understand, you have helped me to find an answer to a riddle. Firstly, at the 'Witch's Mortar'. Yesterday evening I saw a man there whom I know very well. I'd never have suspected him, and that disturbs me. He was very tired, dirty, riding on horseback to the Gap. Seeing me, he came nearer: 'What are you doing here, Mr. Svetsilovich?' I answered jokingly, 'I'm in search of yesterday's day.' And he burst into laughter and asked: 'Does yesterday's day, then, the devil take it, come into today's?' And I said to him: 'Yesterday's day hangs around all our necks.' Then he said: 'However, it doesn't come, does it?' Then I said: 'But the Wild Hunt? Hasn't it come from the past?' He changed in his face. 'Damn it! Don't even mention it.' And he moved on northwards along the quagmire. I went on towards your house, Mr. Belaretsky, but when I turned around I saw that he had turned back and was letting himself down into the ravine. He went there and disappeared."

"Who was it?" I asked. Svetsilovich hesitated. Then he raised his bright eyes.

"Forgive me, Belaretsky, forgive me, Ryhor, I cannot tell you yet. It's too important, and I'm not a gossip. I cannot lay such a terrible accusation on the shoulders of a person who, perhaps, is not guilty. You know that for such a thing a person may be killed simply on suspicion. All that I can say is that he was among the guests at Yanovsky's. I'll think it over in the evening, will weigh everything, will recall in detail the story about the promissory notes and tomorrow I'll tell you. But for the present I cannot say anything more..."

Oh, of course! A dependable alibi. Oh, fools! And what dim thoughts! By analogy I recalled my own indefinite thoughts, too, the thoughts about "the hands", which were to help me in investigating something important.

We decided to have Ryhor sit this night through at the Cold Hollow. It was not far from there to Svetilovich's house where he lived with an old attendant and a cook. In case of need we could find him.

"Nevertheless I don't believe that I'll be able to catch them when they leave. Svetilovich has put them on their guard," Ryhor said hoarsely. "They'll find another road out of the dense forest onto the plain."

ULADZIMIR KARATKEVICH

"But another road into the park they won't find. I'll be lying in wait for them near the broken-down fence," I decided.

"It's dangerous alone," Ryhor lowered his eyes.

"But you, too, will be alone."

"Me? No! I'm nobody's fool. I'm bold, but not so bold as to fight one against twenty."

"But I tell you," I said stubbornly, "that the mistress of Marsh Firs will not live through another appearance of the Wild Hunt at the walls of her house. I must not allow them to enter the park if they intend to come."

"Today I cannot help you," said Svetsilovich sunk in a brown study. "What I must clear up is more important. Perhaps the Wild Hunt won't come today at all. An obstacle will stand in its way."

"Well then," I, rather dryly, interrupted him. "You should have expressed your views and not given us puzzles to answer. I'll go out alone today. They aren't expecting anybody, and on that I am placing my stakes. By the way, they don't know that I have a gun. Twice I met with the Hunt, and also with that man who shot me in the back, and I never used it. Well then, they will see yet... How slowly we are untying this knot! How lazily our brains are working!"

"Only in bad novels things are cleared up easily and logically," Svetsilovich growled, offended. "In addition, we are not detectives from the country police. And thank Lord for that!"

Frowning, Ryhor was digging the ground with a twig. "Enough!" he said with a sigh. "We must act. I'll make them hop about yet, the skunks! And, excuse me, after all you are aristocrats, gentlemen and all. We are together now, following the same path, but if we find them, we muzhyks shall not only kill these savage creatures, we will burn their nests, we will bring utter ruin on their offspring and we'll perhaps put an end to their descendants."

Svetsilovich began to laugh, getting carried away:

"Belaretsky and I are very fine gentlemen! As the saying has it, a gentleman all dressed up in a caftan made of grape vine, and sandals made of bast. Actually, we ought to annihilate them all and their like including their young ones, for with the passing of time, these young ones will grow up to be aristocrats."

"If only it is not a phantom, this Wild Hunt, a vision seen in a dream when asleep. Well, there wasn't, there has never yet been a person to hide his tracks from me, the best of hunters. But phantoms will be phantoms."

We left Ryhor. I, too, agreed partially with his last words. There was something supernatural about this Hunt. This cry that turned one's heart to ice – it couldn't come from a human chest. The thundering hoofs heard from time to time. The drygants are an already extinct breed, and even if they could still be found, who in such a remote corner as ours, is wealthy enough to have been able to buy these horses? Somehow this must be connected with King Stakh's Wild Hunt. Who is this Lady-in-Blue whose ghost disappeared in the night, if her twin – a twin entirely unlike her – is peacefully sleeping in her room? To whom does this awful face belong, the face that looked at me through the window? My head was splitting. Yes, there was something unnatural going on here, something criminal and frightening, a mixture of sorcery and reality.

I looked at Svetsilovich who was walking at my side, merry and playful, as if these questions didn't exist as far as he was concerned. The morning was indeed a beautiful one, although the weather was cloudy and dull, the sun was not far away, and each little yellow leaf on the trees thrilled, and it even seemed that they were turning towards the dew in the warm autumn sun.

Through the glade we saw a level plain far ahead, and farther on – the boundless brown bog and the heather waste land. Marsh Firs was far behind them. And in all this there was a kind of sad, incomprehensible beauty, a beauty that made the heart in every son of these depressing places beat both painfully and sweetly.

"Look, a little aspen tree has run out into the field. It has become shy and begun to blush, reddening all over, poor thing," Svetsilovich said, deeply moved.

Moving forward, he stood at the precipice. His ascetic mouth softened and a timid, wandering smile appeared on his face. His eyes looked into the distance, and he himself, his entire body, seemed to have become weightless, impetuous, ready to soar upward above our dear, poor land.

"This is how such as he ascend from the cross," I again thought. "A beautiful head under the filthy, rotten axe..."

And really, one sensed a kind of thirst for life and a readiness for self-sacrifice in this beautiful face, in these "lilywhite" hands, as our poetic ancestors would have put it, in the fine, slender neck, in the steady brown eyes with their long lashes, but with a metallic lustre in their depths.

"Ah, my land!" he sighed. "My dear, my only one! How cold your attitude towards the little aspens that run out into the field ahead of all the others, and into the light. They are the first to be broken by the wind. Don't be in such a hurry, you little fool... But it cannot help itself. It must."

I put my hand on his shoulder, and quickly removed it. I understood that he was not at all like me, that now he was soaring above the entire Earth, that he was not here. He was not even ashamed of using high-flown speech which regular men usually avoid.

"Do you remember, Belaretsky, your preface to 'Belarusian Songs, Ballads and Legends'? I remember this: 'My Belarusian heart became embittered when I saw that our best, our golden words and deeds had fallen into oblivion.' Wonderful words! For these words alone your sins will be forgiven you. So what then is there to be said, when not only my Belarusian, but my human heart aches at the thought of our neglect and the human suffering, the useless tears of our unfortunate mothers. It is impossible, impossible to live like this, my dear Belaretsky. It is in man's nature to be kind, but he is turned into an animal. Nobody, nobody, wishes to let him be a human being. Simply to cry: 'People, embrace one another!' is, evidently, not enough. And there are people here who keep going to the rack. Not for the sake of glory, but for conscience' sake, to kill the torments of conscience – as a man does when he goes into a dense forest, although he doesn't know the way, to save a friend, because he knows that it is shameful, shameful to stop, to stand still. So they go on, stray, and perish.

They know only that a person mustn't be like that, that it is no good promising him pie in the sky, that he needs to have happiness under these ceilings so covered with smoke. And they are more courageous than Christ, they know that there is no resurrection after the crucifixion. Only crows will fly over them and women will bewail them. And chiefly, their saintly mothers."

At this moment he seemed superhuman to me, so fine, so worthy, that I felt terrified and foresaw his death through the veiled future. Such as he do not live. Where will it be? On the rack in a torture chamber? On the scaffold facing the people? In a hopeless battle of insurgents against the army? At a writing desk hurriedly putting down his last fiery thoughts, breathing his last breath? In a prison hall, shot in the back, not daring to look him in the eyes?

His eyes were shining.

"Kalinowsky went to the gallows. Miss Pyarowsky, a woman you would be willing to die for on the scaffold.

Such beauty – and with a dirty rope around her neck...
You know, Miss Yanovsky resembles her somewhat.
That's why I idolize her, although that's not quite exactly
so. But she was an aristocrat. That means there is a way
out for some of our people, too. Only you must follow
their path, if you do not want to rot alive... They strangled her. You think all can be strangled? Our strength is
growing. If I could hang with them, even by a rib from
the hook, to prevent King Stakh's Wild Hunt tearing
across the land at a mad pace, to stop the horrors of the
past, its apocalypse, the death. I'll leave as soon as I finish
with this. I can't stay here. You know what friends I have,
what we have in mind to do? They shall tremble, those fat
ones, they shall! We haven't all been strangled to death.
This means a great fire. And the years, the years ahead!
How much suffering, how much happiness! What a gold-
en, magic expanse is ahead! What a future awaits us!"

Tears spurted from his eyes, uncontrollable tears. I
don't remember how we parted. I remember only his
fine slender silhouette outlining at the top of the burial
mound. He turned towards me, waved his hat and shouted:

"Years and years are ahead of us! Great expanses! The
sun!"

And he disappeared. I went home. I believed I could
do anything now. Of what significance was the gloom
of Marsh Firs, if ahead were great expanses, the sun and
faith? I believed that I'd fulfil everything, that our nation
was alive if it could give birth to such people.

The day was yet ahead, such a long one, shining, po-
tent. My eyes longed for the new day and the sun which
was hidden as yet behind the clouds.

CHAPTER ELEVEN

That very night at about eleven o'clock I was lying hidden in the lilac tree at the torn fence. I was in an uplifted mood, absolutely without fear, and in this state I remained until the very end of my stay at Marsh Firs. It seemed to me that crows could peck at somebody else's body, that had nothing at all to do with me; but they could not peck at mine that I loved, my strong and slender body. Whereas in the meantime the situation was a sad one. And the time, too, was sad.

It was almost quite dark. Over the smooth, gloomy expanse of the Gap, low black clouds had gathered, promising a pouring rain by nightfall. The autumn in general was a bad one and dreary, but with frequent, heavy showers, as in summer. A wind arose, in the blackish green pyramids of the firs it became noisy, then again became quiet. The clouds swam slowly along, piled over the hopeless, level landscape. Somewhere, far, far away a light flashed and, having winked, went out. A feeling of loneliness crept over my heart. I was a stranger here. Svetsilovich was really worthy of Nadzeya, while absolutely nobody had any need of me here. As of a hole in a fence.

Whether I lay there long or not – I cannot say. The clouds right over my head thinned out, but new ones arose.

A strange sound struck my ears. Somewhere in the distance, and as it seemed to me, to my right, a hunter's horn sounded, and although I knew that was aside from the path the Wild Hunt was on, involuntarily I began to look more frequently in that direction. Yet another thing began to trouble me. White fragments of fog began to appear here and there in marshes. However, with that everything ended. Suddenly another sound flew over towards me – the dry heather began to rustle somewhere. I glanced in that direction, looked until my eyes began to ache, and at last noticed some spots moving against the dark background of the distant forests.

For an instant I shut my eyes for them to "come to", and when I opened them, straight ahead of me and not at all far away, the dim silhouettes of horsemen came into view. Again, as previously, they were flying across the air in great leaps. And complete silence, as if I had become deaf, enveloped them. The sharp tops of their cocked felt hats, their hair and capes waving with the wind, their lances – all this imprinted itself on my memory. I began to crawl back closer to the brick foundation of the fence. The Hunt swung around, then recklessly bunched together in confusion – and began to turn about. I took my revolver from my pocket.

They were few in number, less than ever, eight riders. Where have you put the rest, King Stakh? Where have you sent them to? I placed the revolver on the bent elbow of my left arm and fired. I am not a bad shot and can hit the mark in almost complete darkness, but here something surprising happened. The horsemen galloped on as if nothing had disturbed them. I noticed the last one – a tall, strong man. I fired, but he didn't even stagger.

The Wild Hunt, as if desiring to prove to me it was illusive, turned about and was already galloping sideward at me, but out of reach of my shots. I began to crawl on my back to the bushes and succeeded in coming nearer to them, when someone jumped on me from behind and a terribly heavy weight pinned me to the ground. The last bit of air squeezed out of my lungs, I even moaned. It became clear from the very first seconds of the ordeal that this was not someone I could possibly compete with neither in size nor in strength.

He attempted to twist my hands behind my back and whistled in a husky whisper:

"H-halt, S-s-satan, wait... W-won't get aw-way y-you w-won't, you bandit, murderer... H-hold, you rotten bone..."

I understood that if I didn't employ all my adroitness I'd perish. I remember only that I thought with regret of the spectral Hunt that I had shot at, but hadn't harmed even one of its hairs. In the next instant, feeling some-one's paw sneaking at my throat, I used an ancient well tested manoeuvre to put whoever it was out of action. Something warm came running down my face – he smashed his nose had with his own hand. I grabbed him by the hand and twisted it under my body, rolling to-gether with him on the ground. He groaned loudly and I understood that my second move had also been success-ful. Immediately after this I received such a blow on the bridge of my nose that the bog began to swim before my eyes and my hairs stood on ends. Luckily, I had instinc-tively strained the muscles of my abdomen in time, and therefore the following blow below the belt did not harm me. His hairy hands had already reached to my throat when I recalled my grandfather's advice in case of a fight with an opponent stronger than myself. With an unbe-lievable strength I turned over on my back, pressed my hands hard against the heavy belly of this stranger and drove my sharp, hard knee into the most sensitive spot. Involuntarily he gave way and fell on me with his face and chest. Gathering all my remaining forces, I thrust him up into the air as far as possible with my knee and

ULADZIMIR KARATKEVICH

outstretched arms. I had, evidently, thrust too hard, for, as it turned out, he made a half-flip in the air and his heavy body – oh what a heavy body – struck against the ground. I fainted at about the same time.

When I came to, I heard someone groaning somewhere behind my head. My opponent could not move from his place, while I was making a great effort to stand up on my feet. I decided to give him a hard kick under his heart so he shouldn't be able to breathe, but at first I took a glance at the swamp where the Wild Hunt had disappeared. And suddenly I heard a very familiar voice, the voice of the one who was moaning and groaning.

"Oh, damn it, where is this blockhead from? What a skunk! Our holy martyrs!"

I burst out laughing. The same voice answered:

"It's you, Mr. Belaretsky! I doubt whether I can be a welcome guest with the ladies after today. Why did you crawl away from the fence? That only made things worse. While those devils are now far away, damn you... pardon my French."

"Mr. Dubatowk!" I exclaimed in surprise.

"Damn you again, Mr. Belaretsky... Oh! Excuse me!" The very large shadow sat down, holding on to its belly. "You see, I was on a stake out. I got worried. Rumours had reached me that some nasty events had been taking place at my niece's. And you, too, it seems, were on the look-out? May you get hit by lightning on the day of Christ's birth!"

I picked up the revolver from the ground.

"And why did you throw yourself on me like that, Mr. Dubatowk?"

"The devil alone knows! I saw some worm creeping, so I grabbed it without thinking. May your parents meet you in the next world as you have met me in this one. However, you skunk, how painfully you strike!"

It turned out that the old man had learned by-passing us about the visits of the Wild Hunt and he had decided to take it by surprise, "since the young ones are such weak ones – the wind swings them, and they are such cowards that they cannot defend a woman." The end of this undertaking of his you know now. Hardly able to keep from laughing, which might have seemed disrespectful, I helped the groaning Dubatowk onto his freezing horse standing not far away. He mounted him groaning and swearing, sat sidewise, muttered something like "the devil tugged me to fight ghosts – ran up against a fool with sharp knees" and rode off.

His pinched face, his crooked one-sided figure were so pitiful, that I choked with laughter. He rode off to his house, groaning, moaning, casting curses on all my kin until the twelfth generation.

Dubatowk disappeared in the darkness, and here an indescribable, an inexplicable alarm pierced my heart. A kind of fearful guess stirred in my subconscious, but would not come to light. "Hands?" No, I could not recollect why this word worried me. Here there was something different... Why had there been so few horsemen? Why had only eight ghosts appeared today near the torn fence? What had happened to the rest? And suddenly an alarming thought struck me:

"Svetsilovich! His meeting with a person at Cold Hollow. His foolish joke about the Wild Hunt that might be interpreted as meaning that he suspected someone or had discovered the participants in this dark affair. My God! If that person is indeed a bandit, he will inevitably make an attempt to kill Svetsilovich even today. Why so few of them? Probably the second half made its way to my new friend, and these to Marsh Firs. Maybe they even saw us talking, after all, we, like fools, were standing in view of everybody over the precipice. Oh! If that is true, what a mistake you made today, Andrey Svetsilovich, when you did not tell us who that man is!"

It was clear that I had to hurry! Perhaps I could yet arrive in time. Our success in this affair and the very life of a kind, young soul depended on the speed of my feet. And I ran off so fast, faster than I had run the night when King Stakh's Wild Hunt raced after me. I dashed straight through the park, climbed over the fence and rushed to Svetsilovich's house. I did not fly in a frenzy. I understood very well that I would not last all the way, therefore ran at a measured pace, 300 steps running as fast as I could, and fifty steps more slowly. And I kept to this pace, although after the first two miles my heart was ready to jump out of my chest. Then it became easier. I alternated running with walking almost mechanically and increased the running norm to 400 steps. Stamp-stamp-stamp... and so 400 times, tap-tap... fifty times. Misty, solitary fire swam past. A smarting pain in my chest, my consciousness almost not working, towards the finish my counting mechanical. I was so tired that I'd have gladly lain down on the ground or at least have increased by five the number of such calm and pleasant steps, but I honestly fought temptation.

In this way I came running up to Svetsilovich's house – a whitewashed building, not a large one, in the back of a stunted little garden. Straight across empty beds, crushing the last cabbages popping under my feet, I darted onto the porch decorated with four wooden columns and began to drum on the door.

In the last window a still, small light flickered, then a senile voice asked from behind the door:

"What's brought someone here?"

It was the old man, a former attendant, who was living with Svetsilovich.

"Open the door, Kandrat. It's me, Belaretsky."

"Oh, my God! What's happened? Why are you panting so?"

The door opened. Kandrat in a long shirt and in felt boots was standing before me, in one hand a gun, and in the other – a candle.

"Is the master at home?" I asked, breathing heavily.

"No, he's not," he answered calmly.

"But where did he go?"

"How should I know? Is he a child, sir, that he should report to me where he is going?"

"Lead into the house," I screamed, stung by this coldness.

"What for?"

"Maybe he's left a note."

We entered Svetsilovich's room. The bed of an ascetic, covered with a grey blanket, the floor washed to a yellow colour and waxed, a carpet on the floor. On a plain pine table a few thick books, papers, pens thrown about. An engraved portrait of Marat in his bath, stabbed with a dagger, and above the table a pencil portrait of Kalinowsky. On another wall hung a caricature of Muravyov with a whip in his hand, standing over a heap of skulls. His face that of a bulldog, a frightful one. Katkov, bending low, is licking his behind.

I turned over all the papers on the table, but in my excitement found nothing except a sheet on which in Svetsilovich's handwriting was: "Can it really be he?" I seized the woven wastepaper basket and shook out all its contents on the floor: nothing interesting there except an envelope made of rough paper, on which was written: "For Andrey Svetsilovich".

"Were there any letters today for the gentleman?" I asked Kadrat, who was completely dumbfounded and perplexed.

"There was one, I found it under the door when I returned from the vegetable garden – of course I gave it to the owner."

"It wasn't in this envelope, was it?"

"Just a minute... well yes, in this one."

"And where is the letter itself?"

"The letter? Devil knows. Maybe in the stove."

I rushed to the stove, opened the door – a whiff of warm air came out from it. I saw two cigarette butts at the very door and a small scrap of white paper. I grabbed it – the handwriting exactly the same as that on the envelope.

"Your luck, damn you," I swore, "that you heated the stove early."

But not quite good luck yet. The paper was folded in half, and the side closer to the corners, now covered already with grey ash, had become brown. Impossible to make out the letters there.

"Andrey! I learned that you are interested in the Wild Hunt... Ki... Nadzeya Rom... in danger... my da... (a large piece burnt out) *...Today I spoke with Mr. Belaretsky. He agrees... left for town. Drygants... chie... When you receive this letter, go immediately... to... ain, where only three pines stand. Belaretsky and I will wait... ly ma... is going on this ea... Come without fail. Burn this letter, because it is very dang... for me. You... fir... He is also in mortal danger which only you can ward off...* (again much burnt out) *...me.*

Your well wisher Likol..."

All was obvious somebody had sent the letter to lure Svetsilovich out of the house. He believed every word. He evidently knew very well the person who had written it. Something subtle had been planned here. He shouldn't come to me, they wrote they had spoken with me, that I had left for town, I would be awaiting him somewhere at "ain" where three pines stand alone. What is this "...ain"? At the plain?

Not a minute to be wasted!

"Kandrat, where are there nearby three big pines on the plain?"

"The devil knows," he thought awhile. "Unless it's those near the Giant's Gap. Three enormous pines stand there. It's there that King Stakh's horses – so people say – flew into the quagmire. But what's happened?"

"This is what's happened: Mr. Andrey's life is in grave danger... He left long ago?"

"No, an hour ago, perhaps."

I dragged him out onto the porch, and he, almost in tears, pointed out to me the way to the three pines. I ordered him to remain in the house, and I myself ran away. This time I did not alternate running with walking. I flew, I tore on as fast as I only could, as if I wanted to fall down dead there at the three pines. I threw off my jacket as I ran, and my cap, threw out of my pockets my gold cigarette case, the pocket edition of Dante which I always carried with me. Running became a little easier. I would have removed my boots, if I could have done that without stopping. It was mad racing. As I timed it I should turn up at the pines some twenty minutes after my friend. Terror, despair, hatred gave me strength. Suddenly a wind arose behind me, pushing me ahead. I hadn't noticed the sky become completely cloudy, that something heavy, depressing was felt in the atmosphere. I kept racing on, madly...

The three great pines were already in sight at the distance, and above them such dark clouds, such a pitch darkness, such a dim sky... I rushed into the bushes, trampling them under my feet. And here... ahead, a shot sounded, a shot from an old pistol.

Wildly I yelled, and as if in answer to my yell, the silence was broken by a mad stamping of horses' hoofs.

I jumped out into a clearing and saw the shadows of ten retreating horsemen who turned about in the bushes at a gallop. And under the pines I saw a human figure slowly settling down on the ground.

ULADZIMIR KARATKEVICH

By the time I had run up to him, the man had fallen down face upward, with hands widely outstretched, as if wishing to protect his land from bullets with his body. I had time yet to send a few shots in the direction of the murderers, it even seemed to me that one of them had reeled in his saddle, but this unexpected woe made me throw myself down at once on my knees at the side of the body lying there.

"Brother! Brother mine! My brother!"

As if alive he lay there, and only a tiny little wound from which almost no blood flowed, told me of the truth, a cruel and irremediable truth.

The bullet had pierced his temple and left through the back of the head. I looked at him, at the ruthlessly ruined young life. I held him in my arms, called to him, shook him and howled like a wolf, as if that could help.

Then I sat up, put his head on my lap and began to stroke his hair.

"Andrey! Andrey! Wake up! Wake up, my dear friend!"

He was beautiful in death, unusually beautiful. With his face thrown back, his head hanging down, his slender neck as if carved from marble, he lay in my lap. The long, fair hair had become entangled with the dry yellow grass which caressed it. His mouth was smiling as if death had solved one of life's riddles for him, his eyes were closed peacefully, and his long eyelashes overshadowed them. His hands so beautiful and strong, hands which women might have kissed in moments of happiness, lay alongside his body, as if in rest.

As a mother grieving over her son did I sit there, on my knees my son who had undergone torture on the cross. I howled over him and cursed God who was merciless towards people, towards the best of His sons.

"God! God! All Knowing, All Powerful One! May You perish! You Apostate, having sold Your people!"

Over my head something thundered, and in the following instant an ocean of water, a terrible shower, came pouring down on the swamp and the waste land, so lost and forgotten in the forests of this territory. The firs, bent down under it to the ground, moaned and groaned. Rain drops were beating against my back with which I was sheltering the face of the deceased from all that water, rain went wild, mercilessly slashing at the ground.

I sat, having completely lost my senses, numb to everything. Ringing in my ears were the words that I had heard uttered some hours ago by one of the best of people I had known.

"My heart aches... they go on, stray, perish, because it is shameful to stand still... and there is no resurrection for them after the crucifixion... But do you think that all were strangled? Years and years are ahead! What a golden, magic expanse is ahead! The sun!"

I began to groan. The future, murdered and growing cold in the rain, was lying here in my lap.

I wept, the rain flooded my eyes, my mouth. And my hands continued stroking this youth's golden head.

"My country! Wretched mother! Weep!"

CHAPTER TWELVE

Crows sense a corpse from afar. The following day a police officer, a handsome man with a moustache, appeared in the Yanovsky region. He arrived without a doctor, examined the place of the murder, and with an air of importance that became a murder, said that because of the shower it was impossible to discover any traces of the crime. Ryhor, who had accompanied him, only smiled bitterly into his moustache. After examining the body of the murdered man, the policeman turned the head around with his thick white fingers, and in a solemn voice, said:

"Well-well! Finished him off how? Fell immediately."

Then he drank vodka and had a bite to eat in Svetilpvich's house, in the room next to the hall in which the old servant was bitterly crying, his tears choking him, while I was sitting literally crushed by woe and remorse. At this time nothing existed for me besides the thin candle which Andrey held in his hands. The candle was throwing rosy streaks of light on his white shirt, the front of which was made of lace. It was an old shirt that the servant had dug out from a trunk. But I had to find out what the authorities thought about this murder and what they intended to do.

"Nothing, to our regret, nothing," the police officer answered, his voice pleasant and well modulated, his black velvety eyebrows playing. "This is a wild corner – impossible to carry out investigations here. I appreciate your noble grief... But what can be done here? Some years ago there was a vendetta here." He pronounced it 'vandetta' and it was apparent he liked the word very much. "We were powerless to do anything. Such a forsaken place. For example, we could have made you, too, answerable for this, because, as you yourself say, you applied a weapon against these... say... hunters. We won't do that. It's none of our business, not at all. Perhaps he was murdered because of a person of the beautiful sex. People say he was in love with this – he moved his eyebrows in satisfaction – this lady, the mistress of Marsh Firs. Not bad... Or perhaps, this was a suicide? The deceased was a 'melancholic' fellow, ha-ha, suffered for the people."

"But after all I myself saw the Wild Hunt."

"Allow me not to believe you. Fairy tales have outlived themselves... It seems to me that your acquaintance with him is, in general, somewhat... say... suspicious. I have no desire to complicate matters for you, however... it is also highly suspicious of you striving so stubbornly to shift the attention of the investigation onto others, onto some Wild Hunt."

"I have a paper showing that he was enticed out of his house."

The officer turned purple, his eyes became shifty.

"What paper?" He asked avidly, and he reached his hand out to me. "You must hand it over, and if it is considered that this scrap of paper is worth something, it will be filed with other material concerning this case."

I hid the paper because neither his eyes nor his greedily outstretched hand inspired trust.

"I'll hand it over myself when and to whom I consider it necessary."

"Well, so be it," the policeman swallowed something, "that's your own affair, most respected one. But I advise you not to tempt fate. The population here is a barbarous one," he significantly looked at me, "they can kill."

"I am not very much afraid of that. I can only say that if the police engage in discoursing instead of fulfilling their direct obligations, then it becomes necessary for the citizens themselves to take up their own defence. If the authorities exert all their efforts to hush up an affair, things give off a most unpleasant odour and make people think the most unpleasant thoughts."

"What is this?" The brows of the policeman began creeping smartly somewhere towards his hair, "insulting the authorities, are you?"

"God forbid! But this gives me the right to send a copy of this letter to the provincial centre."

"That's as you like," the police officer said, picking his teeth. "However, my dear Mr. Belaretsky, my advice to you is to reconcile yourself to things. And besides, it will hardly be pleasant for the authorities in the province to learn that a scientist is defending a former dissident in this way."

Gallantly, in a chesty baritone, he was persuading me that a father could not have been more attentive to his son than he was to me.

"Just a moment," I said, "is there any such law that liberals are outcasts and must be outlawed? A villain can murder them and bear no responsibility?"

"Don't magnify things, my dear Mr. Belaretsky," the dandy said, drawing out his words. "You are prone to magnifying life's horrors."

This ridiculous grumbler – and I can't think of any other word – most certainly considered the death of a person only a "magnification of life's horrors."

"And I think," I said vehemently, "that it is necessary to hand this case over to the court, that a legal investigation must be instigated. Here we have to deal with malicious intent. Here people are driven mad, of course with a definite aim in view. This gang holds the entire neighbourhood in terror, scares and murders people."

"Now don't, sir, no good going on like that, sir. This makes the people become more moderate. According to the rumour, the murdered one was a follower of Bacchus, given to drinking and merrymaking. And it is dangerous to manifest obvious sympathy for such fellows. A political suspect, disloyal, not trustworthy and obviously, a separatist, taking the part of the muzhyks, how should I put it... bewailing his younger brother."

I was furious, but for the time being held myself together. To quarrel with the police was the least of my wants.

"You don't wish to intervene in the case concerning the murder of Sir Svetsilovich?"

"God forbid, God forbid!" he interrupted. "It's that we simply doubt whether we can unravel this case, and we cannot compel our investigator to do everything in his power to solve the case of a man whose ideas were directed in quite an opposite direction to those of all honest, loyal sons of our country."

And with a charming smile he waved his hand in the air.

"All right. If the Imperial Russian Court does not wish to force the investigator to establish the truth in the case of the murder of Svetsilovich, who was an aristocrat, then perhaps it will wish to force the investigator to unravel the case concerning the attempt to deprive Nadzeya Yanovsky, the owner of Marsh Firs, of her sanity and her life?"

Comprehensively he looked at me, turned pink at some pleasant thought, and smacked his lips several times, lips fat and moist, and asked:

"But why are you taking such pains for her sake? You've decided, most certainly to make use of her yourself, haven't you? And why not? I approve of that, in bed she is, most probably, not bad."

The blood rushed to my face. The insult to my unfortunate friend, the insult to my beloved, whom even in my thoughts I could not call mine, became united into one. I don't remember how a whip came to be in my hand. I choked with fury.

"You... you... skunk!"

And with all my might I dealt him a blow on his dark-pink face.

I thought he would take out his revolver and kill me. But this strong fellow only groaned. Once again I struck him across his face and threw the whip away in disgust.

Like a bullet he flew out of the room into the yard in great haste and only about half a mile away did he cry: "Help!"

When Ryhor learned about everything, he didn't approve of what I had done. He said that I had spoiled everything, that I'd most certainly be called out to the district on the following day, and would be imprisoned for a week or banished from the region. But I had to be here, for the darkest nights had set in. I had however, no regrets. I had put all my hatred into that blow. And even if the district officials didn't lift a finger to help me, still, now I knew well who had been my friend and who – my enemy.

Other events of this and the following day vaguely imprinted themselves on my memory: good old Dubatowk, bitter tears choking him as he cried over the dead youth, and still hardly able to move after the "treat" I had given him; Miss Nadzeya standing at the coffin, wrapped in a black mantilla, so beautiful, so pure in her mourning.

As if in a day dream I afterwards recalled the funeral procession. I was escorting Lady Yanovsky, holding her by the arm, and against the background of the grey autumn sky people were walking with their heads bared, the twisted birches throwing their dead yellow leaves at the feet of these people. The face of the murdered man was floating over the tops of their heads.

Peasant women, muzhyks, children, old men following behind the coffin, and a quiet sobbing sounding in the air. In front of us Ryhor carrying on his back a large cross made of oak.

Louder and louder, soaring upward over the entire mourning procession, over the wet land, the bewailing voices of the women began:

"But to whom then have you left us? And why have you fallen asleep, our own, our dear one? And why are your clear eyes closed, your white hands folded? And who then shall defend us against the unjust judges? While the aristocrats all around are merciless, no cross on them! Our beloved one, where then have you flown to, away from us, for whom have you deserted us, your poor little children? As if there were no brides for you all around, that you had to go and marry the Earth, you, our darling? And what kind of a hut have you chosen for yourself? No windows in it, no doors, and not the free sky over the roof – only the damp soil. And not a wife at your side – a cold board! Neither girl-friends there, nor a beloved one! Then who will kiss you on the lips, and who will comb your little head?! And why have the little lights grown dim? And why are the conifers reproving? It's not your wife crying, your beloved! After all it's not she who is weeping, wasting herself away. It's people, good people, weeping over you! It's not a little star that's lit up in the sky! It's the tiny wax candle in your little hands that's begun to glow!"

The coffin was accompanied by such sincere lamentations and weeping from the people of the neighbourhood, by moaning and groaning that cannot be bought from professional wailers.

And here was the deep grave. When the time came to leave, Yanovsky fell on her knees and kissed the hand of the man who had perished for her sake. With difficulty I tore her away from the coffin when the people began lowering it into the grave. About three dozen peasants dragged over an enormous grey stone on runners and began to pull it up the hill where the lonely grave had been dug. A cross was carved on the stone and also the name and surname – in crooked, clumsy letters.

Lumps of soil ricocheted against the coffin's cover, hiding the dear face from me. Then the enormous grey stone was placed near the grave. Ryhor and five peasants took old guns and began to shoot into the indifferent sky. The last of the Svetsilovich-Yanovskys had floated off into the unknown.

"Soon the same will happen with me, too," Yanovsky whispered to me. "The sooner the better."

The shots thundered. Like stone were the faces of the people.

Then, in accordance with an ancient custom among the gentry, the family coat of arms was smashed against the tombstone.

The family remained without a future. The family had become extinct.

CHAPTER THIRTEEN

I felt that I would go mad if I did not occupy myself in searching for and finding the guilty ones, and didn't punish them. If there is no God, if there is no justice to be found among the authorities, I myself will be both God and Judge.

And by God, hell itself will tremble, if they fall into my hands. I shall pull out the sinews of them living.

Ryhor said that his friends were searching in the Reserve, that he himself had examined the place of the murder and found there a cigarette butt. He had also found it was a tall, slender man who had smoked the cigarette under the pines while awaiting Svetsilovich.

Besides that, he had found a paper wad from the murderer's gun, and also the bullet that had killed my friend. When I unfolded the wad, I became convinced that the scrap of paper, too thick to be from a newspaper, was most likely a piece of a page from a journal.

I read:

"Each one of them is guilty of some offence when they are led to be executed. Forgive me, Your Highness, you've forgotten the crucifixion... Forgive me, God has deprived me of my reason..."

These words reminded me of something very familiar. Where could I have met something similar? And soon I recalled that I had read just these words in the journal *North-West Antiquity*! When I asked Yanovsky who subscribed there for it, she answered in an indifferent tone, that besides themselves – nobody. And here a blow awaited me. I found out in the library that in one of the numbers of the journal a few pages were missing, and specifically those that I needed.

I grew cold – things had taken a very serious turn. The instigator of the Wild Hunt was here in the castle. But who then was it? Not I nor Yanovsky, nor the foolish housekeeper, who every day now on seeing the mistress began to cry and moreover, it was apparent that she regretted her misdeeds. And this meant that only Bierman–Hatsevich was left.

This was logical. Bierman was a runaway criminal, and was well informed of all ongoing events. It was possible that it was he who had shot at me, who had torn out a page from the journal and had killed Svetsilovich. I couldn't understand one thing only: why had he tried to convince me that the greatest danger was the Wild Hunt and not the Little Man? And also the fact that he, Bierman, could not have killed Roman since it was not he who had invited Nadzeya to the Kulsha's, and during the murder he was at home. However, hadn't Svetsilovich that last day said that it was a man beyond suspicion? And how frightened he became, this Bierman, when I came into his room! And then couldn't he have been simply the one who inspired this abomination? But really, how then in that case explain the existence of the Lady-in-Blue? And this is the most inexplicable fact in the entire affair. And most important of all it was impossible to understand what Bierman had to gain. But such a fiend might think up anything at all.

From Miss Yanovsky I received her father's personal archive and carefully examined the material of his last days. Nothing comforting besides notes that he no longer liked Bierman; he often disappeared from the house somewhere, was too much interested in the Yanovsky genealogy, in old plans of the castle. But this, too, was a significant fact. Why not suppose that he, Bierman, was responsible also for the appearance of the Little Man, more exactly speaking, for producing the Little Man's steps? After all, perhaps he had been able to dig up old plans, to make use of some acoustic secrets of the castle and frighten people every night with the sound of those steps.

I told Ryhor about my findings and stated my views on the subject, and he said that it was quite possible that it was so, he even promised to help, since his uncle and grandfather had been stone masons at the Yanovsky's before serfdom had been repealed.

"Somebody is hiding here somewhere, the scoundrel, but who he is, where the passages are, how he gets into those places, we don't know," Ryhor sighed. "No matter, we'll find out. But take care. I've met in my lifetime only two worthy men among the living. It will be a pity if something should happen to you, too. Then all these rotten people will have no right to eat bread and breathe the air."

We decided not to trouble Bierman as yet, so as not to frighten him prematurely.

Then I began to make a detailed study of the letter written by an unknown person to Svetsilovich. I used many, many sheets of paper before I managed to restore the text of the letter at least approximately:

"Andrey! I learned that you are interested in the Wild Hunt of King Stakh, and also that Nadzeya Romanawna is in danger (further nothing understandable) *...my da...* (again much missing) *Today I spoke with Mr. Belaretsky. He agrees with me and has left for town... Drygants – chief... When you receive this letter – go immediately to... plain where three pines stand by themselves. Belaretsky and I will wait... ly ma... what's going on in this world! Come without fail. Burn this letter,*

because it is very dangerous for me. ...Yo... fr... They are also in mortal danger which only you can ward of... (again much burnt) *...me.*

Your well wisher, Likol..."

The devil knows what this is all about! This deciphering gave me almost nothing. Well, once again I became convinced that the crime had been a planned one. And in addition I learned that an unknown "Likol" – what a heathen name – had cleverly made use of our being on friendly terms, of which only he could have guessed. And nothing, nothing more! Whereas in the meantime an enormous grey stone was laid on the grave of a person who could have been one hundred times more useful for our country than I. And if not today, then tomorrow, such a stone may be weighing down upon me too. And then what will happen to Nadzeya Yanovsky?

That day brought me yet another bit of news – I received a subpoena. On surprisingly bad grey paper in a high-flown language was written an invitation to appear at the court in the chief town of the district. It was necessary to leave. We arranged with Ryhor about a horse, I told him what I thought about the letter, and he informed me that Haraburda's house was being watched, but nothing suspicious had been noticed.

Again my thoughts turned to Bierman.

This quiet evening, not at all typical for autumn, I thought long over what was awaiting me in the district town, and I decided not on any account to remain there for long. I was already about to go to bed and have a good sleep before my trip, when suddenly, on making a turn in the lane, I saw Yanovsky on a bench covered with moss. A dark greenish light fell on her blue dress, on her hands with fingers interlaced her eyes wandering, an absent-minded look in them, such a look that one sees in a person lost in thought.

The pledge which I had given myself did not waver, the memory of my dead friend even strengthened this pledge, and nevertheless for a few minutes I felt a triumphant rapture at the thought that I could have held in my arms this dear slim figure and pressed her to my breast. But bitterly did my heart beat, for I knew that this would never be.

However, I went out to her from behind the trees almost quite calm.

Here she lifted her head, saw me, and how sweetly, how warmly did her radiant eyes begin to shine.

"It's you, Mr. Belaretsky. Sit down here beside me."

She was silent for a while, then she said with surprising firmness:

"I'm not asking you why you beat a person so hard. I know that if you did do such a thing, it means it was impossible to have done otherwise. But I am very uneasy about you. You must know. There is no justice here. These pettifoggers, these liars, these – terrible and thoroughly corrupt people can condemn you. And although it isn't a crime for an aristocrat to beat a policeman, they can exile you from here. All of them together with the criminals form one large union. It will be in vain to beg justice of them, this noble and unfortunate people will perhaps never see it. But why didn't you control yourself?"

"I took the part of a woman, Miss Nadzeya. You know, there is such a custom with us."

And she looked me in the eyes so piercingly that it made me feel cold. How could this child have learned to read hearts, what had given her such strength?

"This woman, believe me, could have endured it. If you are exiled, this woman will pay too high a price for the pleasure you received in venting your feelings on some vulgar fool."

"I'll return, don't worry. And Ryhor will guard your peace during my absence."

Without saying a word, she closed her eyes. After a while she said:

"Ah! You haven't understood anything... As if it is this defence that matters. You should not go to the district town. Stay here for another day or two, and then leave Marsh Firs forever."

Her hands, their fingers trembling, lay on my sleeve.

"Do you hear, I beg you, beg you very sincerely."

I was too much taken up with my own thoughts and therefore didn't quite grasp the meaning of her words, and said:

"At the end of the letter to Svetsilovich the signature is 'Likol'. Is there any such gentleman here in this region whose given name or surname begins like that?"

Her face immediately darkened as the day darkens when the sun disappears.

"No," she answered, her voice trembling as if offended. "Unless it's Likolovich... This is the second part of the surname of the Kulshas."

"Well, it can hardly be that," I answered indifferently.

And having looked at her attentively, only then did I realize what a brute I was. From under her palms with which she had covered her eyes, I saw a heavy, superhuman lonely tear rolling out and creeping down, a tear that would break down a man in despair, not to speak of a young girl, almost a child.

I am always at a loss and become a cry baby on seeing women's or children's tears, while this tear was such a tear, God forbid anyone should see in his life, the tear in addition of a woman for whose sake I'd willingly be turned into ashes, be smashed into pieces, if that would help to stave off sadness from her.

"Miss Nadzeya, what's the matter?" I muttered, and involuntarily my lips formed into a smile, the like of which one can see on the face of an idiot attending a funeral.

"Nothing," she answered almost calmly. "It's simply that I shall never be... a real person. I am crying for Svetsilovich, for you, for myself. It's not even for him that I am crying, but for his ruined youth – I understand that well – for the happiness predestined for us, the sincerity we lack. The best, the most worthy are destroyed. Remember how once you said: 'We have no princes, no leaders and prophets, and like leaves are we tossed about on this sinful Earth.' We must not hope for anything better, lonely are the heart and the soul, and nobody responds to their call. And life burns out."

She stood up, with a convulsive movement broke a twig that she was holding in her hands.

"Farewell, my dear Mr. Belaretsky. Perhaps we shall not see each other again. But to the end of my life I shall be grateful to you... And this is all."

And here something broke within me. Without realizing it, I blurted out, repeating Svetsilovich's words:

"Let them kill me – and as a dead man I shall drag myself here!"

She did not answer me, she only touched my hand, silently looked me in the eyes and left.

CHAPTER FOURTEEN

One might suppose that the sun had turned round once when I arrived in the district town in the afternoon. I use the word "suppose" because as a matter of fact the sun had not shown itself from behind the clouds. It was a small town, flat as a pancake, worse than the most ill-kept of small towns, and it was separated from the Yanovsky region by some eighteen miles of stunted forests. My horse tramped along the dirty streets. Instead of houses there were some kind of hen-coops, and the only things that distinguished this small town from a village were the striped sentry boxes near which stood moustache Cerberuses in patched regimental coats, and also two or three brick shops on a high foundation. Emaciated goats with ironical eyes belonging to poor Jews were looking me over from the decayed, ragged eaves.

Tall, mighty walls of an ancient Uniate Church with two lancet towers over a quadrangled dark brick building stood far in the distance.

And over all this the same desolation reigned as everywhere else. Tall birches grew on the roofs.

The main square sank in dirt.. In front of the grey building of the district court, beside one of the wings, six pigs grouped together, trembling with cold and from time to time trying unsuccessfully to creep under one another to warm themselves. This was each time followed by offended grunting.

I tied my horse to the horse line and, making my way along squeaking steps, came up into a hall that smelled of sour paper, dust, ink and mice. A door, covered with worn-out oilcloth, led into the office. The door was almost torn off and was hanging down. I entered and at first saw nothing, such little light came through the small, narrow windows into this room filled with to-bacco smoke. A bald-headed, crooked little man with his shirt sticking out at the back of his pants raised his eyes and winked at me. I was very much surprised to see how his upper lid remained motionless, while the lower one covered his eyes as if he were a frog.

I said who I was, gave my name.

"So you have come!" the frog-like man was surprised. "And we..."

"And you thought," I continued, "I would not appear at the court, would run away. Lead me to your judge."

The protocol keeper scrambled out from behind his writing desk and with stamping feet went in front of me into the midst of this smoky hell.

In the next room behind a large table three men were sitting. They were dressed in frock coats so bedraggled that it seemed they were made from old fustian. They turned their faces towards me and I noticed identical ex-pressions of greediness, insolence and surprise in their eyes at seeing me actually show up.

These men were the judge, the prosecutor and an ad-vocate, one of those advocates who skin their clients like a plaster and then betray them. A hungry, greedy and corrupt judicial pettifogger with a head resembling a cucumber.

And these were neither the fathers nor the children of judicial reform, but rather minor officials of the days before Peter the Great.

"Mr. Belaretsky," his voice reminding me of pepper-mint, "we expected you. Very pleasant. We respect people with the lustre of the capital." He did not invite me to be seated, kept his eyes fixed on a piece of paper: "You probably know that you have committed something resembling a crime when you had beaten up a district police officer for some harmless joke of his? This is indeed a criminal act, for it is in exact contradiction to the morals and manners of our circuit and also the code of laws of the Russian Empire."

Through his glasses he cast at me a very proud look – this descendant of Shamyaka's was so terribly pleased that it was he who was administering justice and meting out punishment in the district.

I understood that if I did not step on his toes I would lose the game. Therefore I moved a chair up and sat astride it.

"It seems to me that politeness has been forgotten in the Yanovsky region. Therefore I have seated myself without an invitation."

The prosecutor, a young man with dark blue circles under his eyes, common among victims of a shameful disease, said dryly:

"It's not for you, sir, to talk about politeness. No sooner did you appear here than you immediately began disturbing the peaceful lives of our residents. Scandals, fights, an attempt to start a duel ending fatally at a ball in the house of the honourable Miss Yanovsky... And in addition you considered it possible to beat up a policeman while he was on duty. A stranger, but you pry into our lives."

A cold fury stirred within me somewhere under my heart.

"Dirty jokes in the house where you are eating should be punished not with a whip across the face, but with an honest bullet. He insults the dignity of people who are helpless against him, who cannot answer him. The court must deal with such affairs, must fight for justice. You speak of peaceful residents. Why then don't you pay any attention to the fact that these peaceful residents are being murdered by unknown criminals? Your district is being terrorized, but you sit here with your incoming and outgoing papers... Disgraceful!"

"The discussion of the case concerning the murder by an offender against the State, who is, however, a resident here and an aristocrat, will be taken up not with you," hissed the judge. "The Russian Court does not refuse anybody their defence, not even criminals. However this is not the question. You know that for insulting a policeman we can... sentence you to two weeks imprisonment or fine you, or as our forefathers had it, banish you from the bounds of the Yanovsky region."

He was very sure of himself.

I became angry:

"You can do that, applying force. But I shall find justice against you in the province. You shield the murderers. Your police officer discredited the laws of the Empire saying that you don't intend to engage in an examination of the murder of Svetsilovich."

The judge's face became covered with an apoplexic raspberry colour. He stretched his neck as a goose does and hissed:

"And you have witnesses, where are they?"

The solicitor, as a worthy representative of the conciliatory principle of the Russian court of law, smiled bewitchingly:

"Naturally, Mr. Belaretsky has no witnesses. And in general, this makes no sense; the police officer could not have said that. Mr. Belaretsky simply imagines this. He misunderstood."

From a tin box he took out some fruit drops, threw them into his mouth, smacked his lips and added:

"For us of the aristocracy, Mr. Belaretsky's attitude is particularly understandable. We do not want to make you uncomfortable. Indulge yourself, leave from here without a quarrel. Then everything here, how should I say it, will come find its end, and we'll hush up the case. So, *gut*?" He finished in German.

Strictly speaking, the idea would be the cleverest way out for me, but I remembered Yanovsky.

"What will happen to her? For her it can end in death or madness. I'll leave, and she, the silly little thing, can be hurt by anybody and everybody, perhaps only not by a lazy fellow."

I sat on the chair, pressed my lips hard, and hid my fingers between my knees so they shouldn't betray my excited state.

"I will not leave," I said after a silence, "until you find the criminals who conceal themselves in the form of apparitions. And afterwards I'll disappear from here forever."

The judge sighed:

"It seems to me that you'll have to leave quicker than we can catch these... miph...miph"

"Mythical," the lawyer prompted.

"That's it, mythical criminals. And you'll leave not of your own free will."

All my blood rushed to my face. I felt my end had come, that they would do with me whatever they wished, but I staked everything, played my last card, for I was fighting for the happiness of her who was dearest to me of all.

With an unbelievable strength I stopped the trembling of my fingers, took out from my purse a large sheet of paper and threw it under noses. But my voice broke with fury:

"It seems you have forgotten that I am from the Academy of Sciences, that I am a member of the Imperial Geographic Society. And I promise you that as soon as I am free I shall complain to the Sovereign, and not a stone shall remain of your stinking hole. I think that the Sovereign will not spare the three villains who wish to remove me so that they may commit their dirty deeds."

For the first and the last time did I name as my friend a person whom I was ashamed to call my country-man even. I had always tried to forget the fact that the ancestors of the Romanovs, Russian tsars, come from Belarus.

And these blockheads did not know that half the members of the Geographic Society would have given much for it not to be called an Imperial one.

But I almost screamed:

"He will intercede! He will defend!"

I think that they began to waver somewhat. The judge again stretched his neck and... nevertheless whispered:

"But will it be pleasant for the Sovereign that a member of such a respected society had dealings with a State criminal? Many honourable landed gentlemen will complain of this to that very Sovereign."

They had edged me in like borzois, those Russian wolfhounds. I settled myself more comfortably in my seat, crossed my legs, put my hands on my chest and spoke calmly, I was calm, so calm that to drown would have been preferable.

"And don't you know the local peasants? They are, so to say, sincere monarchists. But I promise you, if you banish me from here, I shall go to them..."

They grew green.

"I think, however, that affairs won't take such a turn. Here is a paper from the governor himself, in which he orders the local authorities to give me all the support I need. And you know what can happen for insubordination to such an order."

Thunder at their ears would not have shaken them as did an ordinary sheet of paper with a familiar signature.

ULADZIMIR KARATKEVICH

And I, greatly resembling a general suppressing a mutiny, with teeth set, feeling that my affairs were improving, spoke slowly:

"What's it you want? To be dismissed precipitately from your posts? That's your wish, is it? I shall do that! And for your indulgence towards some wild fanatics performing wild deeds, you shall also answer."

The judge's eyes began to shift from side to side.

"So then," I decided, "as well be hanged for a sheep as for a lamb."

I pointed to the door. The prosecutor and the advocate hurriedly left the room. Clear was the fear in the judge's eyes, the fear of a polecat brought to bay. I saw something else, something secret, wicked. Now I subconsciously felt certain that he was connected with the Wild Hunt, that only my death could save him, that now the Hunt would begin to hunt me, because it was a question of life or death for them, and I would probably even today receive a bullet in my back, but wild anger, fury and hatred gripped at my throat. I understood why our ancestors were called madmen and people said that they continued to fight even after death.

I stepped forward, grabbed the man by the scruff of his neck, dragged him out from behind the table and lifted him up in the air. Shook him.

"Who?" I roared and myself felt how terrible I had become.

It was surprising how correctly he understood my question. And to my surprise, he began to howl.

"Oh! Oh! I don't know, don't know, sir. Oh! What shall I do?! They will kill me, they will!"

"Who?"

"Sir, sir. Your little hands, your little hands I'll kiss, but don't..."

"Who?"

"I don't know. He sent me a letter and 300 roubles in it, demanding that I do away with you because you are interfering. He only said that he was interested in Miss Yanovsky, that either her death or his marriage to her would benefit him. And also that he was young and strong, and if it were necessary he would shut up my mouth for me."

The resemblance of the judge to a weasel became greater because of the stench. I looked at the face of this skunk filled with tears, and although I suspected he knew more than he had told, I pushed him away, disgusted. I could not dirty my hands with this stinking thing. I just couldn't. Otherwise I'd have lost all respect for myself forever.

"You'll answer for this yet," I threw at him from the door. And it's upon such people that men's fates depend! Poor muzhyks!

Riding along the forest road, I was running over in my mind all that had happened. Everything seemed to begin to fit into its place. Of course it was not Dubatowk who had created the Hunt, he had nothing to gain, he was not Yanovsky's heir, nor was it the housekeeper, nor the insane Kulsha. I thought of everybody, even of those whom it was impossible to imagine being involved, but I had become very distrustful. The criminal was young, Yanovsky's death or his marriage to her would benefit him. According to Svetsilovich, this person was present at Yanovsky's ball, had some influence on Kulsha.

Only two persons fit in: Varona and Bierman. But then, why had Varona behaved so stupidly towards me? Yes, it was Bierman, most likely. He knows history, he could have incited some bandits to commit all those horrors. It's necessary to find out how Yanovsky's death could benefit him.

But who are the Little Man and the Lady-in-Blue at Marsh Firs? My head was spinning from these questions, and all the time one and the same word running in my head.

"Hands... Hands..." Why hands? I am just about to re-member... No, it's again escaped my memory... Well then, I must search for the *drygants* and this entire masquerade. And the quicker the better!

CHAPTER FIFTEEN

That evening Ryhor came dirty from head to foot, perspiring and tired out. He sat sullenly on a stump in front of the castle.

"Their hiding place is in the forest," he growled at last. "Today I tracked down a second path from the south, in addition to the path where I had watched them. Only it is up to the elbow in the quagmire. I got into the very thick of the virgin forest, but came across an impassable swamp. And I didn't find a path to cross it. I almost drowned twice... Climbed to the top of the tallest fir-tree and saw a large glade on the other side, and in it amongst bushes and trees the roof of a large structure. And smoke. Once a horse began to neigh on that side."

"We will have to go there," I said.

"No. No foolishness. My people will be there. And excuse me, sir, but if we catch this lousy bunch, we'll deal with them as with horse thieves."

He grinned, and the grin that I saw on his face from under his long hair, was not a pleasant one.

"Muzhyks can suffer long, muzhyks can forgive, our muzhyks are holy people. But here I myself shall demand that with these... we should deal as with horse-thieves: to nail their hands and feet to the ground with aspen pegs, and then the same kind of peg, only a bigger one to stick into the anus up into the innards. And of their huts I won't leave one live coal, we will turn everything into ashes; this rotten riffraff should never be able to set foot here again." He thought a moment and added: "And you beware. Perhaps someday something smelling of a landlord may creep into your soul. Then the same with you... sir."

"You're a fool, Ryhor," I uttered coldly. "Svetsilovich also belonged to the gentry, and throughout all his short life he defended you, blockheads, defended you from greedy landowners and the conceited judges. You heard, didn't you, their lamentations, how they wailed over him? And I can lose my life in the same way... for you. Better if you'd kept quiet if God hasn't given you any sense."

Ryhor grinned wryly, then took out from somewhere an envelope so crumpled as if it had been pulled out from a wolf's jaws.

"All right, no hard feelings? Here's the letter. It was at Svetsilovich's all these days, addressed to his house... The postman said that today he brought a second one to Marsh Firs for you. So long! I'll come tomorrow."

I tore the envelope open immediately. The letter was from the province from a well-known expert in local genealogy to whom I had written. And in it was the answer to one of the most important questions:

"My Highly Respected Mr. Belaretsky, I am sending you information about the person you are interested in. Nowhere in my genealogical lists, as well as in the books of old genealogical deeds did I find anything on the antiquity of the Bierman–Hatsevich family. In one old deed I came across a report not devoid of interest. It has come to light that in 1750 in the case of a certain Nemirich there is information about a Bierman–Hatsevich who was sentenced to exile for dishonourable behaviour – banishment beyond borders of the former Polish Kingdom and he was deprived of his rights to aristocratic rank. This man was the step-brother of Yarash Yanovsky nicknamed Schizmatic. You must know that with the change of power old sentences lost their force, and any Bierman, if yours is indeed an heir of that Bierman, can pretend to the name of Yanovsky if the main branch of this family vanishes. Accept my assurance..." and so on and so forth.

I stood stunned, and although it was growing dark and the letters were running before my eyes, I kept on reading and re-reading the letter.

"Devilish doings! Now all's clear. This Bierman is a scoundrel and a refined criminal – and he is Yanovsky's heir."

And suddenly it struck me:

"The hand... the hand?.. Aha! When the Little Man was looking at me through the window, his hand was like Bierman's! The fingers were just as long as Bierman's, not the fingers of a human being."

And I rushed off to the castle. On the way I looked into my room, but found no letter there. The housekeeper said there had been a letter, it had to be there. She guiltily fawned upon me; after that night in the archive she had become very flattering and ingratiating.

"No, sir, I don't know where the letter is. No, there was no postal stamp on it... Most probably it was sent from the Yanovsky region or perhaps from a small district town. No, nobody was here, save perhaps Mr. Bierman who came in here thinking that you, sir, were at home..."

I didn't listen to her any more. I glanced at the table where papers were lying about scattered, among which someone had evidently been rummaging, and ran to the library. Nobody there, only books piled high on the table. They had evidently been left in a hurry for something else more important. Then I went to Bierman's room. And here traces of haste – the room's door wasn't even locked. A faint light from my match threw a circle of light on the table, and I noticed a glove on it and a slantingly torn envelope, an envelope just like the one that Svetsilovich had received that awful evening:

"Mr. Belaretsky, My Most Respected Brother: I know little about the Wild Hunt, nevertheless I can tell you something of interest about it. And in addition, I can throw some light on a secret, and on the mystery of several dark events in your house. It may simply be a product of the imagination, but it seems to me that you are searching in the wrong place, dear brother. The danger lies in the very castle belonging to Miss Yanovsky. If you wish to know something about the Little Man at Marsh Firs, come today at nine o'clock in the evening to the place where Roman perished and his cross lies. There your unknown well wisher will tell you wherein the root of the fatal events lies."

Recalling Svetsilovich's fate, I hesitated, but I had no time to lose, or to think long – the clock showed fifteen minutes before nine. If Bierman is the head of the Wild Hunt, and if the Little Man is his handiwork, then reading the perlustrated letter must have upset him terribly. Can it be he's gone instead of me to meet that stranger, to shut him up? Quite possible. And in addition, the watchman, when I asked him about Bierman, pointed his hand northwest, in the direction of the road leading to the cross of Roman the Old's.

That is where I ran to. Oh! How much I ran those days, and as people would say today, got in some good training. To the devil with such training together with Marsh Firs! The night was brighter than usual. The moon was rising over the heather waste land, a moon so large and crimson, shining so heavenly, our planet's colour so fiery and such a happy one, that a yearning for something bright and tender, bearing absolutely no resemblance to the bog or the waste land, wrung my heart. It was as if some unknown countries and cities made of molten gold had come floating to the Earth and had burnt up over it, countries and cities whose life was entirely different, not at all like ours.

The moon, in the meantime having risen higher, became pale and grew smaller, and little white clouds, resembling sour milk, were covering the sky. Again all became cold, dark and mysterious, and there was nothing to be done about it, unless, perhaps, to sit down and write a ballad about an old woman on her horse with her sweetheart sitting in front of her.

Having somehow got through the park, I came onto a path and was already nearing Roman's cross. To the left the forest made a dark wall, and near Roman's cross loomed the figure of a man.

And then... I simply did not believe my eyes. From out of somewhere phantom horsemen appeared. They were slowly approaching that man. In complete silence. And a cold star was burning over their heads.

The next moment the loud shot of a pistol was heard. The horses began to gallop, stamping the man's figure with their hoofs. I was astounded. I thought I should meet scoundrels, but became the witness of a killing.

Everything turned dark before my eyes, and when I came to, the horsemen had vanished.

Throughout the marshes spread a frightful, inhuman cry filled with terror, anger and despair – the devil knows what else. But I felt no fright. By the way, I have never ever been afraid of anything since that time. All the most awful things that I met with after those days seemed a mere trifle in comparison.

Carefully, as a snake, I crept up to the dead body darkening in the grass. I remember that I feared an ambush, was myself thirsting to kill, that I crept on, coiling and wriggling in the autumn grass, taking advantage of every hollow, every hillock. I also remember to this very day, how tasty was the smell of the absinthe, how the thyme smelled, what transparent blue shadows lay on the Earth. How good was life even in this awful place! But here a man had to wriggle and coil like a snake in the grass, instead of breathing freely this cold, invigorating air, watching the moon, chest straightened, walking on his hands out of sheer happiness, kissing the eyes of his beloved.

The moonlight was brushing over Bierman's dead face. His large meek eyes were bulging, on the distorted face an expression of inhuman suffering.

But why had they killed him? And why him? Wasn't he guilty? But I was certain that he was.

Oh! How bitter, how fragrant the smell of the thyme! Herbs, even dying, smell bitter and fragrant.

At that very moment I instinctively, not yet comprehending what was wrong, turned back. I had crept rather far away when I heard footsteps. Two persons were walking there. I sneaked under a large weeping willow, got up on my feet, merging with the trunk so as the men would not notice me and, pulling myself up with my hands, climbed into the tree and hid among its branches like an enormous tree frog.

Two phantoms came up to the murdered man. The moon was shining directly on them, but their faces were hidden behind pieces of dark cloth. Strange figures they made. Dressed in very old fashioned boots and coats with long capes over them, with long hair over which they wore some kind of a head gear made of woven strips of leather such as could have been seen in the Vilnia museum. They came up closer and bent down over Bierman's corpse. Fragments of their conversation reached my ears:

"Both fell for one and the same bait... Likol... Ha, ha! How they believed this childish nickname. Both, that brave young one and this pig here. Likol... Likol's paid them."

And suddenly one of them exclaimed in surprise:

"Look, Patsuk, this isn't him!"

"What do you mean, not him?"

"I am telling you this isn't him. This... this is that queer fish, the manager of the Yanovsky's estate."

"What the hell are you saying? Ah, anyway, hardly a problem."

"For this 'hardly a problem', mate," said the second one darkly, "Likol will have our heads cut off. It's bad, brother. Two men dead – horrible! The authorities might become interested in this."

"But why did he show up instead of the other one?"

The second man did not answer. They left the corpse under the tree in which I was sitting. Had I wished it, I could have let my feet down and stood on the head of each one of them, as I chose, or else, I could have shot twice from my revolver. At such a distance a child would have hit the mark. I was trembling with excitement, but the voice of cold reason told me that I must not do that – I would scare away the rest of the gang. To put an end to the Hunt, one must do it with one hit! I had, as it was, already committed too many blunders, and should yet Nadzeya Yanovsky perish in addition to this all – then the only thing left for me would be to go to the Giant's Gap, jump into it, and hear the wild roar of the air escaping from out of the swamp over my head.

"Why does he hate this Belaretsky so much?" asked the one called Patsuk.

"I think because Belaretsky wants to marry young Yanovsky. And then the castle will slip out of Likol's hands."

"What does he need it for anyway? It's a moulding coffin, not a castle."

"Well, it's not that you don't have a point, but... This coffin may be of no use to the Yanovskys even though it's a family estate, still for an outsider the castle has great value. And he is, in addition, in love with antiquity, in his sleep he dreams of being the owner of a tremendous castle, a castle like his ancestors once had."

They stopped talking, then a light flashed and curls of tobacco smoke began creeping up to me. It was already clear to me that those standing there were local aristocrats. Their crude local speech, coarse and infested with words of Polish origin, was hurting my ear. The voices, however, seemed familiar to me.

"It seems," growled Patsuk after a lengthy pause, "that there's yet one more reason for this – the serfs."

"Right you are. And if we kill this one, too, they'll quiet down, like mice under a broom. For they've become too impudent. The recent uprising, the murder of Haraburda's steward. Looks impudent. Look at them, now particularly bold after the arrival of that Svetsilovich. The skunk lived here only one month, but had done more harm than a fire. He got four serfs out of the hands of the court and complained about two nobles. Things got worse since this Belaretsky has appeared here, now no life at all. Belaretsky goes to their huts, writes down foolish stories. Well, no matter, they'll grow quiet, the boors will, if we also strangle this betrayer of our gentry... If only we knew who the leader of these brazen fellows is. I'll not forgive him my burnt haystacks."

"I think that I might know who he is – Ryhor, Kulsha's watchman. What an ugly mug, like a wolf's. He has no respect for anybody."

"Never mind, he'll be belching too, soon."

Again they were silent. Then one of them said:

"Truth be told, I'm sorry for Miss Yanovsky. To drive such a woman to madness or to kill her... stupid, a stupid thing to do. People used to kiss the feet of such a woman like herself. You remember, don't you how she danced at the ball in that very old fashioned dress, floating along like a swan?"

"Yes, and our master regrets it," the other one said. "But it can't be helped."

And he suddenly burst out laughing.

"Why are you laughing?"

"We got the wrong guy! We are out of luck, but he is even more so. You remember how Roman screamed when he was driven into the bog? He said that he would reach us from his grave. But, as you see, he's keeping quiet."

And they walked away from the tree.

I heard Patsuk pronouncing in his bass voice:

"Never mind, we'll soon visit this one, too."

I slipped down from the tree without making any noise and moved on after them. My feet stepped noiselessly on the grass and here and there I again crept.

And, of course, again I turned out to be a fool, having neglected the fact that they might have come on horses. They hid behind the shrubs and in fear of running into them I slowed down. The following instant I heard the tramp of horses' hoofs.

When I came out onto the road, in the distance I saw two horsemen driving their horses madly south-westward away from Roman's cross.

I returned to my sad thoughts. Having learned that they were hunting Lady Yanovsky and me, that no mercy could be expected, I allowed two bandits make their escape, and also I had been so cruelly mistaken about Bierman. I was convinced that his was a suspicious character, he had opened a letter addressed to me, and for some reason or other went to this dreadful place where he met his death. In itself the fact of this death pushed into the background the rest of his sins from me. But I had learned a great deal from the conversation that I had overheard and, first and foremost, now I knew one of the Wild Hunt. The story about the burnt haystacks gave him away. The haystacks that had been burnt had belonged to Mark Stakhievich. I had seen him at the drunken revel at Dubatowk's place. And it was this man who had been Varona's second. Well, let's say I had been mistaken as to Bierman, but there's no mistake, it seems to me, about Varona. And he shall be mine. Only now greater determination is necessary.

And late in the evening King Stakh's Wild Hunt appeared again. Again it howled, wailed, cried in an inhuman voice:

"Roman of the last generation, come out! We have come. We shall put an end to all! Then we shall rest. Roman! Roman!"

And again, lying hidden in the bushes at the entrance, I shot at the flying shadows of horsemen that flashed by at the end of the lane lit up by a misty moon. When I shot the first time, the horses threw themselves into the thicket and disappeared, as if they had never even been. It resembled a horrible dream...

It was necessary to put an end to things. I recalled Mark Stakhievich's words spoken beneath the tree, concerning Roman's promise that after his death he would give away the murderer, and I thought that Roman might have left some clue in the house or at the place of his death. A clue that even Ryhor's vigilant eye had overlooked.

And when Ryhor came we hurried together to the place where Roman had been murdered. I am not a bad walker, but I could hardly keep up with this leggy figure. It might have seemed, looking at him, that Ryhor was walking slowly, but his movements were measured, and his feet he placed not as ordinary people do, but with his toes turned inward: all born hunters walk that way. By the way, it has been observed that this makes every step approximately one inch longer. Along the way I told him about the conversation between Mark Stakhievich and some Patsuk.

"Varona's men," Ryhor angrily growled. And then added: "But we had thought that 'Likol' is the beginning of a surname. You, sir, hadn't asked the right question. 'Likol' is evidently a nickname. You must ask Miss Yanovsky who is called that way. If Svetsilovich knew this nickname and, perhaps, even Bierman, it means that she must also know it."

"I asked her."

"You asked her about a surname, said that 'Likol' was its beginning, but not that it's a nickname."

Long story short, we approached the well known place which I have twice described, the place where Nadzeya's father had perished. We sought all over in the dry grass, although it was stupid to look for anything in it after two years. And finally we came up to a place where there was a precipice, not a large one, over the quagmire.

Over the abyss a rather small stump met our sight sticking out from the ground, the remnant of the trunk of a tree that had grown there long ago, its roots now spreading throughout the abyss like mighty snakes, roots reaching downwards into the quagmire, as if there to quench their thirst, roots simply hanging in the air.

I asked Ryhor to recall whether Roman's hands had been visible over the quagmire.

Ryhor's lowered his eyes, trying to remember:

"Indeed, they were. The right one was even stretched out, he must have wanted to catch hold of the roots, but couldn't reach them."

"But perhaps he simply threw something there where a hole is visible under the roots?"

"Let's look."

And holding onto the roots, and breaking our finger nails, we let ourselves down almost into the very mire, hardly able to hold onto the small slippery ledges of the steep slope. A hole did indeed turn out to be under the roots, but there was nothing in it.

I was about to climb up to the top, but Ryhor stopped me:

"Stupid we are. If there really was something here, then it is already under a layer of silt. He could have thrown something, but you know, two years have passed, the soil there in the hole would have crumbled and buried it."

We began scratching the caked silt with our fingers, emptying it out of the hole, and – believe it or not, soon my fingers hit on something hard. In the palm of my hand lay a cigarette case made of maple wood. There was nothing else in the hole.

We climbed out and carefully wiped off from the cigarette case the reddish silt, mixed with clay. In the cigarette case we found a piece of white cloth which Roman had evidently torn out from his shirt with his teeth. And on this little rag were written hardly decipherable reddish letters: "Varona mur..."

I shrugged my shoulders. The devil knows what this meant! Either evidence that Varona killed Roman, or a request to Varona to kill someone. Ryhor was looking at me.

"Well, so now it's clear, Mr. Andrey. Varona drove him here. Tomorrow we shall take him."

"Why tomorrow? He may come today even."

"Today is Friday. You, sir, have forgotten this. People say: 'Look for the cut throat in the church.' Really too holy and godly. They kill with the name of the Holy Trinity on their lips. They will come tomorrow because

they've lost all patience. They have got to get rid of you."
He became silent, a harsh flame blazed in his eyes. "Tomorrow, at last, I'll bring the muzhyks. With pitchforks.
And we'll give you one, too. If you're with us, then you're
with us to the end. We'll lie in wait at the torn down
cross. We'll finish them off, all of them. To the very roots,
the devil's seed."

We went together to Marsh Firs and there we learned
that Miss Nadzeya was not alone. Mr. Haraburda was
with her. Yanovsky had been avoiding me lately, and
when we met she would turn her eyes away, eyes that
had grown dark and were as sad as autumn water.

Therefore I asked the housekeeper to call her out into
the lower hall where Ryhor was sombrely looking at St.
Yuri, himself as powerful and tall as the statue. Lady
Yanovsky came in and Ryhor, ashamed of his dirty footprints all over the floor, was hiding his feet behind an
armchair. But his voice when he addressed her was as
formerly, rough, though somewhere deep down within
him, something trembled.

"Listen, clever Miss. We have found King Stakh. It's
Varona. Give me a pair of guns. Tomorrow we'll put an
end to him."

"And by the way," I said, "I was mistaken when I asked
you whether you knew a person whose surname began
with 'Likol'. Now I want to ask you whether you know
a person whose nickname *is* Likol, simply Likol. He is
the most dangerous man in the gang, perhaps its leader
even."

"No!" she screamed suddenly, her hands clutching at
her breast. Her eyes widened, frozen with horror. "No!
No!"

"Who is he?" Ryhor asked darkly.

"Be merciful! Have pity on me! That's impossible...
He is so kind hearted and tender. He used to hold Svetsi-

lovich and me on his knees. Our childish tongues at that time couldn't pronounce his name, we distorted it and that gave birth to the nickname by which we called him only among ourselves. Few people knew this."

"Who is he?" adamantly repeated Ryhor moving stone jaws.

And then she began to weep. Cried, sobbed like a child, and through her sobbing finally escaped a brief:

"Mr. Likol... Mr. Ryhor Dubatowk."

I was horror stricken to the very heart. Dumbfounded!

"Impossible! Such a good man! And, most important, of what benefit is it to him? After all, he's not an heir!"

And my memory obligingly reminded me of the words of one of the scoundrels under the tree: "He's in love with antiquity." Even the undeciphered "...ly ma..." in the letter to Svetsilovich suddenly turned naturally into Dubatowk's favourite byword: "Holy martyrs! What's going on here in this world!"

I wiped my eyes driving off my confusion.

Like lightning the solution flashed through my mind.

"Wait here, Nadzeya. And Ryhor, you wait, too. I'll go to Mr. Haraburda. Then I'll have to look through Bierman's things."

Up the stairs I ran, my mind working in two directions. Firstly, Dubatowk might have arranged matters with Bierman, although why had he killed him? Secondly, Haraburda also might have been dependent on Dubatowk.

When I opened the door, an elderly gentleman with Homeric haunches got out from his armchair to meet me. He looked at my determined face in surprise. "Excuse me, Mr. Haraburda," I flung at him sharply, "I must put a question to you concerning your relations with Mr. Dubatowk: why did you permit this man to order you about?"

He had the look of a thief caught in the act of committing a crime. His low forehead reddened, his eyes began to wander. However, from the look on my face, he probably understood that I was in no mood for joking.

"What can one do... Promissory notes..." he muttered.

"You gave Mr. Dubatowk promissory notes secured by Yanovsky's estate, which does not belong to you?"

And again I struck home aiming at the sky.

"It was such a miserly sum. Only 3,000 roubles. The kennel requires so much."

Things were beginning to fall into their places. Dubatowk's monstrous plan gradually became clear.

"According to Roman Yanovsky's will," he mumbled, removing something from his morning coat with trembling fingers, "such a substitution was established. Yanovsky's children receive the inheritance..." and he looked at me pitifully in the eyes. "There won't be any. She'll die, you know... She'll die soon. After her – her husband. But she is mad, who will marry her? Then the next step – the last of the Yanovskys. But there aren't any, after Svetsilovich's death – none. I am Yanovsky's relative in the female line. If there aren't any children or a husband – the castle is mine." And he began to whimper: "But how could I wait? I've so many promissory notes. I'm such an unfortunate person. Mr. Ryhor has bought up most of my notes. And in addition gave 3,000 roubles. Now he'll be the owner here."

"Listen to me," speaking through set teeth, "there was, is, and will be only one owner here, Miss Nadzeya Yanovsky."

"I laid no hope on receiving an inheritance. Yanovsky could get married. So I gave him a promissory note, its security being the castle."

"So! You lack both shame and a conscience. You probably do not even know what they are. But don't you really know that from the financial aspect this act is not valid? That it's criminal?"

"No, I don't. I was glad."

"But you know, don't you, that you drove Dubatowk into committing a terrible crime, a crime for which there is no word even in man's language? Of what is the poor girl guilty that you decided to deprive her of her life?"

"I suspected that it was a crime," he babbled, "but my kennel, my house..."

"You lousy thing! I don't want to dirty my hands on you. The provincial court will busy itself with you. And in the meantime, on my own authority, I'll put you in the dungeon of this house for a week, so you won't be able to warn the other rascals."

He began to whimper and whine:

"That's coercion."

"It's for you, is it, to speak of coercion? You villain! It's for you, is it, to appeal to the law?" I flung at him. "What do you know about that? You who lick people's boots!"

I called Ryhor, and he pushed Haraburda into the dungeon, under the central part of the building where there weren't any windows.

An iron door thundered behind him.

CHAPTER SIXTEEN

The small light of a candle loomed somewhere in the distance behind dark window-panes. When I lifted my eyes, I saw close by the reflection of my face in sharp shadows.

I was looking through Bierman's papers. It still seemed to me that I might find something of interest in them. Bierman was too complicated a character to have lived the life of a foolish sheep.

And so, here I was with the consent of the mistress. I had taken out all the papers from the secretaire and put them on the table, also all the books, letters and documents, and I sat, sneezing from the thick layer of dust on these relics.

There was little of interest, however, in them. I came across a letter from Bierman's mother, in which she asked for help, and the rough draft of his answer, where he wrote that he was supporting his brother, that now his brother didn't interfere with his mother living as she liked, and as for the rest – they were quits. Strange! What brother, where is he now?

I dug out something resembling a diary in which next to monetary expenditures and rather clever remarks on Belarusian history, I found also Bierman's discourses such as these:

"The Northwest Territory as a concept is a fiction. The reason for this possibly lies in the fact that it serves with its blood and brain the idea of the universe as a whole, but not as of five provinces, that it pays off all debts and obligations, and that it is preparing a new Messiah in its very depths for the salvation of mankind, and therefore its lot is to suffer. This, however, does not refer to those who are its best representatives, people possessing energy, strength and an aristocratic spirit."

"Well, just take a look, with the spirit of a knight, a strong man in torn pants," I muttered.

"My only love is my brother. At times it seems to me that all other people are only caricatures of him and there is need of a person who would remake everybody in his likeness. People must be creatures of darkness. Animal beauty appears more clearly in their organisms, a beauty that we must guard and love. Then isn't the only difference between the genius and the idiot the fig-leaf, which man himself revised? Belaretsky's mediocrity irritates me, and, by God, it would be better for him if he disappeared, and the sooner the better."

And yet another note:

"Money is the emanation of human authority over a herd of others, and regretfully so!. We should have learned to perform castration of the brains of all those who do not deserve the life of a conscious being. And the best should be given boundless happiness, for such a thing as justice is not foreseen by nature itself. This applies also to me. I need peace, which we have here more than anything else, and money in order to mature the idea for the sake of which I appeared in the world, the idea of splendid and exceptional injustice. And it seems to me that the first step might be the victory over that towards which my body is striving and which, however, it's necessary to overcome, the desire for the mistress of Marsh Firs. She is anyway condemned by blind fate to be done away with – the curse on her is being fulfilled by the appearance of the Wild Hunt at the walls of the castle. Though she is stronger than I had thought: she hasn't lost her mind yet. King Stakh is weak, and I am ordained to correct his mistakes. I am, nevertheless, jealous of all young men and especially of this Belaretsky. I shot at him yesterday, but was forced to retreat. I shoot badly."

The next sheet:

"It is possible that if I fulfilled the role of God's will, of his highest design, such as has been known to happen with ordinary mortals, the evil spirits will leave this place and I shall remain the master here. I convinced Belaretsky that the Hunt presents the chief danger. But what danger can there be in apparitions? The Little Man is a different story."

"Gold, gold! Thousands of panegyrics could be sung to your power over people's souls. You are everything – the baby's diaper, the girl's body to be bought, friendship, love and power, the brain of the greatest geniuses, even the decent hole in the Earth. And I will achieve all this."

I crumpled the paper and squeezed my fingers until they ached.

"Abomination!"

Suddenly my hand came across a sheet of parchment folded in four among piles of paper. I unfolded the sheet on my lap and could only shake my head – it was the construction plan of Marsh Firs, a plan dating back to the sixteenth century. And in this plan four listening channels were clearly indicated in the walls. Four! But they were so hidden in the plafonds that to find them was simply impossible. One of them, by the way, led from the dungeons in the castle to the room near the library, probably in order to overhear prisoners' conversations, and the second one connected the library, the now abandoned servants' rooms on the first floor and Miss Yanovsky's quarters. The two others remained unknown to me; they opened into the hall where were located the rooms belonging to Yanovsky and myself, but where they led to had been carefully rubbed out.

The villain had found the plan in the archive and had hidden it.

There turned out to be some more interesting things in the plan. The outer wall of the castle contained an empty space, a narrow passage and three small cells of some kind – where I had once torn off a board in the boarded up room.

I swore as never before in my life. Many unpleasant things might have been avoided if I had thoroughly knocked at the walls covered with panels. But it wasn't too late even now. I grabbed the candle, glanced at the clock – half past ten – and ran as quickly as I could to my hall.

I was knocking for half an hour probably, before I hit on a place which answered to my knocking with a resonant sound as if I were knocking on the bottom of a barrel. I looked for a place in the panel that I could catch onto and tear off at least a part of it, but in vain. Then I saw some light scratches on it, made with some sharp thing. I equipped myself with a folding knife and began to prod it into the hardly noticeable cracks between the panels. With a blade of the knife I managed quite soon to find something that gave way. I pressed harder – the panel began to squeak and slowly turn on the side, forming a narrow slit. I looked at the reverse part of the panel at the place in which I had stuck the knife. A hollow board made opening the manhole from the inside impossible. I went down about fifteen steps, but the door behind my back began to squeak so pitifully that I hurried upstairs and managed just in time to hold it back with my foot so that it shouldn't shut. To remain in a rat hole alone under the threat of sitting there till Doomsday with a candle end was foolhardy.

Therefore I left the door half open, put a handkerchief near the axle and myself sat down not far away on the floor, with my revolver on my knees. I had to blow out the candle, for its light might frighten the mysterious creature if it had thought of creeping out of its hiding place. The candle burning round the corner in the hall all night, even though dimly, still gave some light, and an indefinite grey light also poured in through the window.

I don't know how long I sat there with my chin buried in my knees. It was about twelve when drowsiness began to overtake me, my eyes became glued together. No matter how I fought sleep, I nodded; the past sleepless nights were catching up with me. In an instant, my mind slipped away and I fell into a kind of a dark, stuffy abyss.

Have you ever tried to sleep while sited, your back leaning against a wall or a tree? Try it. You will become convinced that the sensation of falling was left to us from our forefather – the monkey. For him it had been necessary to prevent his falling off the tree. And, sitting against the tree, you will, in your sleep, fall very often, awakening and again falling asleep. Finally, wonderful dreams overcome your soul, a million years of man's existence will disappear, and it will seem to you that under the tree a prehistoric mammoth is going to – the water and the eyes of a cave bear are burning from under a cliff.

This was my condition by approximation. Dreams... Dreams... It seemed to me I was sitting in a tree and I was afraid to let myself down, for a pithecanthropus was stealthily making his way along the ground under me. It was night and wolves were moaning behind the trees. At that very moment I "fell" and opened my eyes.

In the semi darkness a strange creature was moving straight in front of me. Green, old fashioned clothes, covered with dust and cobwebs, its long lowered in thought head was stretching out as a bean seed, frog-like eyelids almost covered its eyes, and hands were hanging down, hands with such long fingers they were almost touching the floor.

The Little Man of Marsh Firs moved past and floated on farther, while I followed after him with my revolver. He opened a window, then another one and crept inside. I stuck my head out after him and saw him walking with the ease of a monkey along a narrow ledge the width of three fingers! Here and there he nipped off a few buds from the branches of a lime tree touching the wall, and champed them. With one hand he helped himself to move on. Then he crept back into the hall again, closed the window and slowly moved ahead somewhere. A fearful sight was this inhuman creature! Once it seemed to me that I heard a kind of mumbling. The Little Man beat himself on his forehead and was lost in the dark where the light of the distant candle did not reach. I hurried after him, because I was afraid he would disappear. When I found myself in the dark I saw two fiery eyes that looked from around the corner and were inexplicably threatening.

I rushed to the Little Man, but he began to groan grievously and wandered off somewhere, shaking on his little legs. Turning around, he fixed his gaze on me, threatening me with a long finger. For a moment I was dumbfounded, but collected myself, caught up with the Little Man and grabbed him by the shoulders. My heart began to beat happily, for it was not a ghost.

When I dragged the creature out into the light, it put a finger into its mouth and pronounced in a squeaking voice:

"Aam–aam!"

"Who are you?" I was shaking him.

And the Little Man, the former ghost, answered – his answer well rehearsed:

"I'm Bazyl. I'm Bazyl."

A slyness which exists even in idiots suddenly lit up his eyes:

"I saw you. Ha-ha! I was sitting under the table – under the table, my brother was feeding me. And you suddenly showed up..."

And again he champed with that large mouth of his that was reaching to his ears.

I began to understand everything. Two villains, the ringleader of the Wild Hunt and Bierman, both pursuing one and the same aim – to get rid of Yanovsky – hit upon, as a matter of fact, one and the same idea. Bierman, knowing that he is a relative of Yanovsky, arrived at Marsh Firs and found the listening channels and passages in the walls. After that he secretly went to town, abandoned his mother to her fate, took back with him his brother who avoided people not because he preferred being alone – he was simply a hopeless idiot. Not for nothing had his bad behaviour surprised the people in the club – Bierman had, of course, brought not his actual brother to the club but a random person. Bierman roomed together with his brother at Marsh Firs, taking advantage of the fact that nobody ever came to see him. And he ordered his brother to sit quietly. Once when I happened to come in on them during the Little Man's feeding hour, the invalid, as it turns out, was under the table, and if only had I reached out my hand, I could have grabbed him.

During the night Bierman would lead him out into the secret passages where he walked about. As a result of this activity sounds were created in the listening channels that were heard by all the inhabitants of the house.

From time to time Bierman let the Little Man out into the hall. In that case he'd put on him an old fashioned costume, made specifically for such occasions. While his little brother took his walk, Bierman waited for him at the open door of the passage, for the Little Man couldn't open it himself. Sometimes he allowed him to take a walk in the open air. With the ease of a monkey, or rather with that of a spider, he ran along the ledges of the building, glancing into the windows, and in case of an alarm, disappeared like lightning behind the numerous corners of the castle.

It was very easy for the Little Man to do all this. In fact, nothing could be easier – his caveman mind completely lacked the instinct of self-preservation. He walked along a ledge as calmly as we do when we walk along a railway track for fun.

It was during one such promenade of his that his meeting with me took place. What then happened afterwards? Likol had sent me a letter in which, in order to call me out of the house, he mentioned that he had information about the Little Man. Bierman, who had been watching me closely of late, read the letter and hastened to the meeting spot, hoping to come to an agreement with the author of the letter. There he was mistaken for me and the tragedy occurred, a tragedy to which I had become a belated witness.

The dwarf remained all these days inside the passages, lacking the strength to get out, and had become entirely weakened by hunger.

If I hadn't opened the door, he would probably have died of hunger without having guessed why his brother had left him, his brother who always fed and caressed him.

What was I to do with him? The unfortunate fellow was not guilty of being born such a creature into this world. Here he disappears from our story. I fed him, informed Yanovsky of the death of one of the ghosts inhabiting the castle, and on the following day sent him off to the district hospital for the weak minded.

And for the first time I saw a ray of hope beginning to shine in the eyes of the mistress of Marsh Firs, and although the light in them was tender, it was as yet but weak.

CHAPTER SEVENTEEN

"Is that you, Ryhor?"

"Me, Andrey. More exactly, us."

I held out my hand to Ryhor. This night was the first cloudless and moonlit night that we'd had in a long time. The full moon cast a bluish silver light over the peat bogs, the waste land, the Marsh Firs Park and far, far away it shone in a little window of some lonely hut. The nights turned considerably colder, and now the swamps were "sweating", giving birth to a mobile white fog in the hollows.

Ryhor stepped out from among the bushes that grew along the broken down fence, and people appeared behind him in the darkness, about twelve in all.

They were muzhyks. All of them in leather coats turned inside out, in identical white felt hats.

And they all looked alike in the moonlight, as if the Earth itself had simultaneously given birth to them. I saw that two of them had long guns the same as Ryhor's. A third held a pistol in his hand, the rest were armed with boar spears and pitchforks, and one had an ordinary club.

"Who are they?" I asked in surprise.

"Muzhyks," Ryhor said. "Our patience is exhausted. Two days ago the Wild Hunt trampled to death the brother of this muzhyk. His name's Michal."

Michal, the embodiment of a giant from an urban legend, had deep little eyes, high cheekbones, arms and legs meatier and more impressive than Dubatowk's. His eyes were red and swollen, and his hands gripped his gun so hard that the knuckles of his fingers had even turned white. He looked gloomy and sullen, but clever.

"Enough's enough!" Ryhor said. "The only thing left for us to do is to die. But we don't want to die. And you, Belaretsky, if anything is not to your liking, keep quiet. This is our affair. And God allows the whole world to rise against the horse thief. Today we'll teach them not only not to trample the people, but even not to eat bread. These people with Michal at their head will remain here under your command. Mine are waiting for me at the swamp that surrounds the Yanovsky Virgin Forest near the Witch's mortar. There are twenty more of them there. If the Hunt comes there – we'll meet them, if they take another road unknown to us – you'll meet them. We'll keep watch at the Virgin Forest, the Cold Hollow and the waste lands that are next to us. If you need help, send a man."

And Ryhor disappeared into the darkness.

We arranged an ambush. I instructed six muzhyks to take their places along both sides of the road at the broken fence, and three somewhat farther on, thus forming a sack. In case anything should happen, the three would have to block the way to retreat for the Wild Hunt. I took my place behind the large tree by the very path.

I forgot to say that for each one of us there were three torches. Quite enough, should the need arise, to light up everything around us.

As my people in leather coats lay down, they merged well with the ground – they couldn't be distinguished from the hummocks, their grey sheepskins became one with the beaten down autumn grass.

In this way we waited quite a long time. Above the marshland floated the moon, from time to time some blue sparks flashed there, the fog sometimes became a

ULADZIMIR KARATKEVICH

compact, low sheet up to one's knees, sometimes it slowly moved away again.

They, as always, appeared unexpectedly. Twenty misty horsemen on twenty misty horses. Their approach was noiseless and terrifying. A silent mass moved on us. The bits did not ring, no human voices were heard. Capes were waving with the wind. The Hunt was dashing on, and at its head raced King Stakh, his hat, as previously, pulled down over his face. We had expected them to come flying with the wind, but at about a hundred steps away they dismounted, spent much time near the horses' hoofs. When they moved on again, an altogether unexpected thunder of hoofs reached us, breaking into the silence.

Slowly they came nearer and nearer to us, they were already passing the quagmire and were riding up to the fence, but here they passed round it. Stakh came riding straight towards me, and I could see his face, a face white as chalk.

When he was almost at my tree, I stepped forward, took his horse by the bridle. Simultaneously – with my left hand in which I clutched the riding crop – I pushed his hat onto the back of his head.

I was looking at Varona's face – a face pale as death, eyes without a living light in them, large dead eyes.

Being taken by surprise like that he certainly did not know what to do, but I, to make up for it, knew very well what I should do.

"So you are King Stakh?" I asked quietly, and hit him in the face with the riding crop.

Varona's horse reared and dashed away from me into the group of horsemen.

At that very instant the guns thundered from the ambush, the torches blazed, and everything sank in a whirl into a mad sea of fire. The horses reared, the horsemen fell, someone yelled in a heart rending voice. I still remember only Michal's face as he cold bloodedly took aim. A cone of bullets flashed out from a long gun. Then a young man's face floated in front of me, the face of that man with high cheekbones; his long tresses of hair were falling down his forehead. The fellow was working with a pitchfork as on a threshing floor, then lifted it and with terrific strength thrust it into the belly of the rearing horse. The horseman, the horse, and the man fell down together. I remained standing, and in spite of the fact that shots were already coming also from the Hunt, and that bullets were whistling overhead, I deliberately chose whom to shoot at from among the horsemen energetically surrounding me. Shots came pouring on them also from behind.

"Brothers, treachery!"

"Our galloping is over!"

"Save us!"

"Oh, Lord! Oh, Lord!"

I saw fear on the faces of these bandits, and the joy of revenge took possession of me. They should have thought beforehand that the day of reckoning would come. I saw a muzhyk with a club breaking into the thick of the fight, inflicting violent strokes on his victims. All the old fury, all the suffering now exploded in an attack of unheard of passion and fighting bravery. Somebody jerked off one of the hunters from his saddle and the horse dragged his head by the roots.

Within ten minutes all, in fact, was over. Abandoned horses neighed horribly, the killed and the wounded lay like sheaves on the ground, Varona alone like the devil, cornered by the muzhyks and beating them off with his sword with his revolver clutched between his teeth. He fought splendidly. Then he saw me, his face disfigured with such terrible hatred that even now I still remember it and sometimes see in my dreams.

Having trampled down one of the peasants with his horse, he grabbed his revolver.

"Beware, you villain! You've taken her away from me! But there'll be no caresses for you!"

The peasant with the long whiskers pulled him by his leg and due only to that I didn't crash on the ground with a hole in my skull. Varona understood he would be pulled off his horse now, and firing point blank, he killed the long-whiskered man on the spot.

Having succeeded in reloading my revolver, I sent all the six bullets into him without hesitation. Varona, grasping at the air with his hands, reeled in his saddle, but nevertheless turned his horse around, knocked a muzhyk, the one with high cheekbones and meaty legs, to the ground and dashed off in the direction of the swamp. He was all the time grasping at the air with his hands, but stayed in the saddle and together with it – the saddle girth must have broken – slid down one side until he was hanging over the ground. The horse turned aside. Varona's head struck heavily against a stone post in the fence. His lifeless body flew out of the saddle, struck against the ground and remained lying motionless, dead.

Theirs was a crushing defeat. The terrible Wild Hunt was overcome by the hands of ordinary muzhyks on the very first day that they exerted themselves a little and began to believe that with pitchforks they could rise even against phantoms.

I examined the battlefield. The peasants were leading the horses off to the side. They were real *drygants of the Palessie,* the presumably extinct breed. All striped and with spots, with white nostrils, with eyes ablaze in red flame deep in them. Not surprising then that their capering in the fog seemed so unnatural, for I knew that this breed was distinguished for its remarkably long strides.

And unexpectedly two more riddles were solved. Firstly, four sheepskin bags hung at the saddle of each of the hunters. Should the need arise, they could be put on the horses' hoofs and tied at the pasterns. Their steps became entirely noiseless. Secondly, among the dead and the wounded I saw three scarecrows on the ground, all three dressed like hunters, but they were tied to their saddles with ropes. Evidently, Varona did not have enough people.

However, our losses were also heavy ones. We'd never have conquered this band of professional murderers if our attack had not been so unexpected. But even as it was, our score was bad; the muzhyks just could not fight. The fellow with the prominent cheekbones who was knocked down by Varona's horse, lay with his head smashed. The long-legged muzhyk had a bullet hole darkening in the very middle of his forehead. The muzhyk with the club lay on the ground, his feet jerking – he was dying. Of the wounded there were twice as many. I also received a wound. A bullet at the rebound had flicked me in the back of my head.

We were swearing. Michal was bandaging my head and I was screaming that it was a trifle, rubbish. Soon one man was found alive among the Hunters, and he was led to a blazing campfire. In front of me stood Mark Stakhievich, his hand hanging down at his side like a whip. It was that very same young aristocrat whose conversation with Patsuk I had overheard sitting in the tree. He looked very eye catching in his cherry coloured *chuga*, in a little hat, with an empty sabre scabbard at his side. "It seems you threatened the muzhyks, didn't you, Stakhievich? You will die as these here," I said calmly. "But we can let you go free, because, alone, you are not dangerous. You will depart from the Yanovsky region and will remain alive, if you tell us about all the foul deeds of your gang."

He hesitated, looked at the severe faces of the muzhyks, the crimson light of the campfire lighting up their faces, their leather coats, their hands gripping their pitchforks, and he understood there was no mercy to be expected. Pitchforks from all sides were surrounding him, touching his body.

"Dubatowk is to blame – it's all his doings," he said sullenly. "Yanovsky's castle was to have been inherited by Haraburda, but he was greatly in debt to Dubatowk. Nobody, except us, Dubatowk's people, knew about that. We drank at his place and he gave us money, while himself he dreamed of the castle. He did not want to sell anything from that place, although the castle cost a lot of money. Varona said that if all the things in the castle were sold to museums, a large fortune could be raised. A chance event brought them together. At first Varona did not want to kill Yanovsky even though she had refused to marry him. But after Svetsilovich's appearance, he agreed. The tale about King Stakh's Wild Hunt came into Dubatowk's head three years ago. Dubatowk had stashed money somewhere, although he seems to be living poorly. In general he is a liar, very sly and secretive. He can twist the cleverest man round his little finger, he can pretend to be such a bear you'd be at a loss what to think. And so he went to the best of stud farms owned by a lord who had become impoverished in recent years, and bought all his *drygants*. Then he brought them to the Yanovsky Reserve where we built a hide out for ourselves and a stable. Our ability to tear along through the quagmire, where nobody can even walk, surprised everybody. But nobody knows how long we crept along the Giant's Gap in search of secret paths. And we found them. And studied them. And taught the horses. And then we dashed through places where the paths were up to the elbow in the quagmire, but at the sides all it was an impassable marsh land. And the horses are a miracle! They rush to Dubatowk's call as dogs do. They sense the quagmire, and when a path breaks off, they can make enormous leaps. And we always went on the hunt only at night, when fog creeps over the land. And that's why everyone considered us phantoms. And we always kept silent. It was risky. But what could we do: die of hunger on a tiny piece of land? And Dubatowk paid. And we were not only driving Yanovsky to madness or death, but we even put the fear of God into those impudent serfs and taught them not to have too high an opinion of themselves. It was Dubatowk who got Haraburda to force Kulsha to invite the little girl, because he knew that her father would be anxious about her. And we intercepted Roman on the way and seized him. Oh! And what a chase it was! Ran away like the devil... But his horse broke a leg."

"We know that," I observed caustically. "By the way, Roman did give you away precisely after his death, although you didn't believe his cries. And some days ago you still didn't believe it when you were speaking with Patsuk after Bierman's murder."

Stakhievich was so surprised his jaw fell. I ordered him to continue relating.

"We inspired fear everywhere in the region. The farm hands agreed to the price the owners gave. Our life improved. And we led Nadzeya Yanovsky to despair. Then you appeared. Dubatowk's bringing the portrait of Roman the Old was no accident. If not for you, she would have gone mad within a week. Dubatowk saw that he had made a mistake. She was merry and carefree. You were dancing with her all the time; Dubatowk especially invited you when the guardian's report on affairs was to be made, and his guardianship handed over, so that you should become convinced she was poor. He conducted the estate well – it was, you see, to be his future estate. But Yanovsky's poverty had no effect on you, and then they decided to get you out of the way."

"Speaking of which..." I said, "I never had any intention of marrying her."

Stakhievich was totally surprised.

"Well, never mind. All the same you interfered with us. With you there, she was revived. To be just, I must say that Dubatowk really loved little Yanovsky. He did not want to kill her, and if he could have got along without doing that, he would have willingly agreed. He respected you. He always said to us that you were a real man, only it was a pity that you didn't agree to join us. In short, things became too complicated. We had to get rid of you and of Svetsilovich who had the right to the inheritance and loved Yanovsky. Dubatowk invited you to his place, where Varona was to challenge you to a duel. He played his part so well that no one even suspected that it was Dubatowk, not Varona, who was the instigator, and we in the meantime studied you closely, because we had to remember your face."

"Go on," I said.

Stakhievich hesitated, but Michal poked him with the pitchfork at the place from which our legs grow. Mark looked around sullenly.

"The affair with the duel turned out stupidly. Dubatowk made you drink a lot, but you didn't get drunk. And you even turned out to be so smart that you put Varona to bed for five whole days."

"But how could you then be in the house and chase after me at one and the same time?"

Stakhievich continued reluctantly:

"Behind Dubatowk's farmstead others were waiting, novices as they were. At first we thought of sending them after Svetsilovich, in case you were killed, but Svetsilovich sat with us till the morning, while Varona was wounded. We set them off after you instead. Dubatowk still cannot forgive himself for setting these snivellers on your track. You'd never have escaped from *us*, the real Hunt. Then we thought you'd take the roadway, but you went over the waste land, and you even forced the Hunt to waste a whole hour in front of the swamp. By the time the dogs fell on the scent, it was already too late. We cannot, even now, understand how you had managed to escape from us then, you dodged us so well. But take my word for this – had we caught you, you'd have been out of luck."

"But why did the horn blow from the side? And where are the novices now?"

Stakhievich forced himself to speak:

"One of us played the hunting horn, he rode nearby. And the novices – here they are, lying on the ground. Previously we were fewer in number and took scare-crows with us on spare horses. We supposed that only you and Ryhor were lying in ambush. But we did not think there'd be a whole army with you. And look how we paid for our assumptions. Here they all are, Patsuk, Jan Styrovich, Pawluk Babayed. And even Varona. You aren't worth even a finger nail of his. A clever man was Varona, but he, too, has not escaped God's judgement."

"Why did you throw me that note saying that King Stakh's Wild Hunt comes at night?"

"What are you saying? Phantoms don't throw notes. We wouldn't have done such a stupid thing."

"Bierman must have done it," I thought, but said:

"But it was the note that convinced me you were not phantoms, at the very moment when I had begun to be-lieve you were. Be thankful to the unknown well wisher, for hardly would I have been brave enough to fight with phantoms."

Stakhievich turned pale and hardly moving his lips uttered:

"We'd dealt with that person, had torn him to pieces. As for you, I hate you in spite of the fact that it is beyond my power to do anything. And now I'll keep silent."

Michal's hand grabbed the prisoner by the scruff of his neck and squeezed hard.

"Speak. Otherwise you'll be dealt with too..."

"The deuce take it, you're the powerful ones... You can be satisfied, you serfs... But we taught you a lesson, too. Let anyone try to learn what became of those who complained most in the village of Jarki and whom Antos wiped off the face of the Earth. You can ask anyone you like. It's a pity that Dubatowk didn't order to ambush you in the daytime and shoot you. For that would've been easy to do, especially when you were on the way to the Kulsha's, Belaretsky. I saw you. Even then we realized you had prepared the noose for us. Kulsha, the old woman, even though mad, could still have blurted out something. She had begun to guess that she was a tool in our hands the day of Roman's murder. And we only had to threaten her once with the appearance of the Wild Hunt. Her head was weak, and she immediately went balmy."

The abomination this man was telling us about made my blood boil. It was only now that my eyes were opened to what depths the gentry had fallen. And within me I agreed with Ryhor that it was necessary to destroy this kind of people, who raised a stink across the whole world shaming the spirit of nobility.

"Go on, you skunk!"

"When we learned that Ryhor had agreed to carry out the search together with you, we realized that things would be tough for us. For the first time I saw Dubatowk frightened. His face even turned yellow. We had to stop, and not for the sake of wealth, but in order to save our own hides. And we showed up at the castle."

"Who was it that yelled then?" I asked severely.

"He who yelled is no more. Here he lies... Patsuk..."

Stakhievich was frankly amusing himself in relating everything arrogantly, with such a display of courage, as if he were about to begin to wail at any moment, alternately lowering and raising his voice. I heard the howling of the Wild Hunt for the last time, inhuman, frightening, demonic.

"Roman!" he sobbed and wailed. "Roman! Revenge! We'll come, Roman of the last generation, we'll come for you!"

On and on rolled his voice across the Giant's Gap somewhere into the distance, his voice and its echo shouting to one another, completely filling the air. It made my flesh creep.

But Stakhievich laughed.

"You didn't come out then, Belaretsky. No matter. Anyone else in your place would have died of fright. At first we thought that you got frightened, but the next day something occurred that couldn't be remedied. Svetsilovich ran up against Varona who was on his way to recruit new men for the Hunt and he was late. And Svetsilovich was just near to the paths that lead to the Reserve where our hiding place was. And afterwards, spying on him, we saw that he met you in the forest, Belaretsky. Although at that time he didn't tell you anything as that was clear from your behaviour, we realised that he could crack any minute and we had to put an end to him. Dubatowk sent Svetsilovich a letter to lure him out of the house. Half of our people were directed to the three pines. The other half – three old hunters and the newcomers – rode off to Marsh Firs. Dubatowk himself hurried over to you, sneaking from behind. But you had already managed to make a couple of shots, and our raw fellows, unused to shooting, took to their heels. And yet another surprising thing – Dubatowk got such a hard beating from you that he can't ride a horse as of yet and he is staying in the house. And he is at home today, so you, fellows, beware. But you, Belaretsky, he fooled nicely. No sooner had you come to yourself, than you were already helping him to mount his horse. We got lucky with Svetsilovich. Varona was waiting for him, and when he appeared, said to him: "You've exposed the Wild Hunt, have you?" He spit at Varona. Varona shot him. And at that moment you appeared, shot at us and hit one fellow in the hand. And then you beat up a district police officer, and you were summoned, not without our help, to the district centre. You probably don't know that you were to be arrested and put an end to. But you, you devil, were lucky, you turned out to be too clever, and the governor's letter made the judge refuse us his help. On his knees he begged Dubatowk to hurry up and shoot you. By the way, when Varona shot Svetsilovich, he applied such a ruse that you'll never guess."

"But why do you think so?" I said with indifference. "Dubatowk had torn out several pages from a journal at Yanovsky's, and he made wads from them. You thought that if I managed to escape alive from your paws, I'd suspect Bierman."

Stakhievich was scratching away at his chest, his crooked fingers resembling claws.

"You devil!" he cried hoarsely, choking. "We shouldn't have had anything to do with you. But who could have thought of that? Here they are, those who didn't think, lying here like sacks of excrement."

Then he went on:

"And yet another mistake of ours. We kept a watch on you, but not on the serfs and Ryhor. While they found us out, got to our hide out, our secret paths... And even at Roman's cross you were in luck – we killed a chick, letting you escape from our grip. We killed on the run, without stopping. And only later we returned to check. And even here we ran up against you like a bunch of fools. Then Haraburda disappeared, and we decided not to return home tonight until we caught you. So, here we have found you..."

"That'll do," I said. "It's disgusting to hear you. And although you deserve the noose, we won't kill you. We've given our word. Later we'll investigate, and if you are very much to blame, we'll hand you over to the provincial court and if not – we'll let you go free."

Hardly had I finished, when Stakhievich suddenly pushed two of the muzhyks away, tore off, and with exceptional swiftness made for the horses. With his foot he kicked in the belly the muzhyk guarding the horses, threw himself into the saddle and started to gallop at full speed. He turned about on the way and shouted in a scathing tone:

"Just you wait for the trial in the provincial court! I'm off to Dubatowk's, he'll have the gentry of the whole region rise against you, you skunks, and we'll put an end to all of you. And you, you cad from the capital, there'll be no life for you and that loose woman of yours. But you, you stupid Michal, let it be known to you that it was me who trampled your brother to death, and you'll get the same."

Michal turned the muzzle of his long gun and without taking aim pulled the trigger. Stakhievich silently turned a somersault out of the saddle, rolled over several times on the ground and fell silent.

Michal came up to him, took the horse by the bit, shot Stakhievich straight in the forehead. Then said severely to me:

"Go ahead, Chief. Your kindness to them was a bit too early. Away with kindness! The gypsy wedding will get along without marzipans. Go on, we'll catch up with you. Take the road to the Cold Hollow. And don't turn back to take a look."

I left... And indeed, what right had I to be sentimental? If this bandit got to Dubatowk – they would overflow the whole region with blood. And Dubatowk must be captured all the sooner. Today, this very night, we must take him.

From behind I heard moaning and groaning. The wounded there were being finished off. I wanted to turn back, but couldn't. My throat was parched. But wouldn't they have done even worse with us?

The muzhyks caught up with me half way to the Hollow. They raced on the *drygants* with pitchforks in their hands.

"Mount, Chief," Michal said warmly, pointing to a horse. "With these everything is over. And the Gap won't tell anybody."

I answered as calmly as I could:

"Let bygones be bygones. But now as quickly as possible to Ryhor. Then together with him we'll go to Dubatowk's house."

We hastened to the Hollow, reaching it in the twinkling of an eye, and there we found the very end of the same tragedy. Ryhor kept his word, though they didn't deal with the participants of the Wild Hunt as they did with horse thieves. Horse thieves they simply killed outright. The last of the living hunters here lay on his back in front of Ryhor. He was quite a young fellow. And he, guessing from my clothes that I was not a peasant, suddenly began to scream:

"Mother mine! Mother mine! They're killing me."

"Ryhor," I begged. "You don't need to kill him, he's so young yet."

And I seized him by the shoulder, but my hands were caught from behind.

"Away with you!" Ryhor shouted. "Take him away, this blockhead. Did they have any pity for our children in Jarki? They died of hunger – of hunger! A person, in your opinion, has no right to eat? This one has a mother dear! And haven't we mothers? Or didn't Michal have a mother? Haven't you got one, that you are so kind? You sniveller! And don't you know that this very 'young fellow' shot Symon, Zoska's brother, and killed him? Never mind, we'll commit such outrages as in the song "The Vampires' Night".

Ryhor was referring to the Murashka Rebellion and the slaughter of aristocrats at the hands of the peasants. I didn't need to think twice. And Ryhor, turning around, struck his pitchfork into the man lying prostrate on the ground.

I went aside and sat down.

I was sick and didn't immediately hear Ryhor coming up to me and taking me by the shoulder when the dead were already being thrown into the quagmire.

"You're a fool, you are! You think I'm not sorry? My heart is bleeding. It seems to me I'll never again in my life be able to sleep calmly, but suffering must be endured, and once we've begun, then on to the end. Not a single one to be left, only we alone by mutual guarantee should know... 'A young one!' You think this young one wouldn't have grown into an old skunk? He would, certainly! Especially when recalling this night. His 'pity' for our people, bondsmen, will be something only to marvel at. Let him go – and we'll have the law here. For me and you – the noose, for Michal and the rest – penal servitude. The region will overflow with blood, they'll beat so hard that the flesh from our backsides will come off in rags."

"I understand," I said. "Not a single one of these must remain alive, but I've just recalled Svetsilovich and his dream... We must go to Dubatowk – to the last one left alive."

"Well," Ryhor grumbled, though tenderly. "Lead the way."

With our detachment behind us, we moved on towards Dubatowsk's house. We flew at a gallop, our horses raced as if wolves were after them. The moon dimly shone on our cavalcade, on the muzhyks' leather coats, the pitchforks, the dark faces, the scarecrows on some of the horses. We had to skirt the marsh round the Yanovsky Reserve. The road seemed a rather long one till we came to where we saw the linden tree crowns near Dubatowk's house. The moon flooded them with a deathly pale light; although it was very late, a light was burning in three windows.

I ordered the people to dismount about fifty metres away from the house and surround it in a close circle. The torches to be held in readiness and to light them when the signal was given. The command was fulfilled in silence. I crept over a low fence and walked through rows of almost bare apple trees lit by a flickering uncertain moonlight.

"Who's with the horses?" I asked Ryhor who was walking behind me.

"One of our boys. In case anything should happen, he will signal us. He whistles very well."

We stole on farther, and our boots stepped softly on the wet surface. I came up to a window. Dubatowk was nervously walking from one corner of the room to another, glancing often at the clock on the wall.

He was unrecognizable. This was an altogether different Dubatowk, and alone by himself, the real one, of course. What had become of his kindness, cordiality and tenderness? Where had that rosy face disappeared to, a face as healthy and merry as the face of Santa Claus?

The face of this Dubatowk was yellow, the corners of his mouth were abruptly lowered and sharp wrinkles outlined his nostrils. His sunken eyes looked dead and dark. I was horrified at seeing him like that, as a person becomes horrified when on awakening in the morning after a night's sleep he finds a snake in his bed having crept into it to warm itself, and then spent the night with him there.

"How could I have been so clueless?" I thought.

Yes, the sooner we put an end to him, the better. We just had to do it. He, alone, is more dangerous than ten Wild Hunts. It's well that during our fight I deprived him for a while of the possibility of riding his horse, for otherwise it would have been tough for us. He would not have placed himself right in front of a bullet, he would not have split up his detachment – he would have run us down like kittens with his horse's hoofs, and we'd have been lying now at the bottom of the Gap with our eyes put out.

"Ryhor, send seven men here. Have them break down the door of the entrance, while I'll try to tear off a board from the shed and make an unexpected attack on him from there. But see to it, everybody together..."

"Perhaps we could pretend we are the Hunt and knock at the window, and when he opens it, we'll grab him. He's sent his relatives somewhere, he's at home alone," Ryhor suggested.

"Nothing will come of that. He's a sly fox."

"Nevertheless, let's have a try. You understand, a pity to lose so much blood..."

"See that it doesn't turn out to be for the worse," I said, shaking my head.

The horses were led up to the house. I was happy to see Dubatowk's face in the window brightening up. He went up to the door with a candlelight, but suddenly stopped, stood stock still, on his face a puzzled expression. In a twinkling he blew out the candle and the room was drowned in darkness. The plan had fallen through.

"Come on, fellows," I shouted. "Break down the door!" Hasty footfalls and cries were heard. They began beating on the door with something heavy. A shot rang out from the attic. Following the shot, a voice full of fury echoed from the top tower:

"Surrounded! Just wait, you dogs! The gentry does not give in so easily!"

And from another window in the attic a cone of bullets came flying. Dubatowk was running, evidently, from one window to another, shooting at the advancing attackers from all sides.

"Oho! He must have a whole arsenal there," Ryhor said quietly.

His words were interrupted by yet another shot. A young fellow, standing beside me, fell on the ground with a hole in his head. Dubatowk shot better than the best hunter in Palessie. And yet another shot.

"Flatten yourselves against the walls!" I shouted. "The bullets won't reach there."

The bullets of our men, standing behind the trees, broke off the boards from the attic and the plastering. It was impossible to guess at which window Dubatowk would appear. Our victory promised to be a Pyrrhic one.

"Andrey!" Dubatowk's voice thundered. "You, too, will get what's coming to you. You devils have come after my soul, but you'll be giving up yours."

"Light the torches," I commanded. "Throw them onto the roof."

In the twinkling of an eye, scores of fires burst out surrounding the house. Some of them describing an arc in the air fell on the roof and sprayed tar, and tongues of flames were gradually reaching the windows of the attic. In answer to this, a howl was heard:

"Forty against one! And using fire! What nobility!"

"Be quiet!" I shouted. "Sending twenty bandits against one girl – that's nobility? There they are, your Hunters, lying in the quagmire and you will be there, too."

In answer a bullet clicked at my head, striking against the plaster.

Dubatowk's house was ablaze. Moving farther away from the walls of the house, I made for the trees and almost perished – a bullet from King Stakh sang at my ear. My hair even stirred.

Flames penetrated into the attic, and there, in the fire, guns loaded in good time, began to shoot by themselves. Our minds set at ease we had left the house behind, now that it had become a candle, when suddenly the fellow near the horses began to shout. We looked in his direction and saw Dubatowk creeping out from his dungeon, over a hundred metres away from the house.

"Ah!" Ryhor gritted his teeth. "We forgot that a fox always has an extra passage in his burrow."

And Dubatowk ran in loops in the direction of the Giant's Gap. His right hand was hanging. We had, obviously, given the skunk a good treat.

He raced at a surprising rate for a man as stout as he. I shot from my revolver – far off. A whole volley from my people was like water off a duck's back. Dubatowk crossed a small meadow, leaped rashly into a bog and began to jump from hummock to hummock like a grasshopper. Finding himself at a safe distance, he threatened us with his fist.

"Beware, you rats!" his frightful voice came flying to us. "Not one of you shall remain alive. I swear in the name of the gentry, I swear by my blood to slaughter you together with your children."

We were stunned. But at this moment such a loud whistle was heard that it deafened my ears. And I saw a young fellow sticking a bunch of stinging dry thistle into one of the horses right under his tail. And again a piercing whistle...

The horses neighed. We understood this youth's plan and rushed to the horses, and began to whip them. In a twinkling the herd dashed off, panic stricken, to the Giant's Gap. The figures of the scarecrow hunters were still sitting on some of the horses.

The wild stamping of hoofs broke into the night. The horses raced like wind. Dubatowk, apparently, also understood what it meant, and after a wild scream, ran off; the horses rushed in pursuit, having been taught to do that by this very man who was now running away from them.

We watched the mad race of King Stakh's Wild Hunt, now without horsemen on their backs. Their manes waved with the wind, mud flew from under their hoofs, and a lonely star burned in the sky above the horses' hoofs.

Nearer and nearer they came! The distance between Dubatowk and the furious animals was growing less and less. In despair he turned away from the paths, but the horses, having gone mad, also turned away.

A scream full of deathly fright came flying towards us. "To my rescue! Oh! King Stakh!" At that very moment his feet fell recklessly into the abyss, and the horses, having caught up with him, also began to fall into it. The first horse smashed Dubatowk with his hoofs, pushing him deeper and deeper into the stinking swamp, and began to neigh. The quagmire began to bubble.

"King Stakh!" reached our ears from there. Then an enormous thing turned over in the depths of the abyss, swallowing water. The horses and the man disappeared, and only the large bubbles whistled at the top as they burst. Like a candle burned the house of the last of the "knights", knights who like wolves marauded in the night. The muzhyks in leather coats turned inside out, with pitchforks in their hands surrounded the house, a crimson and alarming light illuminating them.

CHAPTER EIGHTEEN

I came home dirty and tired and, when the watchman opened the door for me, I immediately went to my room. At last, everything connected with these horrors was quite over and finished with; we had run down and crushed the cast iron Wild Force. I was so exhausted that after lighting the candle, I almost fell asleep in the armchair, with one boot pulled off half way. When I finally got into bed, everything was swimming before my eyes: the swamp, the flames over Dubatowk's house, the measured stamping of the horses' hoofs, the frightful screams, Ryhor's face as he lowered a heavy fork on somebody's head. I fell asleep only after some time had elapsed; a heavy sleep overcame me. I pushed my head into my pillow as the horse had pushed Dubatowk's head. Even in my sleep, I was experiencing the events of the night all over again. I ran, shot, jumped, and felt my feet moving, in my sleep.

My awakening was a strange one, although the state I was in could hardly have been called an awakening. Still sleeping, a feeling of something heavy arose, as if the shadow of some great and last misfortune were threatening me. It seemed that someone was sitting on my feet, so heavy had they become. I opened my eyes and saw Death nearby with Dubatowk laughing boisterously. I understood that this was all a dream, but the misfortune was tangible and alive in the room, it was moving, it was coming nearer and nearer.

The canopy was threatening me, was floating down to me, choking me, its tassels were swinging right in front of my eyes. My heart was thumping madly. I felt something mysterious approaching me, its heavy steps sounding along the passages, but I was weak and helpless, nor was there any need for strength, the evil monster was about to catch me now, or rather, not me, but her; and her thin, weak little bones were about to crack. I hadn't the strength to prevent what was coming; I shook my head and mumbled something, unable to shake off this horrible nightmare.

And suddenly the flame of a candle turned towards the ceiling, began to grow smaller and, weakened by its struggle with the darkness, finally died out altogether.

I looked at the door – it was ajar. The moon had cast a deathly light along the walls of the room and made window squares on the floor. In going out, the candle-light gave off a puff of smoke that rose upward as if in a blurred fog.

Suddenly I saw two very large eyes looking at me through the transparent curtain. It was awful! I shook my head. A woman was looking at me. But her eyes did not see me, they were staring somewhere behind me, as if they were looking through me, not noticing me at all.

Then she floated away. I looked at her, at the Lady-in-Blue of Marsh Firs, and my hair stood on end, though I knew not whether it was reality or a dream, a dream of my weakened mind.

It was reality, the woman from the portrait, resembling Nadzeya Yanovsky, and at the same time not at all like her. The face elongated and calm, as peaceful as death – the expression altogether a different one. She herself was taller and stronger. The eyes looked lifeless but penetrating, deep as a pool.

The Lady-in-Blue came floating over, was already here in her amazing attire, which in the moonlight fog played like shining waves; she was floating into the middle of the room, reaching out with her waving hands.

I felt that I had finally quite awakened, but my feet were in chains. The surprising apparition was moving towards me.

"What can have happened to the lady of the house, perhaps she is dead now and that is why such an indescribable fright took hold of me just now in my dream?"

This thought gave me strength. I threw off the blanket with my feet and prepared for an attack. When she floated up closer, I grabbed her outstretched hands. In one hand I held the sleeve of her magic attire, some kind of a veil slipped out of my fingers; in the other was something surprisingly weak and warm.

With a strong jerk I pulled her towards me and I heard a scream. I understood the essence of the phenomenon when I saw a look of fright on her face again, as if she had awakened from sleep; in her eyes there appeared a meaningful light, an expression of pain, alarm and something else comparable to what one can see in the eyes of a dog awaiting a blow. The Lady-in-Blue began to tremble in my arms, unable to utter a sound, and then broke into convulsive weeping.

The resemblance of this creature to Nadzeya Yanovsky was so startling that I, forgetting myself, screamed:

"Miss Nadzeya, calm yourself! What's the matter? Where are you?"

She couldn't say a word. Then the pupils of her eyes filled with horror.

"Ah!" she screamed and shook her head in fright.

Awakened while sleepwalking, she as yet understood nothing except the fear in her tiny, trembling little heart. Indescribable fear overtook me, too, for I knew that from such a fright people often lose their minds or remain dumb.

I was slow to grasp what I was doing, how to save her, but I began to cover her with kisses, kissing her sweet smelling long hair, frightened, trembling eyelids, her cold hands.

"Nadzeya, my beloved! My dearest! Don't fear! I'm right here, I'm with you. I've destroyed King Stakh! Now nobody will disturb your peace, your rest. Now you are safe."

Slowly, very slowly, consciousness returned to her. She opened her eyes again. And I stopped kissing her.

Although that was harder than death itself.

"What is it? What room is this? Why am I here?" her lips whispered.

I was still holding this little reed, without which I, a strong man, would instantly be broken. I held her because I knew that if I let go of her, she would fall.

And in the meantime, fright rushed into her eyes, fright mixed with such distraction that I regretted having awakened her.

"Miss Yanovsky! For God's sake, calm yourself! There's no need to be afraid any longer. All, all will be well and bright for you in this world."

She did not understand. A black shadow was creeping towards her from somewhere in a corner – a cloud had evidently floated across the moon. She looked at it and the pupils of her eyes became wider and wider and wider.

Suddenly a wind began to rattle some half broken shutters somewhere; it howled, it whined and whimpered in the chimney. So striking was its resemblance to the distant thunder of the hoofs of the Wild Hunt, to its inhuman yell: "Roman! Come out!" that I shuddered.

She suddenly began to scream, pressing herself to me. I felt her breasts and her knees under the thin fabric, and I, overcome by an irresistible desire, held her hard in my arms.

"That accursed money! Damned money! Take me away, take me away from here, take me away! You are a big and strong man, my master, take me away from here! I cannot, I cannot... It's so frightening here, so cold, so dark and gloomy! I don't want to die, don't want to die!"

And still pressing herself to me, on catching my look hid herself on my breast.

I turned my face away, I was choking, but I couldn't help myself. The sensation overpowered me, a weak man, and I gave in – everything became fused in a fiery whirlpool and she forgave me even the pain.

The moon hid behind the house, the last gleams fell on her face, on her hair that had fallen on my hand, on her happy and peaceful eyes looking into the dark.

I was ready to burst into tears of happiness, happiness that binds two virgins coming together, tears because nobody had ever touched my hand with her face like that before, and I thought with horror that she, my first and only one, forever mine, might have become like that woman in the Kulsha's house if those villains had achieved their aim.

That will not be. With tenderness, kindness, with everlasting gratefulness, I shall do whatever may be necessary to cure her somnambulism. Not a single stern word will she hear from me. For was it not unimaginable fright, the expectation of death, a mutual desire for ordinary warmth which brought us together, married us? Had we not risked our lives for each other's sake? Did I not then receive her as the greatest gift a man can have, a gift I had not hoped for?

CHAPTER NINETEEN

And that is all. On the following day, for the first time, the sun together with slight hoarfrost fell on the mossy castle walls. The tall grass was bestrewed with a cold white powder and was reddening under the first sun rays. And the walls were rose coloured, they had even become younger, awakened from a heavy sleep that had reigned over them for three years. The bright window panes looked young, pale rays shining on them, the Earth at the walls was moist, and the grass was damp.

We were leaving. The carriage was standing in front of the castle and our modest belongings were being tied on behind it. I led Lady Yanovsky out of the house. She was wrapped up in a light fur coat and I sat beside her. We cast a last glance at the castle in which we had experienced such suffering and unexpectedly for us had found love, such love that a man could, without regret, give up even his life for its sake.

"What do you think you will do with all this?" I asked. Yanovsky winced as if it were cold.

"The antique things will go to museums, the rest let the muzhyks take, the muzhyks who rose in defence of their huts and saved me. The castle – let it be turned into a hospital, a school, or something like that." And she smiled an ironical smile. "An entailed estate! How much blood, such a tangle of meanness, sordid crimes and intrigue. And for the sake of what? For a handful of gold... No, let's forget about it, about this entailed estate."

I put my arms round her narrow shoulders.

"I thought as much. That's the way. We don't need all this, now that we have found each other."

In the castle we left a new housekeeper – that widow I had once found with her child along the road. The other servants remained as they were.

And we sighed slightly when the castle disappeared behind the turning in the lane. The nightmare was over.

When we rode out of the park onto the heather land along the Giant's Gap, with the gates closed behind us for the last time, and in the distance the burial mounds were already coming into sight, I saw a man standing at the roadside.

The man making long strides came up to meet us. He took the horse by the bridle, and we recognized Ryhor. He was standing in his leather coat, his entangled hair falling on his face and on his kind, childish eyes.

I jumped out of the carriage.

"Ryhor, my dear fellow, why didn't you come to see us off?"

"I wanted to meet you alone. It's hard for me after all we've done. You are right to leave. Here everything would remind you of the past."

He stuck his hand in his pocket, blushed, and took out a clay doll.

"This is for you, Miss Nadzeya... Maybe you'll keep it near you... you'll remember..."

Nadzeya drew his head to her and kissed him on the forehead. Then she took off her earrings and put them in the dark wide palm of the hunter.

"For your future wife."

Ryhor grunted, shook his head.

"So long... So long... The quicker you leave the better... or else you may see me whimpering like an old woman... You are children. I wish you the best of everything, the very best in the world."

"Ryhor! My friend! Come away with us, you'll stay with us a while, while they're looking for Dubatowk and the others. Some good-for-nothing fellow might kill you here."

Ryhor's eyes became severe, he chuckled:

"Huh, just let anyone try!"

And his hands gripped his long gun, his veins even swelled.

"I've a weapon in my hands. Here it is. Just let them try to take it! I won't leave. My domain is this forest. And this domain must be a happy one."

"And I believe in that," I said simply.

When we had ridden away, I again saw from the edge of the forest his big silhouette on the mound. Ryhor was standing against the background of a crimson sky with his long gun in his hands, the gun reaching above his head, and on him his closely fitting leather coat that he wore turned inside out. The wind was playing with his long hair.

We rode through the woods day and night. The following morning we were met by the sun, by wet, tall grass and by joy! It was only now that I began to understand the difference between the Yanovsky region and this other land.

Enormous nests of storks and a sky blue silence over the clean huts.

Then how was my lady from the eighteenth century to look at this new world, if even I, during such a short period, had forgotten all this?

I glanced at her who was to be my wife. Her eyes were wide open and happy. She pressed herself against me and from time to time sighed, as a child does after tears. I much desired that she should feel even better. And I bent to kiss her hand.

What worried me at this time and later, too, was her illness. Therefore I rented a small house with a garden on the outskirts of the city. The doctors said that everything would pass while living a peaceful life. And indeed, it did pass, when we had been living together two months and she told me that we should have a child.

We surrounded each other with such a sea of kindness and attention, with such love, that even after seventy years I wonder whether it was all a dream. Everywhere life was kind to us, even in Siberia where I found myself in 1902. She was more than just a wife to me – she was a friend until death.

We lived long and happily, as in the song:

While over the land
Sunshine did reign...

But even now I sometimes see in a dream the grey heather and the stunted grass of the waste land, and King Stakh's Wild Hunt leaping, dashing through the marshes. The horses' bits do not tinkle; the silent horsemen are sitting up straight in their saddles. Their hair, their capes, their horses' manes are waving in the wind, and a lonely star is burning overhead.

King Stakh's Wild Hunt is racing madly across the Earth in terrifying silence.

I awaken and think that its time is not yet over. Not as long as gloom, cold and darkness, injustice and inequality, and this dark horror that had created the legend of King Stakh, exists on Earth. Across the land, half drowned in fog, still rovers the Wild Hunt.

ABSOLUTE ZERO

by Artem Chekh

The book is a first person account of a soldier's journey, and is based on Artem Chekh's diary that he wrote while and after his service in the war in Donbas. One of the most important messages the book conveys is that war means pain. Chekh is not showing the reader any heroic combat, focusing instead on the quiet, mundane, and harsh soldier's life. Chekh masterfully selects the most poignant details of this kind of life.

Artem Chekh (1985) is a contemporary Ukrainian writer, author of more than ten books of fiction and essays. *Absolute Zero* (2017), an account of Chekh's service in the army in the war in Donbas, is one of his latest books, for which he became a recipient of several prestigious awards in Ukraine, such as the Joseph Conrad Prize (2019), the Gogol Prize (2018), the Voyin Svitla (2018), and the Litaktsent Prize (2017). This is his first book-length translation into English.

OLANDA

by Rafał Wojasiński

I've been happy since the morning. Delighted, even. Everything seems so splendidly transient to me. That dust, from which thou art and unto which thou shalt return — it tempts me. And that's why I wander about these roads, these woods, among the nearby houses, from which waft the aromas of fried pork chops, chicken soup, fish, diapers, steamed potatoes for the pigs; I lose my eye-sight, and regain it again. I don't know what life is, Ola, but I'm holding on to it. Thus speaks the narrator of Rafał Wojasiński's novel *Olanda*. Awarded the prestigious Marek Nowakowski Prize for 2019, *Olanda* introduces us to a world we glimpse only through the window of our train, as we hurry from one important city to another: a provincial world of dilapidated farmhouses and sagging apartment blocks, overgrown cemeteries and village drunks; a world seemingly abandoned by God — and yet full of the basic human joy of life itself.

Buy it > www.glagoslav.com

Leo Tolstoy – Flight from Paradise
by Pavel Basinsky

Over a hundred years ago, something truly outrageous occurred at Yasnaya Polyana. Count Leo Tolstoy, a famous author aged eighty-two at the time, took off, destination unknown. Since then, the circumstances surrounding the writer's whereabouts during his final days and his eventual death have given rise to many myths and legends. In this book, popular Russian writer and reporter Pavel Basinsky delves into the archives and presents his interpretation of the situation prior to Leo Tolstoy's mysterious disappearance. Basinsky follows Leo Tolstoy throughout his life, right up to his final moments. Reconstructing the story from historical documents, he creates a visionary account of the events that led to the Tolstoys' family drama.

Flight from Paradise will be of particular interest to international researchers studying Leo Tolstoy's life and works, and is highly recommended to a broader audience worldwide.

Buy it > www.glagoslav.com

THE FANTASTIC WORLDS OF YURI VYNNYCHUK
by Yuri Vynnychuk

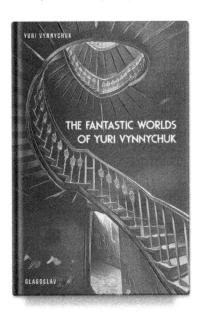

Yuri Vynnychuk is a master storyteller and satirist, who emerged from the Western Ukrainian underground in Soviet times to become one of Ukraine's most prolific and most prominent writers of today. He is a chameleon who can adapt his narrative voice in a variety of ways and whose style at times is reminiscent of Borges. A master of the short story, he exhibits a great range from exquisite lyrical-philosophical works such as his masterpiece "An Embroidered World," written in the mode of magical realism; to intense psychological studies; to contemplative science fiction and horror tales; and to wicked black humor and satire such as his "Max and Me." Excerpts are also presented in this volume of his longer prose works, including his highly acclaimed novel of wartime Lviv *Tango of Death*, which received the 2012 BBC Ukrainian Book of the Year Award. The translations offered here allow the English-language reader to become acquainted with the many fantastic worlds and lyrical imagination of an extraordinarily versatile writer.

Buy it > www.glagoslav.com

Someone Else's Life

by Elena Dolgopyat

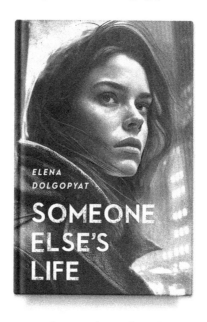

Elena Dolgopyat was born and raised in the USSR, trained as a computer programmer in a Soviet military facility, and retrained as a cinematographer post-perestroika. Fusing her diverse experiences with her own sensitivities and preoccupations, and weaving throughout a colourful thread of magic realism, she has produced an unsettling group of fifteen stories all concerned in some way with the theme of estrangement. Elena herself, in an interview given at the time of the book's launch, said, "Into each of these stories is woven the motif that one's life is 'alien'. It is as if you are separate from your own life and someone else is living it. You feel either that your own life is 'other', or you experience a yearning for a life you have not led, an envy for some other life." In his introduction to the collection, Leonid Yuzefovich writes, "Each of Elena Dolgopyat's stories ... painfully stirs the soul with a sense of the fragility, the evanescence, even, of human existence ... in her quiet voice, she is telling us of "the multicoloured underside of life". She is telling us of things that matter to us all."

Buy it > www.glagoslav.com

Ravens before Noah

by Susanna Harutyunyan

This novel is set in the Armenian mountains sometime in 1915-1960. An old man and a new born baby boy escape from the Hamidian massacres in Turkey in 1894 and hide themselves in the ruins of a demolished and abandoned village. The village soon becomes a shelter for many others, who flee from problems with the law, their families, or their past lives. The villagers survive in this secret shelter, cut off from the rest of the world, by selling or bartering their agricultural products in the villages beneath the mountain.

Years pass by, and the child saved by the old man grows into a young man, Harout. He falls for a beautiful girl who arrived in the village after being tortured by Turkish soldiers. She is pregnant and the old women of the village want to kill the twin baby girls as soon as they are born, to wash away the shame...

Buy it > www.glagoslav.com

- *A History of Belarus by Lubov Bazan*
- *Children's Fashion of the Russian Empire by Alexander Vasiliev*
- *Empire of Corruption: The Russian National Pastime*
  by Vladimir Soloviev
- *Heroes of the 90s: People and Money. The Modern History*
  of Russian Capitalism by Alexander Solovev, Vladislav Dorofeev
  and Valeria Bashkirova
- *Fifty Highlights from the Russian Literature (Dutch Edition)*
  by Maarten Tengbergen
- *Bajesvolk (Dutch Edition) by Michail Chodorkovsky*
- *Dagboek van Keizerin Alexandra (Dutch Edition)*
- *Myths about Russia by Vladimir Medinskiy*
- *Boris Yeltsin: The Decade that Shook the World by Boris Minaev*
- *A Man Of Change: A study of the political life of Boris Yeltsin*
- *Sberbank: The Rebirth of Russia's Financial Giant by Evgeny Karasyuk*
- *To Get Ukraine by Oleksandr Shyshko*
- *Asystole by Oleg Pavlov*
- *Gnedich by Maria Rybakova*
- *Marina Tsvetaeva: The Essential Poetry*
- *Multiple Personalities by Tatyana Shcherbina*
- *The Investigator by Margarita Khemlin*
- *The Exile by Zinaida Tulub*
- *Leo Tolstoy: Flight from Paradise by Pavel Basinsky*
- *Moscow in the 1930 by Natalia Gromova*
- *Laurus (Dutch edition) by Evgenij Vodolazkin*
- *Prisoner by Anna Nemzer*
- *The Crime of Chernobyl: The Nuclear Goulag by Wladimir Tchertkoff*
- *Alpine Ballad by Vasil Bykau*
- *The Complete Correspondence of Hryhory Skovoroda*
- *The Tale of Aypi by Ak Welsapar*
- *Selected Poems by Lydia Grigorieva*
- *The Fantastic Worlds of Yuri Vynnychuk*
- *The Garden of Divine Songs and Collected Poetry of Hryhory Skovoroda*
- *Adventures in the Slavic Kitchen: A Book of Essays with Recipes*
  by Igor Klekh
- *Seven Signs of the Lion by Michael M. Naydan*

- *Forefathers' Eve by Adam Mickiewicz*
- *One-Two by Igor Eliseev*
- *Girls, be Good by Bojan Babić*
- *Time of the Octopus by Anatoly Kucherena*
- *The Grand Harmony by Bohdan Ihor Antonych*
- *The Selected Lyric Poetry Of Maksym Rylsky*
- *The Shining Light by Galymkair Mutanov*
- *The Frontier: 28 Contemporary Ukrainian Poets - An Anthology*
- *Acropolis: The Wawel Plays by Stanisław Wyspiański*
- *Contours of the City by Attyla Mohylny*
- *Conversations Before Silence: The Selected Poetry of Oles Ilchenko*
- *The Secret History of my Sojourn in Russia by Jaroslav Hašek*
- *Mirror Sand: An Anthology of Russian Short Poems*
- *Maybe We're Leaving by Jan Balaban*
- *Death of the Snake Catcher by Ak Welsapar*
- *A Brown Man in Russia by Vijay Menon*
- *Hard Times by Ostap Vyshnia*
- *The Flying Dutchman by Anatoly Kudryavitsky*
- *Nikolai Gumilev's Africa by Nikolai Gumilev*
- *Combustions by Srđan Srdić*
- *The Sonnets by Adam Mickiewicz*
- *Dramatic Works by Zygmunt Krasiński*
- *Four Plays by Juliusz Słowacki*
- *Little Zinnobers by Elena Chizhova*
- *We Are Building Capitalism! Moscow in Transition 1992-1997 by Robert Stephenson*
- *The Nuremberg Trials by Alexander Zvyagintsev*
- *The Hemingway Game by Evgeni Grishkovets*
- *A Flame Out at Sea by Dmitry Novikov*
- *Jesus' Cat by Grig*
- *Want a Baby and Other Plays by Sergei Tretyakov*
- *Mikhail Bulgakov: The Life and Times by Marietta Chudakova*
- *Leonardo's Handwriting by Dina Rubina*
- *A Burglar of the Better Sort by Tytus Czyżewski*
- *The Mouseiad and other Mock Epics by Ignacy Krasicki*
- *Ravens before Noah by Susanna Harutyunyan*
- *An English Queen and Stalingrad by Natalia Kulishenko*

- *Point Zero by Narek Malian*
- *Absolute Zero by Artem Chekh*
- *Olanda by Rafał Wojasiński*
- *Robinsons by Aram Pachyan*
- *The Monastery by Zakhar Prilepin*
- *The Selected Poetry of Bohdan Rubchak: Songs of Love, Songs of Death, Songs of the Moon*
- *Mebet by Alexander Grigorenko*
- *The Orchestra by Vladimir Gonik*
- *Everyday Stories by Mima Mihajlović*
- *Slavdom by Ľudovít Štúr*
- *The Code of Civilization by Vyacheslav Nikonov*
- *Where Was the Angel Going? by Jan Balaban*
- *De Zwarte Kip (Dutch Edition) by Antoni Pogorelski*
- *Głosy / Voices by Jan Polkowski*
- *Sergei Tretyakov: A Revolutionary Writer in Stalin's Russia by Robert Leach*
- *Opstand (Dutch Edition) by Władysław Reymont*
- *Dramatic Works by Cyprian Kamil Norwid*
- *Children's First Book of Chess by Natalie Shevando and Matthew McMillion*
- *Precursor by Vasyl Shevchuk*
- *The Vow: A Requiem for the Fifties by Jiří Kratochvil*
- *De Bibliothecaris (Dutch edition) by Mikhail Jelizarov*
- *Subterranean Fire by Natalka Bilotserkivets*
- *Vladimir Vysotsky: Selected Works*
- *Behind the Silk Curtain by Gulistan Khamzayeva*
- *The Village Teacher and Other Stories by Theodore Odrach*
- *Duel by Borys Antonenko-Davydovych*
- *War Poems by Alexander Korotko*
- *Ballads and Romances by Adam Mickiewicz*
- *The Revolt of the Animals by Wladyslaw Reymont*
- *Poems about my Psychiatrist by Andrzej Kotański*
- *Someone Else's Life by Elena Dolgopyat*
- *The Riven Heart of Moscow (Sivtsev Vrazhek) by Mikhail Osorgin*
- *Liza's Waterfall: The hidden story of a Russian feminist by Pavel Basinsky*
- *Biography of Sergei Prokofiev by Igor Vishnevetsky*

  More coming ...

GLAGOSLAV PUBLICATIONS

www.glagoslav.com